Very hard to find

.Nacho, the homeless man, wore the same clothes he'd worn the night before and had the same black garbage bag tucked under his arm. As he approached, his gaze fell on Nina's red Impala, and he froze in place.

"What . . . ?" Gretchen began, confused by his response. Nacho hadn't seen her in the passenger seat yet. He was reacting to the car as though he knew it. She jumped out when she saw him running away.

"Stay here," she commanded Nina, slamming the car door and breaking into a run. He turned a corner. Gretchen's pulse throbbed as she gave pursuit but Nacho had a wide lead. He cut across the street against the lights. Horns blew. Someone shouted.

Gretchen looked ahead just as he left the sidewalk and disappeared between two commercial buildings. Nacho was the path to her mother, the key to Martha's murder. She felt sure of it. This might be her only chance, and she wasn't about to blow it.

He ran like a desert coyote, like his life depended on it, his arms pumping hard and his eyes, when he glanced back, frightened.

Gretchen remembered the alcohol on his breath from the night before and wondered where his stamina came from. Maybe his fear was greater than hers, and his fear drove his momentum. Although he had nothing at all, he might have more to lose than she did. If that were possible . . .

Dolled Up

FOR Murder

DEB BAKER

BERKLEY PRIME CRIME, NEW YORK

Cathy
Enjoy Baker

THE BERKLEY PUBLISHING GROUP
Published by the Penguin Group
Penguin Group (USA) Inc.
375 Hudson Street, New York, New York 10014, USA
Penguin Group (Canada), 90 Eglinton Avenue East, Suite 700, Toronto, Ontario M4P 2Y3, Canada
(a division of Pearson Penguin Canada Inc.)
Penguin Books Ltd., 80 Strand, London WC2R 0RL, England
Penguin Group Ireland, 25 St. Stephen's Green, Dublin 2, Ireland (a division of Penguin Books Ltd.)
Penguin Group (Australia), 250 Camberwell Road, Camberwell, Victoria 3124, Australia
(a division of Pearson Australia Group Pty. Ltd.)
Penguin Books India Pvt. Ltd., 11 Community Centre, Panchsheel Park, New Delhi—110 017, India
Penguin Group (NZ), Cnr. Airborne and Rosedale Roads, Albany, Auckland 1310, New Zealand
(a division of Pearson New Zealand Ltd.)
Penguin Books (South Africa) (Pty.) Ltd., 24 Sturdee Avenue, Rosebank, Johannesburg 2196, South Africa

Penguin Books Ltd., Registered Offices: 80 Strand, London WC2R 0RL, England

This is a work of fiction. Names, characters, places, and incidents either are the product of the author's imagination or are used fictitiously, and any resemblance to actual persons, living or dead, business establishments, events, or locales is entirely coincidental. The publisher does not have any control over and does not assume any responsibility for author or third-party websites or their content.

DOLLED UP FOR MURDER

A Berkley Prime Crime Book / published by arrangement with the author

PRINTING HISTORY
Berkley Prime Crime mass-market edition / October 2006

Copyright © 2006 by Deb Baker.
Excerpt from *Goodbye Dolly* copyright © 2006 by Deb Baker.
Cover art by Teresa Fasolino.
Cover design by George Long.
Interior text design by Kristin del Rosario.

ISBN: 0-425-21263-7

BERKLEY® PRIME CRIME
Berkley Prime Crime Books are published by The Berkley Publishing Group,
a division of Penguin Group (USA) Inc.,
375 Hudson Street, New York, New York 10014.
The name BERKLEY PRIME CRIME and the BERKLEY PRIME CRIME design are trademarks belonging to Penguin Group (USA) Inc.

PRINTED IN THE UNITED STATES OF AMERICA

10 9 8 7 6 5 4 3 2 1

ACKNOWLEDGMENTS

Thanks to Jacky Sach, the most amazing and talented agent on the planet, and to Chris Roerden, good friend and editorial wizard extraordinaire, for giving this manuscript extra pizzazz. Without her, I'd still be in the slush pile.

Thanks to Anita Husby, who welcomed me into her doll workshop and answered questions throughout the writing process. Any mistakes I've made regarding doll repair are strictly my own.

Thanks to poet and playwright Anne Godden-Segard for never losing her enthusiasm, and to best friends, Mary Goll, Mary Korkor, and Lee Wolfs, for forcing me away from the computer when I thought I might assimilate into it.

Special thanks to my kids for never complaining about all the frozen pizzas, and to my husband, who gave me the space I needed to follow my dream and who taught me to never, ever give up.

*Antique dolls have histories much like their human counter-
parts. They have beginnings, and they have endings. Occasionally a doll collector is fortunate enough to acquire a doll with a
hand-written history dating back to its creation. The collector
can trace the doll's journey through its past owners and its travels. It is up to the new owner to continue writing the history, to
keep a detailed record of the doll's lifetime.*

—From *World of Dolls* by Caroline Birch

Head buried under a mound of pillows, Gretchen Birch
struggled to ignore the phone's incessant ringing. She had
stopped answering the phone at midnight, and it had rung
every hour on the hour since. Gretchen lifted a corner of
the pillow and squinted at the clock on the nightstand.
Three in the morning. The answering machine would pick
up after one more ring, and Nina's urgent message, the
same hour after hour, would reverberate in her head until
the woman called again at four.

What was the use? She wasn't sleeping anyway.

Gretchen fumbled in the dark for the phone and
knocked it to the floor. Tangled in a sheet, she yanked herself free and lunged for the phone.

"What now?" she said. "Don't you ever give up?"

"You have to come to Phoenix." Aunt Nina, her mother's
sister. Bold, bigger-than-life Nina. The dramatist. "Martha
Williams is dead, and your mother is missing."

Gretchen rubbed her red, sleep-deprived eyes. "Drunken Martha tripped and fell from a mountain ledge. That's what you told me when you called the first time. Again, I extend my sympathies to you, even though you hardly knew her."

"Your mother is missing." Nina's husky voice strained upward, hitting a high soprano note. "How many times do I have to tell you that?"

"According to you, she's been missing . . ." Gretchen checked the clock again. ". . . approximately fifteen hours. That isn't missing. That's out power shopping or taking a personal day to recharge. Knowing her, she's probably in Vegas, finishing up at the blackjack table as we speak."

"She didn't take her lucky bracelet. She would never go without it. And she wouldn't leave without telling me."

Gretchen's cat, Wobbles, brushed against her bare toes, demanding attention. The stray's leg had been smashed in a hit-and-run outside Gretchen's apartment two years earlier. She witnessed the accident as she stood waiting for the traffic light to change; the car traveling too fast on the winding street, the cat lying at her feet. Shocked and outraged, she scooped the injured stray into her coat, ignoring the blood soaking her clothes, and rushed to the vet. Too late to save his back leg, but a partnership developed between them. Wobbles, the three-legged cat, had stayed.

Gretchen ran her hand along the cat's silky black fur. She sighed and tried another tactic. "I lost my job last week. Downsizing, remember? I was terminated without warning along with several other startled, soon-to-be-starving souls. I don't even have the money for rent, much less airfare."

Not to mention that July in Phoenix is like the inside of a blast furnace. You cook from the inside out. Roasting, suffocating, charring heat. But Boston, home sweet home, is at its peak. Green, leafy trees, breathable salty air, foghorns calling in the harbor.

"A ticket is waiting for you at the airport," Nina replied. "You have to get moving. Check in by seven, or you'll lose your seat."

Gretchen shot upright, startling Wobbles. "I need more time to think about this. If I decide to come, I need to make arrangements for Wobbles's care, and I need to pack. I need to stop the paper for a few days and water the plants." A to-do list formed in Gretchen's head. "Impossible. I can't come tonight. Tomorrow. I'll come tomorrow. Maybe."

Nina's voice was tense. "Not seven P.M., Gretchen. Seven A.M. your time. You have four hours. Throw a few things together and dig out the pet carrier I sent you for Christmas."

"But, but . . ." Gretchen searched her repertoire of excuses for the perfect response, but Nina had disconnected.

"I have to look for a new job," Gretchen said aloud to no one in particular. What day of the week was it, anyway? Friday. With luck, she'd be back in Boston by Monday, following more weak leads to full-time employment.

Gretchen flung aside the covers and began throwing cosmetics into her travel case. Three fifteen in the morning. What was she thinking? She was as crazy as her aunt Nina and, for that matter, her mother. All three were wildly impulsive and disorganized, and Gretchen secretly attributed the anomaly to a renegade gene passed down through generations of Birch women. A strong matriarchal line with a few crossed wires.

I have to learn to say no, Gretchen thought, considering another genome gone askew, afflicting her but having passed up her mother and Nina. Skipping generations, like twins. She could think *no*, shake her head back and forth *no*, and shout *no* in her head, but when it came to forming the word with her lips and emitting the actual sound, she froze. This inability to refuse a request had landed her in many murky situations. This one, for example.

She threw shorts and tank tops into a suitcase and sorted through a pile of laundry in her closet. Nearly all her clothes needed washing, but she tossed in the cleanest of the dirty clothes. She could wash them at her mother's house. Before she closed the suitcase, she remembered one other essential item: her hiking boots. How could she forget her gear?

Phoenix had few redeeming qualities in mid-July, but it did have Camelback Mountain, and its most challenging series of steep inclines, Summit Trail, was Gretchen's favorite. Before closing the suitcase, she added a Western states bird book and a pair of binoculars. Traveling to Arizona in July was on a par with arriving in northern Michigan in January, but she planned on making the most of it.

The first call from Nina flashed into Gretchen's mind. Martha, a casual acquaintance of her mother, had fallen from Camelback Mountain. Found by a group of hikers. Broken. Dead. A destitute alcoholic with the bad judgment to leave the trails and wander along the rock outcroppings.

What could you expect from a crazy, onetime doll collector who roamed the streets and lived inside a bottle? Certainly not a gentle passing.

Gretchen struggled to remember more, but she'd been too tired at the time to listen to the details. Nina sounded concerned about her mother, but Nina tended to overreact to everything.

Gretchen, loaded down with luggage and a drowsy, medicated Wobbles, entered a taxi. While the cabby expertly maneuvered through winding streets and roared toward Callahan Tunnel, which led to Logan Airport, Gretchen called Steve on her cell phone and explained the events of the last few hours.

She tried to keep her voice even, hiding the hurt she felt at his recent betrayal.

"We had dinner reservations for tonight," Steve said when she finished, sounding groggy and confused.

The taxi flew into the tunnel, and reception on the cell phone began to break up.

Steve's voice cracked. "This is sudden. And early. What time is it?"

"You don't want to know," Gretchen said, watching the tunnel walls, listening to the rapid clack-clack of the tires on the pavement. "I wanted to catch you before I boarded.

It's only for a few days. Nina's concerned about my mother, but she'll turn up soon. She might reappear before my plane even lands."

"How is your mother connected with that woman's death?"

"She's not. Nina should be in theater. Mom's off someplace, and Nina's doing her sixth-sense routine. No two events can be coincidence according to her. The universe flows into and onto itself."

"Your family is too weird," Steve said.

Too weird for what?

Gretchen felt impatient with Steve, a gathering cloud of annoyance. *Just nerves,* she thought. *And lack of sleep.* She was about to lighten the moment by asking him what was so weird about a mother who restores dolls and an aunt who trains purse dogs, but the cell phone beeped and displayed the message Call Lost. She flipped it closed and tossed it into her purse just as the cab burst through the tunnel into the early morning sunlight.

Gretchen stood on the curb for a moment before entering the terminal, hoping to breathe the crisp Atlantic Ocean air. One last cleansing breath. But all she could smell was auto exhaust from the heavy traffic jamming the lanes leading to check-in. She considered calling Steve again but decided against it. Later, when she felt more rested, she'd call from Phoenix.

She knew she would sleep on the plane, catch up after last night's lost battle of wills with Nina. She'd have to find a special therapy group when she returned to Boston for people like herself, people who couldn't say no.

As the plane backed away from the gate, her thoughts turned to Steve. After seven years of dating, their relationship operated more by rote than by reckless abandon. Seven years without progress, without commitment. Gretchen brushed away feelings of rejection.

She thought Steve had been preoccupied with the law firm. He would make partner this year, and that involved a deep commitment to the firm, leaving little emotional energy for a commitment to her. She had tried to remain supportive in spite of a growing sense of resentment and unease.

Then an anonymous phone call had revealed the real cause of his distraction: another woman. It only happened one time, he explained when she confronted him. No, he didn't know the woman's name, he said. And it didn't matter because it would never happen again. He loved Gretchen and would do anything to make it up to her, he said. Anything.

Gretchen felt a sharp pain in her chest every time she thought about it.

Well, others had made it through rough times; so could they.

A few days apart might do them some good.

Caroline Birch was in trouble. Every nerve ending shouted, *Warning! Warning!* The Phoenix airport terminal's harsh lights and mechanical sounds felt surreal to her; intense, irrational, the day like a long, complex bad dream. She rushed now, holding her laptop close to her chest, frequently looking behind her, afraid she might be followed.

She knew that the note found in Martha's hand could be her death sentence. What a foolish thing to overlook, considering the seriousness of the circumstances. If Martha had trusted her with more information, she would possess a name and know what her next move should be. But her enemy was cloaked in obscurity. Invisible and, therefore, deadly.

Instead of standing her ground, the author of *World of Dolls* was racing across the country chasing one, betting her life that the doll would give her the answers she needed. A risky gamble.

Whatever it took, she had to get her hands on that doll.

A disembodied voice announced final boarding, and Caroline broke into a run, gasping for air but reaching the gate in time. Not a runner. Usually. But running now. Boarding pass checked, gates closed, cell phone turned off, she sighed in relief as the plane rolled from the terminal and gained speed, lifting into the air.

When the seat belt sign blinked off, Caroline stumbled down the aisle to the rear of the plane and entered a lavatory, clutching her laptop, her lifeline. She splashed cold water on her face and pressed her wet hands softly against her tired eyes. A few wisps of hair had come free from her cap, hanging across her bent face. She straightened and dried her hands, then removed the baseball cap, releasing her shoulder-length silver hair. "Foxy hair," her sister called it, her trademark. A distinguishing, telling feature, when Caroline needed more than anything to blend in. She ran her fingers roughly through her hair, coiled it on top of her head, replaced the cap, and returned to her seat.

• 2 •

Casual collectors collect dolls for sentimental reasons—they owned a certain kind of doll as a child, or they are adding to a collection that has been in the family for years. The serious collector enjoys the hunt, the taste of triumph, the sweet scent of success. Many serious collectors are dealers and are motivated by the monetary aspects rather than sentimentality.

—From *World of Dolls* by Caroline Birch

The July heat scorched the desert landscape. Gretchen could feel its heavy grip weighing on her body. She could smell the dust. Nina had picked her up at baggage and now drove through Phoenix traffic, weaving in and out of lanes in her red vintage Chevy Impala. Wobbles was stowed in his carrier on the floor in the backseat, relatively calm thanks to the continuing effect of a tranquilizer. Nina's dog, Tutu, was wrestling with Gretchen for the front seat while keeping one beady eye on the travel carrier.

"Tell me about Tutu," Gretchen said.

"A rescue dog. I saw her picture on the Internet and couldn't resist. She's absolutely perfectly behaved. I can't imagine what sort of person would abandon such a wonderful pet."

Gretchen tried to pry herself free from Perfectly Behaved without success.

"How's Steve?" Nina asked, ramming through gears like a NASCAR driver. "Has he proposed yet?"

Gretchen, unwilling to ponder Nina's question, dug sunglasses out of her purse, quite a feat with the miniature schnoodle jumping on her lap. She locked eyes with the comical experiment in dog breed crossings. Schnauzer and poodle, minis at that. What would inventive breeders think of next? Pitt bulls and corgis could be called piggis or pittis or corbulls or . . .

Gretchen stomped on her imaginary brake as Nina raced up to a red light, slowing at the last moment.

"Well," Nina insisted. "Has he popped the question?"

"We've discussed it," Gretchen said evasively.

"Discussed it?" Nina shrieked. "It's been seven years. One of you has a commitment problem. Or maybe both of you do. Living together yet?"

"No. We're comfortable the way things are." Talking about Steve and their stalled forward progress made Gretchen uncomfortable. Lately she'd been hearing her internal clock ticking louder than it once had. Ticking clocks, even those firmly attached to the wall, made her nervous.

The desperation she'd been feeling recently didn't thrill her either. She hated paging through the wedding announcements in the *Boston Globe*. Pages and pages ad nauseam.

One month and three days until she turned thirty. Chances of wearing an engagement ring were growing slim since her latest discovery.

"Humph," Nina snorted. "I'd give him an ultimatum in spite of his good looks. Pop the question or hit the road. That tactic works, you know. At least there would be some kind of action."

Gretchen couldn't imagine Steve's reaction to that sort of pressure. His imported Italian shoes would curl up at the toes.

Nina turned right onto Lincoln and sped toward Camelback Mountain, its prominent humps towering over the city. Caroline's home, their destination, nestled at its base.

Gretchen felt a familiar sense of wonder as she absorbed the mass of the mountain and the scope of the city.

The dry, enormous clumps of reddish rock were visible throughout Phoenix and the surrounding suburbs of Paradise Valley and Scottsdale.

For all Phoenix's exotic beauty and its reputation as a haven in the winter months, it turned forbidding and hostile in July.

She had dozed fitfully on the plane. Thoughts of her mother had been disjointed and intrusive, allowing her only a light, uneasy sleep. Now she bounced new ideas off Nina. "Maybe she heard about a great estate sale and she's on a doll-buying spree."

"Must be in Timbuktu," Nina replied, refusing to catch the ball. "She would be back by now."

"Maybe she's mixing business and pleasure. She's probably sightseeing at the same time. No car in the carport, you said. Right?"

"Right."

"So we know she has it with her. And does this dog have to be on my lap?" Gretchen was annoyed with the schnoodle digging her sharp back nails into Gretchen's legs while planting groomed front paws on the side window, her nose leaving gooey streaks on the glass. Tutu wore a red lacy collar the size of a neck brace. Having sensed competition for Nina's attention the moment Gretchen opened the car door, the schnoodle insisted on the seat of command, which is exactly where Gretchen thought she should sit.

"You're in her spot," Nina said, sliding into Caroline's driveway and turning off the ignition. "You have to learn to share. See how nicely Tutu shares. Good Tutu."

Tutu wagged her tail and barked, a shrill, nerve-piercing sound.

Gretchen's opinion of dogs—groveling, dependent creatures with lofty attitudes and bad manners—hadn't changed upon meeting Tutu. Wobbles, like most cats, had a superiority complex, but at least he could clean himself. And he was quiet. Yapping dogs drove her crazy.

Nina produced a key to the door of Caroline's adobe-style home and stood back with Tutu to allow Gretchen to enter. "After you," she said with a sweeping gesture.

Standing in the doorway holding Wobbles's carrier, Gretchen felt like an intruder. The house was too quiet, disconcertingly vacant. It smelled, not fragrant and earthy like her mother, but like a closed-up, abandoned space. Her mother's spirit, which usually infused a room, was gone.

Dishes from a morning breakfast were scattered on the counter, and a newspaper lay open on the table. A box of maple buckwheat flakes had fallen next to the paper, the top left open. A few pieces of cereal had spilled from the box.

Her mother, in spite of her lack of organizational skills, was meticulous about keeping her kitchen clean, fanatical almost. She wouldn't have left the table like this unless something unforeseen had happened.

For the first time since Nina began calling yesterday, Gretchen believed it might be possible that her mother really was missing.

"See her bracelet." Nina pointed to a pink band lying on the counter. "She always wears it."

Gretchen picked up the bracelet designed to support cancer research and fingered the engraving, Share Beauty Spread Hope. The bracelet matched the one on her own wrist. Their common bond was her mother's triumph over breast cancer, her mother, a five-year survivor: sickened by chemotherapy, bald, her once dark brown hair growing back a monochromatic silver. Their bond continued to strengthen through her long, frightening recovery and the sudden death of Gretchen's father in an automobile accident. Then came her mother's compelling need for a new life, ripping out established roots, the move to Phoenix to be near her sister, abandoning her life in Boston. And Gretchen.

"She left in a rush," Nina whispered.

"Yes," Gretchen muttered, studying the contents of the kitchen. "She didn't take the time to clean up, and that's not like her." She slipped her mother's bracelet onto her wrist next to her own pink band. For good luck.

Gretchen wandered through the house. Her mother's workshop was exactly the same as she remembered it from her last visit. A perpetual work in progress: dolls hanging from lines, dolls scattered over workbenches, heads, bodies, repair tools. Gretchen had helped her mother with the simpler repairs such as cleaning and restringing before the move to Phoenix. Gretchen smiled to herself. She had lived every little girl's fantasy, rooms full of dolls and dresser drawers filled with doll clothing.

Nina made iced tea while Gretchen tugged Wobbles out of his carrier. He lifted his head and emitted a feeble meow, while Tutu's nose twitched, catching his scent. Tutu tried to climb Gretchen's leg.

"Call Tutu," she said to Nina, doubting that Tutu even knew the *come* command. How could Nina train dogs to stay in purses when she couldn't train Tutu in the basics? Yet her mother had insisted that Nina was the best purse dog trainer in the Valley of the Sun. Probably the only one, thought Gretchen, holding Wobbles in both arms. She'd never heard of the profession until Nina announced her new career move.

Nina picked up Tutu. Gretchen carried Wobbles down the hall to her mother's bedroom and wrapped him in the bedding. He seemed to smile gratefully and was fast asleep before she walked out, leaving the door slightly ajar.

Nina's iced tea smelled wonderfully fruity, and Gretchen sipped it slowly at the kitchen table. Nina plopped down beside her. "Tell me everything again," Gretchen said. "I want to hear it all."

"Early yesterday morning, hikers found Martha's body at the base of a ridge on the mountain," Nina began. "Information travels fast through the doll community, and by noon everyone knew about it, including your mother. In fact, I'm the one who told her."

"What did she say when she found out?" Gretchen asked.

"Very little, small exclamations of shock, I suppose. We were all gasping at the suddenness of her death." Nina picked up her glass with both hands and placed her elbows on the table, cradling the glass against her lips. "Then I told her the rest."

"The rest?"

"Bonnie Albright's son is a detective with the Phoenix Police Department. You remember Bonnie? She's president of the local doll club, the Phoenix Dollers."

Gretchen remembered. Red hair shellacked into an exaggerated flip, red-smeared lips, penciled lines where eyebrows used to be. "The Kewpie doll collector."

Her mother had a few Kewpies in her own collection. The original ones had blue wings fanning from their necks. Gretchen liked the chubby dolls, each with a small lock of hair and cherubic grin.

"That's Bonnie," Nina said. "She collects Action Kewpies. Farmers, drummers. Her son, Matt, called her right away because Martha didn't have any identification with her, and he needed Bonnie's help figuring out who she was."

Gretchen frowned. "I don't understand. How did he know Bonnie could help?"

"Because Martha had a doll parasol in the pocket of her shorts, and since his mother collected dolls, he thought she might know her. As it turns out, she did. Bonnie went down to the morgue, and sure enough, it was Martha Williams."

Nina, a solemn expression on her face, set the glass on the table. "Poor Martha."

"It sounds like she had a hard life," Gretchen said.

Nina nodded, then noticed Tutu dancing at her feet. "Let's take Tutu outside. The little dear needs to go."

Tutu started yapping.

Gretchen watched Nina dig through a pouch as big as a baby diaper bag. Out came a white folded pad.

"What's that?"

"You'll see. Follow me."

Gretchen smiled inwardly. Aunt Nina was as quirky as

quirky comes. Stores her shoes on top of the refrigerator so scorpions can't climb in. Had all the silver fillings removed from her teeth so she wouldn't get mercury poisoning. Believes she has special psychic power and can see auras emanating from people. Gretchen wouldn't be surprised if Nina believed that space ships flew out of holes in Antarctica.

The sweltering late morning heat hit Gretchen with enough force that she took a step back before willing her body into forward motion. After the relief of the house's air-conditioning, her skin felt on fire. Motion took superhuman effort. Even her breathing became labored.

They paused next to Caroline's swimming pool rimmed with Mexican tile and gazed up at Camelback Mountain. Gretchen could see a few die-hard hikers weaving upward among the rocks. She wondered how many of the mountain's casualties were accidents and how many were calculated ends. What drove people over the edge? What did they think about in that final moment during the deadly plunge?

She shivered in spite of the heat. Even Tutu paused for a moment of silence.

"Where did she fall?"

Nina pointed to one of the highest peaks. "She must have been standing right about there. See that ledge close to the top? Bonnie thinks they found her about there."

"She must have been an experienced hiker to climb that high. Summit Trail isn't easy."

Summit Trail was strenuous. Not a trail for beginners. Halfway up to the peak of the mountain, the trail steps ended, and the real climb began. Gretchen had climbed it many times and loved the challenge, but the majority of amateur hikers preferred to follow the gentler Bobby's Rock Trail.

Nina shrugged. "As far as I know, she never climbed a mountain in her life. She was afraid of heights. She couldn't even climb a ladder."

"Maybe she was trying to conquer her fear." Gretchen knew there were plenty of opportunities to overcome fear on this mountain.

"Bonnie said Martha was wearing sandals. Who climbs a mountain in sandals?"

Tutu began yapping again. Nina unfolded the small white pad and placed it on the ground. "Here you go, sweetie. Now do your business."

And Tutu squatted on the pad.

"This is the best invention ever designed," Nina said. "I call it the wee-wee pad. See how well Tutu is trained to go on it. No more accidents in the house if you lay one of these where you want your precious pet to go. No more rushing home to let the dog out. Not that I'd ever leave you home alone, Tutu dear."

Gretchen rolled her eyes. Nina needed an outside interest, something that didn't include Tutu.

"The only problem is that Tutu likes the pad so much she won't do what she has to do outside. No grass or desert ground for her. She refuses to pee-pee without her wee-wee pad. I would spread it out in the house, but Caroline says it isn't natural for a dog to go in the house, and she won't allow it."

Nina bundled up the used pad and handed it to Gretchen. Holding it delicately between two fingers, Gretchen walked to the far side of her mother's swimming pool and deposited it in a trash receptacle outside of the cabana.

Instead of returning right away, Gretchen leaned against a barstool and admired the earthy Mexican tile decorating the cabana. Its open front faced the swimming pool with a circular cocktail area, and it had a small living space for guests in back. Gretchen stayed in the cabana on many visits, preferring its intimate coziness to staying in the main house.

Nina watched her from a lounge chair in the shade of a large umbrella. "Whatever happened up on the mountain, Gretchen, I'm afraid it wasn't an accident."

Gretchen sat on a lounge chair next to Nina and stared in bewilderment at her aunt. "What do you mean?"

"For starters, Martha didn't have any dolls. The bank

repossessed her home three years ago, and she lost her entire collection, which, I heard, was one of the finest antique collections in Phoenix."

"You never saw it?" Gretchen eyed up the inviting blue water of the pool.

"No, she was an odd woman, reserved and not particularly friendly. I didn't know her well enough to have the opportunity. But that's not the point. The point is—why did she have a doll parasol in her pocket when she no longer owned any dolls? Martha was homeless at the end of her life. And that's not all. Brace yourself, Gretchen. I couldn't tell you this on the phone."

Nina reached over and placed her bejeweled hand over Gretchen's. "Bonnie told me the police found a note of sorts clenched in Martha's fist."

Nina might be hopelessly melodramatic, but she was pulling it off with style this time. Gretchen felt the hairs on her arm rising. "What? Tell me."

"The piece of paper had your mother's name on it. It read, 'Caroline Birch—put her away.' "

Gretchen stared at her aunt.

"My psychic ability is a curse sometimes," Nina continued, leaning back on the lounge chair and crossing her arms. "I sense something dark happened up there. Martha Williams was pushed from Camelback Mountain and, I'm afraid, your mother is involved."

"Impossible," Gretchen said with conviction.

"That's when your mother vanished. Right after I called her and told her what the authorities found." Nina snapped her fingers, her voice urgent. "Poof. Like smoke, she was gone."

Nina roared away in her red Chevy to pick up her latest purse dog trainee, leaving Gretchen with time to herself. She made a peanut butter sandwich and a salad using slightly wilted lettuce from her mother's refrigerator. While she ate at the kitchen table, she adjusted her watch for the three-hour time difference between Boston and Phoenix, turning the hands back. Noon instead of three, a mere twelve hours since she'd given in to Nina's demands.

Instead of unpacking, she laced up her hiking boots and slipped her cell phone in her pocket. She rubbed sunscreen on her exposed flesh, hung her binoculars around her neck, and selected a bottle of water from a well-stocked supply in the refrigerator.

As an afterthought, she checked her mother's closet. Then she opened the hall closet. Her mother's set of luggage lay empty on the floor. A more thorough search produced a toothbrush in the bathroom. As far as Gretchen could tell, Caroline hadn't taken anything other than the car.

She braced herself for the explosion of afternoon heat and set off, leaving palm trees and bougainvillea behind. She walked up the hill toward Echo Canyon, where the trailhead to Camelback Mountain began.

Hikers, mostly sightseers and casual walkers, tramped up and down the footpath between the trailhead and a large boulder, where they perched like flocks of birds to admire the view of Phoenix in the valley below and to drink from lukewarm water bottles.

The serious hikers, many training for longer hikes, continued moving up where the footpath ended and the handrails began. Gretchen could see the dry washes below and cacti sprouting from impossibly sheer cliff ledges. Birds flitted through the sparse shrubbery, calling to each other.

Gretchen felt light-headed as she trudged upward. Nina's words played over in her mind. Her mother. Vanished. A dead woman. Her mother's name in the woman's pocket. *"Put her away."*

What could it mean?

A message? A warning? An accusation?

The timing of Martha's death and Caroline's disappearance wasn't coincidental, and she knew it. She felt a quick flash of anger at her mother for leaving without notifying anyone. The anger dissipated and steamed into fear. Was her mother safe? Why hadn't she called Nina? Twenty-four hours and counting since Nina had spoken with her sister, the time slowing to an agonizing pace.

Gretchen paused in her sweaty climb to admire the desert scenery. Her mother had taught her the names of the plants growing along the trails: saguaros, ocotillos, barrel cacti, and palo verdes. Rattlesnakes, scorpions, and gila monsters also liked the mountain environment, three poisonous reasons to wear hiking boots and to stay on the designated trails.

Gretchen didn't think she could handle an encounter with any of these three creatures. But spiders were her worst nightmare. A black widow would provide a perfectly good reason to jump off a cliff. It was a good thing they liked dark, remote holes and rarely ventured near humans.

Cautiously she moved over the rocks, well above the cluster of tourists milling around on the boulder below. She forged ahead, picking her way up, using the binoculars to scan the cliffs, remembering with each step the warnings about lizards and snakes. Sweat soaked her shirt and glistened on her face. Gretchen stopped to catch her breath and get her bearings. She could see the top of her mother's house in the valley below. Using the ledge that Nina had pointed out as a guide, Gretchen calculated that Martha had fallen from a ridge directly above her.

Gretchen's heart pounded against her chest cavity, and her throat felt tight and dry. She looked down at her feet, searching for signs that she stood where the woman's body had been discovered, but all she saw were clumps of red rock and a few straggly desert plants.

What if her mother lay injured somewhere up here? Could she be crumpled in the shadows beneath a rock outcropping? Gretchen continued climbing upward, sweeping the binoculars along the far reaches of Camelback until she was satisfied that she'd thoroughly covered the climbable part of the mountain.

She slowly began her descent, pausing again where she thought Martha had fallen.

When she raised the binoculars and spotted a small patch of color in the rocks above her, she thought she'd stumbled across her first sighting of a Gila monster. Her mother had shown her pictures of the venomous reptiles: massive heads and small, beady eyes, with orange, pink, or yellow blotches covering their bodies. She knew they moved sluggishly and couldn't chase her down the mountain, but she was nervous nevertheless as she edged closer for a better look. And closer. Until she stood a few yards away.

The orange coloring wasn't the scaly back of a lizard.

She was looking at a French fashion doll's paisley shawl.

Despite adrenaline pumping through her veins, Caroline fell asleep, a dreamless and heavy retreat from the world. The flight attendant gently placed a hand on her shoulder, startling her awake. "Please return your seat to its original position," she said quietly. "We'll be on the ground in a few minutes."

Groggy and disoriented, Caroline adjusted the seat and noticed for the first time that her bracelet was missing. Her lucky bracelet. Where could it be? She fought back the feeling of panic threatening to overcome her and forced a weak smile. *It's only a bracelet,* she thought. *You're getting superstitious in your old age, like Nina.*

She wondered what was happening at home right now. Were they hunting for her? Had they searched the house yet? She smiled to herself, feeling stronger and more confident.

No one could match her ability for concealing things.

Thanks to her daughter's inherited competitive nature, their games had been played at a highly skilled level. Scavenger hunts. The traditional Easter basket searches. The challenge, each time, to be better than the last time.

Caroline grinned at the memories.

Let them look. They would never find it.

· 3 ·

*Paris was the birthplace of the first fashion doll. The doll's attire
imitated the leading dress styles of the time. Since middle- and
upper-class Parisiennes changed their outfits throughout the
day, some fashion dolls came with trunks filled with gowns, ankle boots, tortoiseshell dressing sets, and other accessories.*

*Because little French girls played with these miniature ver-
sions of their mothers, few dolls survived in good condition.
Most of the trunks and accessories were lost or destroyed.*

*A French Bru fashion doll in mint condition, with no cracks
or repairs and in original costume, sold on eBay sans trunk.
Starting bid: $24,950. An original trunk would have made
the doll worth much, much more.*

—From *World of Dolls* by Caroline Birch

"Ohh, isn't it cute," Nina cooed, holding up the multicol-
ored cotton shawl. It was about the size of a baby's terry
washcloth.

"I wonder what this is worth?" Gretchen said in disbelief. "I've never seen anything like it before. It's in perfect
condition except for a tiny bit of ground-in dirt where it
must have hit the rocks and settled in. It's a miracle I
found it."

Nina looked up from admiring the shawl. "A miracle?
No. This is a sign. You know that most of my psychic predictions come to me in dreams. Well, last night I dreamed
about this very thing." Nina frowned. "In my dream your

mother was the size of a doll and wore the shawl over her shoulders with a dress from this exact historical period. I wonder what the dream means."

"The problem with your dreams," Gretchen said, "is that you can't interpret them. You should take a class on dream analysis." *Preferably one that doesn't allow dogs in the classroom,* Gretchen thought with a watchful eye on Tutu.

Nina scanned a creased photograph lying on the table. "You found this next to the shawl?"

"The shawl must have been in this bag," Gretchen said, holding up a brown paper lunch bag. "It was lucky that it had fallen out so that the colors caught my eye. The picture was inside the bag, and I almost missed finding it because the bag blended so well with the rocks."

Gretchen gazed at the photograph. A French fashion doll with startling blue eyes, wearing a green silk gown, smiled serenely up at her from a compartment inside an open doll trunk. A straw hat with a green ribbon and white flowers rested in her arms, and she wore glistening black earrings.

She noted the trunk's domed shape, its brass-headed tacks, and brass handle.

Nina sat fingering the doll shawl, surrounded by her entourage, Tutu and her latest purse dog trainee. The trainee, a white fluff ball puppy named Rosebud, peered out from a large cloth purse slung over the workshop doorknob. Occasionally it emitted a shrill bark.

"Maltese like this one are so easy to train," Nina said, leaving the table to give Rosebud a little attention. "Especially little females." The tone of Nina's voice curved upward. "Don't feel jealous, little Tutu. You're smarter than all of them put together."

Nina looked at Gretchen. "Everyone thinks they can just buy a little dog and stick it in a purse. They don't realize it has to be trained to stay there. That's where I come in. Most of my clients are easy to work with, but Chihuahuas?" Nina shuddered for emphasis. "They're more like vicious little purse attack dogs. I charge extra for them."

"Can't you take time off from dog training?" Gretchen asked. "Considering the circumstances."

Nina gasped. "I'd lose my clients. I'm in the early, most important stage of my new career. If I started canceling training sessions, word would get around, and no one would come to me anymore. That would be the kiss of death."

Wobbles, wide-awake after his long nap, was cautiously exploring every corner of the house. He made a brief appearance at the workshop door. Tutu's ears perked up.

"Watch Tutu," Gretchen warned Nina, reaching down and hooking a finger through Tutu's red collar to restrain her. "She's mesmerized by Wobbles, and she's licking her lips."

"Tutu won't hurt your kitty."

Gretchen shrugged knowingly. "I'm not worried about Wobbles. He could eat Tutu for lunch. It's Tutu I'm worried about. I'm not sure that Wobbles has had much experience with dogs." She smiled. Wobbles wasn't paying attention to either dog. Arrogant indifference suited him. He cared much more about his own investigation in progress and the new smells around him. After one smug glance at the dog hanging from a doorknob, he turned and stalked off.

"He's remarkably agile on three legs," Nina observed.

The doorbell chimed. Gretchen released Tutu and watched her race for the front door, yapping loudly. The purse trainee trembled, full-body tremors created by the sight of the three-legged stalking tiger and the ensuing commotion.

"That must be April." Nina rose from the table. "I forgot to tell you in all the excitement. I called her right after you called me. We should make sure the shawl is authentic. You remember April?"

Without waiting for an answer, Nina followed Tutu's lead and headed for the door. Gretchen lifted the Maltese

out of the purse, holding her close and stroking her. In spite
of her feelings about canines, she couldn't stand to see any
animal in a state of fear or in pain. Rosebud, fitting easily
into her palm, licked her little lips nervously, but the
tremors began to ease away.

Gretchen remembered meeting April Lehman briefly on
one of her visits to Phoenix, but she didn't need a doll appraiser to examine the shawl. She sensed that it was the
real thing. According to her mother, who was a well-
respected doll expert and published author, doll heads were
much easier to replicate than period clothing. The shawl
couldn't be mistaken for anything other than an intricate,
antique doll accessory.

It was the picture of the doll that interested Gretchen the
most.

April lumbered into the workshop wearing a muumuu
the size of a Volkswagen Beetle. White crew socks and
beige sandals completed her ensemble. "Hey, Gretchen,"
she called and heaved herself onto a stool.

"April can tell a fake doll from the real thing at twenty
paces," Nina said, following April.

Gretchen knew that swindlers roamed the doll world
waiting to dupe unsuspecting beginners. A good appraiser
could tell an original by the number of eyelashes or the
slant of an eyebrow or a marking in just the right spot. April
and her kind were the backbone of the doll collecting community.

"What ya got here?" April adjusted her reading glasses
and bent over the table to study the doll shawl. "My, my.
Where'd you find this?"

"Hiking on the mountain. I found it in the rocks."

April peered at her over the top of her glasses. "You
don't say."

Then she went to work. The silence beat across the
room while they waited for a verdict. Gretchen continued
to stroke Rosebud, who snuggled closer and closed her

eyes. After a few minutes, Nina began drumming her fingers on the table. April gave her a stern look, and Nina crossed her arms to still her impatient fingers.

Gretchen gently returned Rosebud to the purse, where she curled contently into a tiny ball.

Finally, April sat back, moved her reading glasses from the end of her nose to the top of her head, and sighed with pleasure.

"It's a wonderful example of a mid–eighteenth-century French fashion doll accessory," she said. "No question about it."

"I'm assuming it fell from the ridge with Martha," Gretchen said. "Is that a safe assumption?"

April nodded.

"My exact thought," Nina agreed.

"Bonnie's son, that police officer," April said. "What's his name? Matt? He asked me to appraise the parasol they found in Martha's pocket. Same historical period, same size. From the same doll, I'd be willing to bet."

Gretchen held out the photograph she saved for last. "I found this at the same time."

April whistled when she saw the picture.

"The tray is removable, and her trousseau is stored under it," April said, running her finger over the image of the trunk with something approaching reverence. "See how the tray is lined with striped fabric? Wow."

"I'm pretty sure the doll is a Bru," Gretchen said.

April nodded. "A classic smiley Bru. She's worth a ton of money."

"How much?" Nina asked.

April thought for a moment. "I wouldn't want to venture a guess without examining the doll," she said. "What I can say with surety is that the doll is about seventeen inches high. I can base that estimate on the size of the shawl. The trunk would be about twenty inches long and fifteen inches high."

"That's a large trunk," Nina said, reminding Gretchen how little Nina knew about dolls.

"Most fashion dolls were designed to fit right inside the trunks like this one does."

"Why would Martha have an antique doll shawl and a photograph of a priceless Bru with her?" Gretchen wondered aloud. "Did she steal the shawl and the parasol?"

"Logical conclusion." April's voice was cold. "Personally, I never cared for the woman. Shifty, I thought, and unscrupulous. She certainly could have stolen it. But I'm not aware that any of the club members around here own an original Bru with accompanying trunk."

"She had only a picture and a few accessories," Nina said. "That doesn't mean she's a thief. Let's not snap to any rash conclusions."

Gretchen picked up the photo of the fashion doll and turned it over. On the back, she read the date that the film had been processed. Four years ago.

"Gretchen, is it possible Martha was at your mother's house the night she died?" April asked, ignoring Nina's defense of the dead woman.

Gretchen was surprised. "Why would you think that?"

"Camelback Mountain is right in Caroline's backyard. I'm simply exploring the possibility." She arched a brow. "The police won't overlook that, you know."

Gretchen shrugged. "I have no way of knowing for sure. But my mother never mentioned Martha to me." She turned to Nina. "Did Martha ever come here for repair work?"

"Caroline never mentioned it to me," Nina said. "But everyone knew Martha. She used to be a member of the Phoenix Dollers."

April shifted on the stool, her large form completely hiding the seat. "The next obvious question is . . . Where is the doll? And why did Martha have a picture of it?"

"That," Gretchen replied, "is the prizewinning question."

A find like this would be of great interest to her mother, and some of that curiosity had rubbed off on Gretchen.

She'd love to see an antique doll of such quality with its own personal trunk of original clothes.

"We don't have to notify the police, do we?" Nina said, scrunching her nose in distaste at the idea.

April swung around to look at Nina. "Martha's death was an accident or a suicide, regardless of a few doll accessories and an old picture," she said. "The investigation is routine. Bonnie's son is the only one working it, and I'll mention the shawl next time I see him, but it won't change anything. In the meantime we should keep this our little secret. What will we accomplish by exposing Martha as a thief after her death?"

"The note found with Martha was rather mysterious." Nina said.

Gretchen, standing slightly behind April, shook her head at Nina. Nina wrinkled her brow in confusion. The last thing Gretchen wanted was the contents of the message found in Martha's hand known by the entire doll community.

"Yes, the note," April agreed. "It does beg an explanation."

"Does everyone know about the note?" Gretchen demanded.

"News travels fast when it's riding Bonnie's lips," Nina said.

"That's the truth," April said.

Gretchen checked her watch and left the two women chatting in the workshop. Six o'clock in Boston. Steve would probably still be at the office, even though it was Friday and most Bostonians would be on their way to happy hour.

From her mother's bedroom, she dialed his business number. While the phone rang, she studied a Shirley Temple doll posed on the nightstand and ran her fingers across its white taffeta skirt. A receptionist answered and mechanically informed her that Steve was in a meeting and unavailable. Her harried voice reminded Gretchen that Steve's commitment to the firm took other prisoners as well, some not nearly as well compensated.

"Would you like to leave a message?" the receptionist asked.

"No. No message." Gretchen hung up and tried his cell phone. No answer. She left a voice message saying she had arrived safely, her mother was still missing, and she would call later.

The bed looked inviting, but Gretchen knew she'd have trouble getting up again if she gave in to its beckoning comfort. She must look a fright by this time. Long ago, a few doll collectors had compared her features to the Shirley Temple doll next to her. Right now she was sure she looked more like a freaky Chucky doll.

Nina appeared behind her.

"Let's go," Nina said. "The day's still young."

Gretchen wondered at her aunt's stamina. Neither of them had gotten much sleep the night before, thanks to Nina's persistence. Gretchen felt weary, her body still on Boston time. She ran her hands through her unruly brown hair in a futile attempt to restore order.

"Food," Nina said. "You need some fuel. Let's go out and get something to eat. April can follow in her car, and we'll drop off my purse trainee on the way."

"Where is the doll shawl? We can't just leave it on the workbench."

"I've wrapped it up in a wee-wee pad along with the picture, and I'll stow it in the trunk of my car until we find out who owns them. The Impala trunk is more secure than a safe-deposit box." She laughed. "You'd need more than a crowbar to break into it."

Nina had wrapped it in a wee-wee pad?

"I can find something more appropriate," Gretchen said, heading for the workshop. She transferred the shawl and photograph to a long sheet of bubble wrap and rolled it up, securing it with packing tape and placing it inside a small box.

"Ready?" Her aunt said, and Gretchen picked up the box and nodded.

Nina drove like a woman possessed by flying demons. April's white Buick, which was noticeably dented on both the front and back bumper, fell behind and disappeared altogether when Nina gunned the Impala through a yellow light.

"We've lost April," Gretchen said, looking back.

"She knows where we're going. Let's hope she makes it there without an accident. You saw the condition of her car. She's crash prone," Nina said. "Don't worry about her. Worry instead . . ." she ground through the gears, ". . . about Wobbles and Tutu alone in the same house. I can't believe restaurants won't allow dogs. In France everyone dines with their dogs."

"Paris streets are also dotted with clumps of doggy doo-doo. It's everywhere like goose crap around a pond."

"That's why we have to introduce the French to wee-wee pads. A fortune could be awaiting us." Nina peeled into a driveway and deposited Rosebud with the pup's anxious owner.

When they arrived at Richardson's Restaurant and entered the cool and dimly lit interior of the restaurant, they found that April had already made herself comfortable in a deep-seated booth. They sipped margaritas and ordered tomatillo toast and green chile stew.

Gretchen dug in her purse for her cell phone. She checked for voice messages, hoping for word soon from Steve or her mother. Nothing.

"Nina tells me Caroline is missing," April said through a mouthful of tortilla chips.

"I really expected a call from her by now," Gretchen muttered, absently playing with her mother's bracelet on her wrist.

"Call your answering machine in Boston," Nina suggested. "Maybe she's trying to reach you. She couldn't know you're in Phoenix."

Gretchen called her apartment to check for messages. Nothing. She hid her disappointment. She was on the verge

of a full-scale search for her mother, and her mother's silence wasn't making her choices easy. She keyed in her
mother's cell phone number and left a message on her
voice mail asking her to call back immediately.

"I've been leaving messages all day," Nina said.

"Maybe you should file a missing person report," April
suggested.

Gretchen had considered going to the police but quickly
rejected the idea. What if Caroline didn't want to be
found? That thought and its implications had played
through Gretchen's mind most of the day.

Apparently Nina had been thinking the same thing.
"No," she said. "It's too soon. We'll ask around on our own.
Someone has to know where she is."

"The police must already know that she's gone,"
Gretchen said. "Haven't they been to the house?"

"I don't know," Nina said, shrugging. "I'm avoiding
getting involved with the police and their barrage of annoying questions. They're always trying to blame the first
person they stumble across."

"Try the China Doll Shop," April suggested. "Julia and
Larry hear a lot of scuttlebutt at the shop."

"We're headed there next," Nina said.

Steaming bowls of stew arrived filled with green chiles,
chunks of tenderloin, potatoes, cheese, and a rich and fla-
vorful sauce. Gretchen ate with renewed appreciation for
Southwestern cuisine. She had forgotten how wonderful the
exotic flavors could be.

After dinner April left with a promise to make discreet
inquiries about the assortment of doll paraphernalia found
with Martha, and Nina wandered off to the ladies' room.
Gretchen walked outside into the early evening heat and
stood on the curb.

She smelled him before she saw him. The same odor of
unwashed clothing that she remembered from working in
homeless shelters during summer breaks from school. The

memory of that smell of human decay and rancid hopelessness never left her.

He must have been lurking on the side of the restaurant. When Gretchen whirled, she stared directly into his blood-shot eyes. Saw his scruffy beard and dark patches of dirt ground into his face. She wasn't afraid. From her experience, she knew most of the homeless were harmless, tortured souls who shunned the responsibility of their existence, preferring isolation. Their only wish was to be left alone.

Gretchen moved aside to let him pass, but he stood motionless and stared at her. She could smell alcohol on his breath, and she noticed he clutched a filled garbage bag. All his belongings carried in his arms.

He staggered forward a step and spoke, so low Gretchen almost missed what he said. "Get out," he hissed. "Right now. While you still can."

Gretchen watched in astonishment as he trotted away with his bundle, casting one last menacing look back at her.

Caroline made her way through O'Hare's crowded terminal. Herded along toward baggage, she warily studied the travelers around her. No one looked familiar. She clutched her laptop securely against her chest and turned on her cell phone with one hand, hearing its reassuring beep.

She stopped at a vacant gate, sat down in a quiet corner, and dialed a number she had committed to memory. After four rings, a voice answered.

"I'm at the airport," Caroline said. "May I come right away? It's important."

"I'm sorry," the voice said. "But Mr. Timms was called away on business. I'm afraid he can't meet with you."

"That's impossible." Caroline clutched the phone, staring out at the vast concrete runways. "I've come so far."

"He asked me to express his regrets. Good day."

"No! No! Don't hang up."

Caroline stared at the cell phone. The connection termi-nated. Then she seemed to crumple across her laptop like a broken marionette doll, her head touching her knees.

And Caroline Birch began to sob.

· 4 ·

Doll shops offer an array of services for the doll aficionado: appraisals, repairs, dolls, clothing, wigs, and doll-making classes. Since modern molds are made from actual antique heads, many casual collectors are content to own a well-executed reproduction. Doll shops offer classes in porcelain doll making to those who find it an enjoyable hobby and to doll dealers who hope to establish a profitable business in reproductions.

—From *World of Dolls* by Caroline Birch

Gretchen leaned against the exterior wall of the restaurant for support. She heard the rush of diners' voices as the door swung open, and Nina appeared at her side.

"No rest for the wicked," Nina said lightly, breezing by. "Onward and upward." She marched toward the Impala. Her steps slowed when she realized Gretchen wasn't behind her. She swung around. "What? What is it?"

"A man," Gretchen stammered. "A man just threatened me."

"Where is he?" Nina said, rushing back.

"Gone." Gretchen gestured down the sidewalk. "He told me to get out while I still can. Then he ran away down the street."

"What did he look like?" Nina asked. "Did you recognize him?"

Gretchen shook her head. "He was unkempt, dirty, a street person, I think. Shabby clothes. Hairy cheeks. He had a growth of some sort on the side of his head above his ear." She cupped her hand over her ear to show Nina what she meant. "Like a knob."

She didn't say that he looked like he had lost himself inside his head, that he had the tormented eyes of the mentally ill. The homeless. The renegades of society, unequipped for the demands of everyday life. She would never understand their choices to live without the steady assurance of food, water, and a safe place to sleep.

"Sounds like a ranting lunatic to me," Nina said. "Unfortunately, even Phoenix has its share of crazies. Who knows what he meant. He probably doesn't know himself. Forget about it."

"I'm sure you're right," Gretchen said, not sure at all but moving in step with Nina toward the car.

Nina tucked her arm through Gretchen's. "Let's stop at Starbucks on the way to the China Doll Shop. You look like you could use a little caffeine boost."

Gretchen laughed weakly. "Any more surprises like the one I just had, and I won't need jet fuel to keep me going." She was uneasy about the encounter with the stranger. Under the circumstances, she couldn't discount anything that might lead to her mother. His sudden appearance on the sidewalk challenged Gretchen's resolve to remain calm and focused. Tomorrow, in the light of day, she would try to find the man and question him.

"It's cooling off," Nina observed as they sped away.

Gretchen felt hot and sticky. She didn't think the evening temperature had changed much since the sun vanished in a fiery orange blaze. Night descends quickly in the desert. The sun is high and hot one minute, gone the next. Gretchen thought the desert should cool off at sunset. It certainly wasn't true tonight. The Impala's thermometer registered ninety degrees outside, and Gretchen was grateful when the car's air-conditioning kicked in.

Armed with two fully leaded espresso frappuccinos, they zipped along through the Arizona night with a steady running commentary from Nina on life's mysteries.

"For example," Nina said. "Can you tell me why teddy bear collectors look just like the bears they collect?"

"Nope," Gretchen said, slurping the iced coffee. "I never noticed."

"It's true, you know. Next time we're at a doll and bear show, pay attention to the bear collectors. And men . . ."

"Let's not go there." Gretchen tugged her cell phone from her purse and checked for missed calls while Nina wove expertly through traffic. She sighed heavily when she saw that no one had called. Not Steve. Not her mother.

"I don't mean men in general, I'm talking about male doll collectors," Nina continued. "They spend more money than women do. They demand good quality and are very detail-minded. Why is that? Your mother loves to work with male clients on restoration projects." Nina downshifted for a traffic light. "Your current abode is on the way, well nearly on the way. I called the shop from the restaurant, and Julia promised to stay open tonight until nine, so we have time to pick up Tutu. Let's see what the two new friends are up to."

At the house someone had obviously had a rip-roaring good time, with special emphasis on rip. The first clue that something was amiss was Tutu's lowered head and down-cast eyes when she greeted them at the door. A sure sign of guilt. Gretchen, leading the way, stepped in the second clue.

"Yuck," she said, lifting her foot. She glared at the perpetrator and slipped out of her shoes. "You can clean this mess, Nina. And my shoe. You forgot to put down one of those dog pads before we left. I'm checking on Wobbles."

"I'm sure this isn't all Tutu's fault," Nina called after her.

Without responding, Gretchen stalked past an overturned lamp and stepped around globs of stuffing pulled from a sofa pillow. She found Wobbles in the laundry room, buried in a pile of her folded clothes on top of the dryer. The bowl of dry cat food she had left on the washing machine was almost empty.

"Did you have anything to do with that mess?" she asked him.

Wobbles stretched luxuriantly and meowed a soft hello.

Gretchen stroked his back. "I'm glad you didn't cave in to peer pressure," she said. "The canine is in big trouble."

She could hear Nina reprimanding Tutu. "Naughty Tutu. Shame on you."

Gretchen dialed Steve's home number from the laundry room to allow Nina plenty of time to clean up. "Hey," she said brightly when he answered. "Finally, I found you."

"It's been a long day," Steve said. "You know the drill. Work around the clock. How's it going?"

"Things here are complicated. I don't know where to begin explaining the situation to you."

"It's late here, you know, and I have an early morning meeting," Steve said, yawning. "Maybe we can talk tomorrow."

"Sure," Gretchen said, disappointed. She had waited all day to speak with Steve, and now he was putting her off. That seemed to happen more and more these days. "How was dinner?"

"Schmoozing and boring."

"Who went with you?"

There was a pause on the other end.

"A few partners, one of the interns."

"An intern?"

"Courtney. Why?"

Gretchen felt her old nemesis, jealousy, roaring through her veins and zapping her system like an electrical shock. *Zip. Zap. Alert. Attention.* She tried to ignore it. "No reason," she said.

"Gretchen, I know what you're thinking. But it's nothing like that. She's a kid. You met her, remember? It was strictly business, Gretchen. She rounded out the table."

Gretchen remembered Courtney. The dumpling with the broad, beaming, innocent smile and the glint of determined ambition in her eyes. Gretchen was good at reading eyes, and Courtney's said, *I'm on the prowl, and I'm looking for the man who will help me get ahead.*

Was she the woman Steve had slept with whose name he had conveniently forgotten?

Gretchen heard background music playing through the phone gripped at her ear. She closed her eyes and willed herself to stay cool and composed. She could hear Nina calling her name from the front of the house.

"I've got to go," she said. "We'll talk tomorrow. Call me when you have a chance."

"Will do," Steve said and disconnected.

Nina peeked into the laundry room. "Oh, oh," she said when she saw the expression on Gretchen's face and the phone in her hand. "What happened?"

"Steve took his summer helper to the charity dinner tonight."

"I thought you had conquered the jealousy issue years ago."

"Apparently not." Gretchen stabbed the power button on her phone, and it beeped off.

Nina grinned. "You had it worse than anyone I ever knew. You couldn't share your dolls or your friends. You always thought someone would steal them away. Any time other little girls tried to play with you and . . . What was your best friend's name? . . . Oh yes, Katie Hachett, you'd figure out how to get rid of them. Remember?"

"How does my shoe look?" Gretchen said, changing the subject.

"Like brand-new."

"Then let's go." Gretchen pulled on her shoes. "And please take Tutu with us. She's banned from the house until further notice."

"I missed my little poochy poo," Nina cooed while Tutu again attempted to usurp the front seat of the Impala.

Without new job prospects in the foreseeable future, a

rental car wasn't an option. If she was forced to share transportation with Nina, she had to work out a compromise with Tutu. Based on Tutu's recent antics, Gretchen felt she had the upper hand. She refused to take a backseat to a dog, literally.

She lifted the red-collared dog and deposited her in the rear seat.

Nina pulled out of Caroline's driveway, geared up, and slid a sideways glance at Gretchen.

"My shoe," Gretchen reminded Nina before she could complain about Gretchen's treatment of Poochy Poo. "Don't forget my shoe and my mother's pillow. Tutu crossed the line, and there's no going back."

Nina, for once, had nothing to say.

After several failed attempts to jump into the front and a stare-down contest that Gretchen almost lost, Tutu yawned in defeat and turned her attention to the world whizzing by outside the rear window.

The China Doll Shop was located on Thirty-fourth Avenue, nowhere near Caroline's house, as Nina had implied earlier. "It's almost nine," Gretchen said, checking her watch. Almost midnight in Boston. She needed sleep soon. "We better hurry, or the shop will close."

Gretchen knew Julia and Larry Gerney, the shop's owners, through her mother, who considered them friendly competitors. Caroline made very little money cleaning and restringing dolls, rebuilding fingers, and replacing eyes. The work that allowed her mother to live in relative monetary comfort at the base of Camelback Mountain was the details she could furnish: providing the perfect antique shoes, making new mohair wigs, and replacing teeth. The wealthy doll collectors of Scottsdale and Paradise Valley paid whatever it took to round out their collections, so competition for their business and the ensuing financial rewards was fierce.

Nina slid into a small strip mall and turned off the ignition. She attached a pink leash dotted with tiny red hearts to Tutu's lacy collar.

Gretchen noticed that two of the shops in the mall were vacant. Untenanted shops, she knew, meant empty parking spaces and a feeling of decline that would keep customers away. The mall seemed to be slowly dying. Not a good sign for Larry and Julia, who counted on business from casual drop-ins as well as from established clientele.

"How is their business doing?" Gretchen asked Nina. They were waiting by the side of the car for Tutu to take advantage of a wee-wee pad.

"They put on a good front," Nina said. "But business is dropping off. The developers overbuilt, and as Phoenix expands west, everyone wants to set up shop in the new malls. I don't think Larry and Julia can afford to pay those kinds of rents." She balled up the used pad and tossed it on the floor of the backseat. "Watch what you say in front of them. They feed on gossip like buzzards on dead meat."

Julia Gerney met them at the door. She looked like a bulldog, short and stout, with an oversized lower jaw and a personality like artificial sugar. Not the real thing. "Sweet as snake venom," Gretchen's mother once said in the true spirit of gameswomanship.

"Gretchen, how goooood to see you," Julia gushed, every vowel exaggerated. Abruptly her broad smile faded and her eyes narrowed. "Does Tutu really have to come in?"

"It's too hot in the car," Nina said, watching Tutu prance ahead on the tips of her hairy toes. "She'd roast to death."

Julia's steely glare seemed to say that roasting Tutu would be a solution, not a problem. "Keep her on the leash, and don't let her bother my customers. If my allergies kick up, she'll have to go."

Two gray-haired women sat at a large studio table painting doll heads. Large display cabinets lined the sales counter and contained doll supplies: paints, brushes, patterns, and books. More cabinets framed the room and held samples of Julia's reproduction dolls: American Indian dolls, china dolls, and a variety of fashion dolls from the 1950s.

"Our doll-making classes have been a huge success,"

Julia said, heading for the back storage room, which doubled as an office. "But it's been a trying week." She arranged herself on a folding chair with her feet tucked neatly under it. "The air-conditioning unit isn't keeping up. Larry needs to call the repair service before our customers start complaining. He's been out of town attending a few doll auctions, but I expect him back any minute."

Julia didn't ask them to sit down, although Gretchen realized, scanning the room, there wasn't an inch of extra space. Every corner was crammed with boxes; every tabletop was stacked high with doll parts and clothing.

"Caroline is gone," Nina said from the doorway, shortening Tutu's leash to keep her close. "She didn't say a word to me before she left, and we're hoping you have some idea where she might be."

"I certainly don't know," Julia said. "I haven't seen her in weeks. Last time I saw Caroline, probably three weeks ago, now that I think about it, we were both bidding at an auction in Apache Junction."

Yes, Gretchen thought, her mother put a lot of miles on her car chasing deals. Was she simply following another sale? Had Nina overreacted? Nina tended to incite hysteria at will, and this wouldn't be the first time she had led Gretchen astray.

"Caroline would never have gone off without telling me," Nina insisted.

Julia laughed lightly. "She's a grown woman, Nina. She doesn't have to report in to you." She glanced at Gretchen. "Your mother is a very spontaneous woman, prone to rash impulses in spite of what Nina says." Julia looked pointedly at Nina. "She's chasing a bargain. Don't worry about it."

"I don't know what's going on," Gretchen said. "Or why she isn't here. But she disappeared after Martha was found dead, and I have to find her."

Julia gasped. "You don't think there's a connection between Martha's death and your mother's disappearance, do you?"

Too late, Gretchen remembered Nina's warning about Julia, the turkey vulture.

"Most of the Phoenix Dollers weren't very fond of Martha, and I'm sure your mother was part of that group," Julia went on. "Martha had a bad habit of alienating people with disparaging comments. For example, she called me the Tasmanian Devil behind my back."

"Maybe she meant it in an endearing way," Gretchen suggested.

"You remember the cartoon character," Julia said. "It had an enormous mouth and, when it wasn't whirling out of control, it slobbered and made grunting noises. I can't find anything endearing about that."

Before Gretchen could respond, Larry's booming voice filled the doorway behind Nina. "What am I missing? Is this a club meeting?"

He wore standard Southwestern attire: shorts, polo shirt, and leather sandals. He'd lost the paunch Gretchen remembered from her last visit to Phoenix, and he looked fit and trim. But he still had the involuntary facial tic that caused him to squint and blink as though the sun was shining directly in his face.

"Caroline is missing," Julia said to him. "And Gretchen thinks she was involved in Martha's death and is running from the police."

Gretchen stared in astonishment at Julia. "That wasn't what I suggested at all. Please don't repeat that to anyone. It isn't true."

"Of course not," Julia said. "There's a logical explanation in spite of the incriminating note the police found in Martha's hand." Julia smiled sweetly.

Larry squeezed past Nina and Tutu, blinking rapidly, and bent to kiss his wife on the cheek.

Tutu chose that moment to tug the leash out of her owner's grasp. She ran through the shop trailing the leash, with Nina in hot pursuit.

Julia shot out of the folding chair, squealing. She scurried after Nina and Tutu. "That's it. My eyes are beginning to itch. Out of the shop with Tutu!"

Gretchen started to follow, but Larry put a hand on her arm. "Wait, tell me what's going on," he said. "How long has your mother been missing?"

"Only since yesterday. But the timing isn't good."

"You mean because Martha died yesterday?"

Gretchen nodded. She felt weary and wanted nothing more than to go to sleep and wake up to a new day and fresh energy. Maybe tomorrow everything would be clearer.

"Your mother is fine," Larry reassured her. "She'll turn up, and she'll wonder what the fuss is about."

Gretchen idly fingered a stack of doll clothing lying on Julia's desk. She picked up a doll with a repair tag around its wrist—a Schoenhut wooden doll—and admired the expertly carved face. The enamel face paint was slightly cracked around the nose, but the doll was in good condition.

"Nice," she said, noting the spring joints and maneuverability of the parts before she carefully returned the doll to the desk. She glanced up and saw Larry studying her. She looked away. His eye spasms seemed worse than she remembered. "I better find Nina," she said.

The shop was empty when Larry and Gretchen joined Julia in the studio. Nina was nowhere in sight. Julia stood like a guard dog at the front door, blowing loudly into a tissue.

"She takes that animal everywhere she goes," Julia complained. "I know she's your aunt, Gretchen, but others don't appreciate Tutu as much as Nina does. She's waiting outside for you." Julia fanned her face with her hand. "Martha's suicide has taken quite a toll on me. What a terrible tragedy."

"Martha's entire life was a tragedy," Larry said. A hardness edged in his jaw. "She turned into a bitter, pathetic drunk. She used to come into the shop, but she scared away business with her alcoholic theatrics. Julia eventually threw her out." Larry pulled the plug on the Open sign in the window. "I'll stop by in the morning. Maybe something in your mother's workshop will give us some idea where she went. What about her customers?"

"To tell you the truth, I haven't answered her business line. Anyone calling about repairs will get her machine."

"We'll figure it out," he said. Julia nodded and kissed her on the cheek, and Gretchen walked slowly into the parking lot, where Nina waited in the coolness of the running car.

"What an absolutely horrible woman Julia is," Nina said. "And did you see that face problem Larry has? Your great grandmother had one of those tics, and it got worse when she was tired or excited or under a lot of pressure. Poor Larry has to be constantly stressed living with that woman. His eye was blinking like one of those airplane warning lights on top of a cell tower."

Gretchen struggled to stay awake on the ride home, not even caring that she shared her seat with Tutu. When she was dropped off in her mother's driveway, she muttered good night and stumbled inside. She fumbled for the light switch and saw Wobbles peeking at her from the laundry room.

"Bedtime," she said to him, too exhausted to think anymore. She shed her clothes and collapsed into her mother's bed. The last thing she remembered before falling into a dreamless sleep was Wobbles snuggling up to her bare feet, purring loudly.

Caroline wanted to use a credit card, but she couldn't take the risk. She hunted through her purse and found a twenty dollar bill folded inside a side zipper. She added it to the bills in her wallet. Sixty-six dollars left after paying cash for her airfare. Not nearly enough to rent a hotel room for the night and still have enough for a cab and a meal tomorrow. Three credit cards, all useless to her, but invaluable to a pursuer if she was foolish enough to charge anything.

This wouldn't be the first time she'd slept in an airport terminal. Once, on a Midwestern flight, a blizzard had shut down flights and stranded her overnight.

Caroline bought a Chicago-style hot dog from a kiosk and devoured it while she searched for a quiet, unused gate to spend the night.

At precisely ten o'clock her cell phone played Pachelbel's Canon, and she answered after checking the caller ID. Calls from her sister and her daughter had gone unanswered all day, but she took this one.

Caroline listened, and what she heard caused her to reel. She felt weak with shock. It couldn't be possible. What was her daughter doing in Phoenix? Was it a calculated trick to lure her back? No. She sensed Nina's hand in this turn of events, and she mentally chastised herself for failing to anticipate her sister's response to her disappearance. Caroline's lack of foresight would get someone else killed if she wasn't more careful.

"Get her out of there," she said into the phone. "Whatever it takes, get her out of the way before something happens to her."

The doll was more important now than ever. Tomorrow she would find it, even if she had to resort to drastic measures.

· 5 ·

What makes one doll more valuable than another? Top prices are paid for swivel-head dolls created between the 1860s and the early 1900s by famous dollmakers such as Bru, Jumeau, and Kestner. Collectors look for European dolls with swivel heads made from an unglazed porcelain called bisque. Add a kid-leather body and original wardrobe, and the value climbs significantly.

Closed-mouth dolls are worth twice as much as open-mouthed dolls.

—From World of Dolls *by Caroline Birch*

The man standing at her mother's front door wore khaki cargo shorts and a "Running Strong for American Indian Youth" T-shirt. Poking her head through the partially open door and hiding behind it in cotton boxer shorts and a skimpy camisole, she did a quick mental check of her appearance: no makeup, hair in its usual early morning tangle, sleep lines probably creasing her face. Perfect. Great start to the day.

Gretchen had to squint in the radiant light shining from his smile. She shaded her eyes with her hand and caught a whiff of Chrome cologne, one of her favorites.

"Yes?" Gretchen produced a weak smile.

He flipped a badge and held it close to her face. Her tentative smile faded.

"Detective Albright," he said. "I'm looking for Caroline Birch."

"You're Bonnie Albright's son. Matt."

He flashed another dazzling smile. "And you must be Gretchen Birch from Boston."

"News travels fast." Gretchen raked her fingers through her unruly hair. "Did my watch stop?"

"No, it's six."

"Six o'clock on Saturday morning?"

"Correct."

Gretchen edged further behind the door. "Seems a little early for official business. My mother isn't home right now."

"I've heard that news, too," he said. "I was hoping it was a rumor."

"You aren't what I expected." Gretchen imagined his mother. Bonnie of the red flip hairdo and uneven penciled eyebrows. The man looming on the other side of the door had dark wavy hair and a body builder's biceps. He must take after his father.

"What did you expect? Bald and beastly?"

"Where's your uniform?"

"I'm undercover." His eyes slid past her head. "Can I come in?"

"I don't think so." She wedged a bare foot against the door. "Do you have a search warrant?"

He grinned. "Do you have something to hide?"

His smile was disarmingly charming, but Gretchen felt sure that he was acting. She had an overwhelming urge to protect her mother. The role reversal seemed awkward and unnatural. Her mother had always been *her* shield against potential danger.

"Look," he continued, sliding his badge into his wallet. "I'm investigating a death, and your mother's name came up. This is all very routine. If she didn't do anything wrong, you have nothing to hide."

Gretchen hated logic, especially from a cop. "Who said I have anything to hide?"

"You did."

"I did not." *See how a cop will twist your words until you don't recognize them anymore,* Gretchen thought, glancing past his shoulder and watching a neighbor walk her dog past the house. Six A.M. Didn't these people sleep in on Saturdays? She lowered her eyes and met his gaze. Neither one of them flinched or looked away.

"If you know where she is, you should tell me," he said. "I'm trying to help. She's one of my mother's friends."

Gretchen carefully considered the possible reasons why he would be searching for her mother. She thought she detected a hard, determined glint behind the detective's sunshine eyes. After the note found with Martha's body, the police would want an explanation, and Gretchen wasn't sure her mother had one.

"Come back when you have a warrant," she finally said and closed the door. A few minutes later she heard his car drive off.

Wobbles was talkative, meowing and rubbing against her leg. Gretchen poured cat food and water into two bowls she found in the cupboard, made a piece of toast, and started a pot of coffee. She ate the toast while she waited for the coffee to perk, then poured a steaming cup and called Nina.

"What time is it?" Nina's husky voice sounded thick with sleep. *Payback time,* Gretchen thought.

"After six. I need to borrow your car today." Gretchen sipped the fragrant coffee and felt it coursing through her body, rejuvenating her spirit in spite of her early morning visitor. "I'd like to do a little shopping. I brought only a small amount of cat food with me, and there isn't much people food in the house either."

"Six in the morning?"

"You can go back to sleep in a minute, but I need your car later."

"We're having our hair done at eleven," Nina said, yawning. "You can drop us at the salon. That will give you a few hours."

"We?"

"Tutu and I."

Gretchen choked back a chortle, but a small titter slipped out. Nina could make her laugh even in the most trying situations.

"Go ahead," Nina said. "Laugh all you want."

The light moment passed, and Gretchen related the conversation she had with Matt Albright. When she paused, Nina asked, "Did you tell him about the doll shawl and photograph you found on the mountain?"

"I didn't even think of it. I was more concerned about why he was here."

"That's good," Nina said. "He doesn't need to know right now."

"Is the shawl still in your car?"

"Still wrapped up and stowed away," Nina said. "I've been thinking this through. According to April, the French fashion doll is worth a lot of money on its own, but it's worth twice as much with the trunk. If we can find them, we might have our answer to Caroline's whereabouts. I'm still convinced that Martha didn't jump willingly, and Detective Albright snooping around means that the police aren't so sure either. I'll give Bonnie a call and find out if she knows anything more."

Gretchen poured another cup of coffee. "Remind April to keep the news of the trunk to herself, at least for a few days."

"April keeps everything close to her chest."

There was a discernible pause. Nina broke the silence. "This doesn't look good for your mother. You know that, don't you? What if she has the doll? What if she's involved in something dangerous?"

Or deadly. Gretchen couldn't express the thought aloud. Her emotional strength came from believing that Caroline would reappear and explain her absence. That Martha had committed suicide. That there was a logical explanation in spite of Gretchen's growing sense of distress.

After finalizing plans to borrow Nina's car, Gretchen changed into shorts and a tank top and pulled on her hiking boots for a brisk walk up Camelback. She again checked for messages on her answering machine in Boston and on her cell phone. Other than a few greetings from friends, she found nothing from Steve or her mother.

Sliding open the glass patio door leading to the pool, Gretchen was surprised to find the door unlocked. She must have forgotten to lock it yesterday before she left with Nina. She scolded herself for her carelessness.

The morning temperature was tolerable, and Gretchen wondered if she was already acclimating to the harsh desert summer. She loped easily up to the trailhead and slowed to a steady jog, appreciating the sanctuary around her.

Gretchen had learned long ago that the natural world could bring her needed serenity when her thoughts were troubled, and hiking trails had provided the perfect solution. In the area around Boston she had discovered the Blue Hills and Skyline Trail, then Middlesex Fells. After that, she delighted in every quest to find interesting and unique paths to explore.

Even in the center of a densely populated city like Phoenix, she could find refuge.

Summit Trail reminded her of Martha's fall, so she stayed on more accessible paths, jogging along Bobby's Rock Trail. Mesquite and staghorn lined the path. She heard the chatter of birds, and catching movement from the corner of her eye, she spotted a roadrunner on an old, overgrown trail.

As she ran she felt all her worries and anxiety falling away on the path behind her. After the refreshing and mind-clearing exercise she would be ready to face the uncertainty of a new day.

When she returned to the house, Larry Gerney was waiting in his red convertible in the shade of a blue palo verde tree. He unfolded his long legs from the tiny car and greeted her with a paper bag in his hand. "Thought I'd

bring breakfast," he said, following her into the kitchen. He
didn't remove his sunglasses, which saved her the effort of
pretending that she didn't notice his tic. "Have you heard
anything yet?"

Gretchen shook her head and poured a cup of coffee for
each of them. Larry sliced bagels and heaped them with
cream cheese, smoked salmon, and alfalfa sprouts. Wobbles, smelling the salmon, joined them and was rewarded
with a slice of his own.

"I never saw a cat with three legs before," Larry said.
"But he seems to get around fine."

"He's amazing," Gretchen agreed. She nibbled at the
bagel. It tasted wonderful.

"I think we should check your mother's business line
and listen to her messages." Larry wrapped the leftovers
and stored them in the refrigerator.

Of course, he would want to check her messages. Was
his request a sincere offer of help or a devious way to gain
a client list? She studied his features, hoping for a clue to
his motives. Reluctantly, she nodded and led the way.

Gretchen experienced a sense of loss when she entered
her mother's workshop, the same sense of emptiness she
had felt the day before. *It is so easy to forget how much you
love someone,* she thought, *until you realize that you might
lose them.*

Gretchen and Larry listened to twelve messages, each
caller inquiring about the progress on various doll repairs.
Several expressed concern about their dolls being ready at
a specific time, and all wanted return phone calls. None
gave Gretchen the impression they knew that Caroline was
unavailable.

"This is hopeless," Gretchen said. "What am I going
to do?"

Gretchen hadn't worked on a doll since college, when
she'd spent summers in her mother's workshop performing
the simpler repairs. She could disassemble, clean, and re-
string an antique doll, but her mother was the expert when

it came to restoring eyes, refurbishing wigs, and sealing cracks. Not only did Gretchen lack the expertise to satisfy these customers, she didn't have the time.

"You are going to let me handle it," Larry said firmly. "I'll work on the most immediate problems and delay the rest."

Gretchen wondered what her mother would say if she knew her competition had access to her workshop, but his offer would free her mind and would keep the customers happy. If he ended up stealing customers, it was a small price to pay. "I couldn't possibly impose . . ."

"This won't be entirely free," he said, clinching the deal. "I'll expect to be paid for my services."

Larry was returning phone calls before Gretchen left the room. She showered and dressed, and looked around for her mother's cancer awareness bracelet. She found it on top of the dresser and frowned. Hadn't she placed it in the bathroom next to her own last night? Well, she had been exhausted and under pressure yesterday. Gretchen slid her mother's bracelet on her wrist next to her own bracelet, vowing to wear it until she personally handed it back to its owner.

The doorbell rang as she finished, and she opened it to see Matt Albright standing on the porch with two uniformed police officers behind him. "Search warrant," he said, waving a document and handing it to her.

"That was fast." *Bravado, Gretchen. Face your adversary with confidence.*

"I had it earlier, but I decided that I needed backup. You looked scary."

"Is that what they taught you in detective school? How to be as annoying as possible?"

Gretchen examined the warrant. Her words were light, but she swallowed through an enormous lump in her throat. She felt sure that they wouldn't find anything incriminating in their search, because her mother hadn't done anything wrong.

"May I ask what you are looking for?"

Matt slid past her and gestured to the officers to follow
him. "You may, but I can't tell you. Where does your
mother repair dolls?"

"Through there." Gretchen pointed to the back of the
house, and her uninvited guests thundered off in that direction. She walked into the kitchen and sat down hard, her
heart skipping.

From her vantage point in the kitchen she saw the two
cops stride into the workshop, the detective watching them
from the hallway. Gretchen heard Larry's voice, questioning and bewildered. Then he joined her in the kitchen.

"What's going on?" he asked. "They're tearing everything apart."

Gretchen shrugged and shook her head. "I don't know."
She slumped deeper into the chair and waited. Larry paced
in front of her.

Fifteen minutes later, Detective Albright entered the
room, and Gretchen noticed that he'd lost his authoritative
pose. Instead, he was several shades paler than earlier. The
officer behind him held an antique doll in one latex-gloved
hand and a sheet of paper in the other. "Put them on the
table," the detective said to the cop. "Check the bedrooms
next."

"You're going to search the entire house?" Gretchen
knew something was seriously awry when she saw the doll
on the table.

"It's covered in the warrant," he answered, a professional tone in his voice much different from the casual
banter of earlier. More abrupt. "Do you know anything
about these?"

He motioned to the doll on the table and took a step
back, and Gretchen reached to pick it up.

"Don't touch that," he bellowed. Gretchen jerked her
hand away.

Gretchen, hands in her lap and a sick feeling in her stomach, leaned forward to observe the doll. It was an excellent

white-faced parian, sixteen inches high, with a beige dress and leather shoes. "My mother restores dolls professionally," she said. "She has many dolls in her care."

"How about the document?"

Gretchen stood up and leaned forward to scrutinize the paper, while Larry read over her shoulder. Its contents shocked her. "It's ah . . . it looks like an inventory of Martha Williams's doll collection. At least that's what it says."

"And this," Detective Albright said, pointing to the doll, "is one of the dolls on that list. We found the doll and list buried together deep in a supply cabinet. The clothing on the doll matches the description. Don't you agree?"

"But Martha Williams lost her doll collection years ago. At least that's what Nina said."

Larry pulled off his sunglasses and blinked rapidly, "That's right. She didn't have a single doll. She lived on the street. The inventory is clearly an old, invalid list."

The detective's shiny smile was missing. "How much is this doll worth?"

"We aren't appraisers," Gretchen said, coldly, understanding the implications of the question.

"April Lehman will answer that for me," Detective Albright said.

"You can't take the doll," Gretchen insisted.

"Oh, but I can." The detective suddenly noticed Larry squinting and blinking. "Something in your eye?"

"No," Larry said. "A nervous twitch. It comes and goes." He put the sunglasses back on.

Gretchen again surveyed the list of dolls. It was an impressive inventory of antiques, although not particularly large for a serious collector. Poured wax dolls, bisque dolls, wooden dolls, china dolls. Each, she guessed, worth a dollar figure well into the thousands.

The parian doll found in the cabinet matched the one on the list. But Gretchen didn't find an entry for a French fashion doll.

And no doll trunk.

"I'd like a copy of this list," Gretchen said. "And a picture of the doll before you take it."

Detective Albright nodded and stepped away, clasping his hands behind his back. "That's a reasonable request." He motioned to one of the officers. "I noticed a copy machine attached to the computer printer in the workshop," he said as the officer approached. "Get a copy, and be careful."

Gretchen looked at the doll on the table, then at the detective. She watched a thin line of moisture gather above the detective's brow as the other officer moved past him, snapped a picture, and took the doll. In fact, Albright flattened against the wall, allowing the officer more room to maneuver than he actually needed.

The officers found nothing else out of the ordinary. The rest of the search seemed perfunctory and ended abruptly, as though the parian doll and the inventory list had been the true purpose of their mission all along.

An obsolete inventory of dolls and the discovery of a doll that had once belonged to a dead collector. What was going on?

Caroline awoke stiff. Her muscles ached from lying on the hard seats in the passenger waiting area of gate C79. A flight attendant stood behind a counter nearby and readied the gate for an early morning flight. The flight board read Orlando, 6:35 A.M., On Time. Travelers lugging carry-on bags began to arrive.

Caroline sat up and stretched her cramped limbs. She made her way to the women's restroom, where she attempted to freshen up. She bought a sweet roll and hot tea from a vendor, grudgingly parting with a few dollar bills.

She hurried out of the main terminal, searching among the throng of transportation vehicles. She didn't notice the overcast sky and the drops of rain splattering around her.

She stepped solidly into the center of a large puddle as she boarded a shuttle for downtown Chicago, immersed in her own thoughts.

It was now or never. Time for action. She would see the doll today, one way or another.

Whatever it took.

· 6 ·

The wise collector has an extensive inventory list of the most significant dolls in the collection. A complete description would include the doll's maker, height in inches, body construction, overall condition, costume details, and type and color of wig, eyes, and mouth. This list should be stored with the collector's will or other important legal documents to aid an appraiser in evaluating the collection's value. Pictures of each doll are another priceless asset that the collector will never regret taking the time to include.

—From *World of Dolls* by Caroline Birch

Nina teetered on the edge of hysteria. She stomped back and forth on the Mexican tile that bordered Caroline's swimming pool and had come precariously close to tipping into it on her last turn. Tutu followed on her heels, and Gretchen suspected that the latest dog trainee in the poodle-embroidered purse on her shoulder would soon succumb to motion sickness.

"Nothing makes sense anymore." Nina continued her frenzied pacing. "Something's happened to your mother. I can feel it."

"She isn't dead," Gretchen said, finally broaching the inevitable subject.

Nina, her lower lip trembling, whirled. "We don't know that."

"Yes, we do. I searched the mountain and didn't find her. No one has discovered her body."

"She could have been murdered, too," Nina cried. "And her body . . ."

"No, she's alive and hiding," Gretchen said firmly.

"I refuse to believe that my sister killed Martha Williams. And what do the police think? That she killed Martha for a doll?" Nina snorted. "Please. They need to come up with a better motive than that."

"We need to find her and the French fashion doll."

"All these different dolls are confusing me. The Parisian doll and the French doll. Aren't they the same thing?"

"Parian, not Parisian. Parian refers to the type of finish given to the porcelain. A parian's face is white. Tell me what happened to Martha's doll collection. Where is it?"

Nina, the dramatist, flung her arms out wide, then bent and slapped them on her thighs, causing the purse trainee to duck inside for cover. "Martha wouldn't tell us. April Lehman even offered to buy several dolls from her collection at fair market prices. In fact, they had a little falling-out over that. Martha refused to sell until it was too late, and I think the bank auctioned them off with the rest of her possessions, including the house. She really did lose everything."

Gretchen watched the black pup venture to poke its curly head out of the purse, its ears flattened against its head.

"Give the little curly mutt a break, Nina. It's going to upchuck in the purse."

Nina gasped. "This isn't a mutt. He's a teacup poodle."

She released the tiny poodle. It shook its body and ran off around the pool with Tutu. At ten pounds Tutu towered monumentally over the puppy. "Nimrod will be with me for the next two days. His owner is out of town, and he's in immersion training. He loves his purse already."

Gretchen sat down on the edge of the pool and slid one bare foot along the surface. "I couldn't find a work order for the doll the police confiscated," she said. Her mother kept pink copies of all her work orders in the top drawer of the workbench. "The records aren't well-organized, though."

"Your mother is rather disorganized. That doesn't mean much." Nina glanced at her watch. "It's almost eleven. We'll miss our hair appointment if we don't leave right now. Tutu. Nimrod. Let's go."

Nina packed up her entourage while Gretchen checked on Wobbles, who had disappeared during the search but reappeared briefly to voice his objections to the intrusion as soon as the police left. She found him curled in a ball in the center of her mother's bed, sound asleep.

She carefully secured the house, not about to forget to lock up again.

Nina headed for Scottsdale Road, zipping through traffic, making up for lost time. "I should cancel my hair appointment and help you. After all, I'm the one who insisted that you come to Phoenix."

"It's absolutely fine," Gretchen assured her, wanting some personal space to consider the problem on her own. "You can help me this afternoon."

"Matt Albright has a dreadful fear of dolls," Nina said, swerving into another lane. "There's even a name for it—pediophobia."

"That explains why he backed away whenever someone approached with the doll." Gretchen remembered his discomfort. "And that explains why he wouldn't enter the workshop."

"Bonnie had to keep all her dolls in a spare bedroom with the door closed." Nina screeched to a halt at a red light and turned to check on the dogs in the backseat, making sure no one had fallen forward.

"It started when he was a young boy. Every time he saw one of her dolls, he'd feel faint and nauseous," Nina continued. "He had trouble breathing and broke out in a sweat. I saw it happen once, and it was awful. We could never have meetings at her house. And she's the president of the club."

Gretchen suddenly thought of the French fashion doll's shawl in Nina's trunk. "It's a good thing you have the shawl. What if the police had found it at the house?"

"A little piece of fabric? It wouldn't have meant a thing to them," Nina said. "Besides, you said the Bru and the trunk weren't on the list."

"Which makes it more puzzling. We have to find out why she had doll accessories and the picture with her when she died."

Nina brought the car to a stop under a sign reading Scottsdale Solutions and opened the car door. "You have at least two hours, maybe three. I'll call you on your cell when we are almost finished. Can I leave Nimrod with you?"

Gretchen reluctantly looked at the miniature black fur ball sitting in the backseat. Hearing his name, Nimrod tipped his head to the side and took a step forward, wagging his tail. Gretchen looked doubtful as she walked around to the driver's side of the car and slipped in.

"I wee-weed him before we left your mother's house," Nina said, as if that would make all the difference.

"I'd rather not," Gretchen said, attempting a firm *no*, but barely managing the watered-down version that always begged a challenge.

"He won't be a bother," Nina insisted, clipping a leash on Tutu's collar and standing aside while the canine jumped to the ground. "Oh, I almost forgot to leave you his poodle purse."

Wouldn't that be a serious fashion faux pas? Gretchen thought. *A dog without his purse.*

Nina tugged the dog purse from her shoulder and quickly threw it on Gretchen's lap. "Have fun."

Gretchen and Nimrod pulled away and turned toward the center of the city of Phoenix, situated on the opposite side of Camelback Mountain. Three hours didn't give her much time. She drove to the older part of downtown, west of Central Avenue, and slowly cruised up and down each street, moving to First Avenue then Second Avenue in a quest to find the homeless man.

Her encounter with him on the street in front of the restaurant wasn't chance, and Gretchen didn't think he was a ranting madman. She was convinced that he had a compelling reason to threaten her, and she needed to know why.

The midday heat had driven most of the homeless to seek shelter from the sun, but a few directionless people wandered the sidewalks. She weaved through the endless lines of cars. Phoenix traffic was perpetually in gridlock every hour of the day including late evening rush hour.

Gretchen didn't see the man.

After several passes, she eased to the curb, reached in the backseat, and lifted Nimrod into the front seat. His tiny feet spun in anticipation, and once she opened the purse he lunged eagerly inside.

"You're an old pro at this, aren't you," she said, adjusting dog and purse on her shoulder.

She walked along First Avenue, Nimrod peeking out from the safety of his mobile home. He felt weightless on her shoulder. The noon sun scorched the pavement. Gretchen made an effort to stay in the shadows of the buildings, but they offered little comfort from the oppressive heat.

A woman walked slowly toward her, pushing a shopping cart piled with clothes and a variety of personal treasures most people would have discarded. Gretchen had read somewhere that women were the fastest-growing segment of the homeless population. A sad statement.

Gretchen heard the woman mutter as she neared.

"Excuse me," Gretchen said. "Can you help me?"

The woman stopped and stared at Gretchen with suspicion until her gaze shifted to the purse. She saw Nimrod and visibly softened.

"I'm looking for someone," Gretchen said.

"Nice doggy." The woman reached out with dirty hands and ragged fingernails to stroke Nimrod, and Gretchen willed herself not to flinch or pull the purse away. Nimrod sniffed curiously and allowed her to pat his little head.

"I'm looking for a man with a growth on the side of his head," Gretchen said. "It's important that I find him."

"I'm Daisy," the woman said, not looking up from Nimrod, stroking his curly black fur. "Have you come to see me? I've been waiting years to be discovered. I'll be famous, you know, very soon."

"I'm sure you will. But today I'm looking for someone else."

Daisy sighed. "Always someone else. I'm always passed over. Too short for the part, they say, or too tall. Always wrong for the casting." She gave Nimrod a final pat, hung her head, and began pushing her cart.

"Do you know the man?" Gretchen followed, walking in step with her. "I don't know how else to describe him. The lump on his head is sizable. Do you know him?"

"Nacho," Daisy muttered. "Macho Nacho. What's the doggy's name?"

"Nimrod."

"Ah, the mighty hunter."

Gretchen felt frustrated. The woman's delusions must have been caused by mental illness or by the infernal, suffocating desert heat. The weight of the sun burned down on Gretchen as she slowed her steps and fell behind Daisy, soon coming to a complete stop. Nimrod waited patiently at her side as they watched the homeless woman walk away, pushing her cart.

"His name is Nacho," Daisy called loudly without looking back.

Gretchen ran to catch up, forgetting about the heat. "Where can I find him?"

"You look like a nice lady. Can you spare a dollar?"

Gretchen moved Nimrod to her other shoulder and fished a five dollar bill out of her purse.

"A fiver is just right. High-five," Daisy exclaimed.

She extended her open palm, and Gretchen hesitantly

followed her lead. Daisy slapped their hands together briskly. "He sleeps some nights at the Rescue Mission. Later today he'll eat at St. Anskar's Parish. The soup kitchen opens at five. You can find him there."

Maybe Gretchen had misjudged her mental capabilities.

She thanked Daisy for the information and hurried back to the car.

Nimrod woofed from the purse, reminding her abruptly that she had a purse dog to worry about as well as her mother.

Gretchen stopped at a grocery store to stock up on a few days' worth of supplies and was relieved that Nimrod slept at the bottom of the purse while she shopped. She doubted that a food store would welcome a teacup poodle.

Gretchen arrived at the hair salon in time to escort the freshly shampooed duo. Nina and Tutu wore identical candy-striped bows in their hair.

After Nina reclaimed her position in the driver's seat, Gretchen related her meeting with Daisy. "You never said you were looking for that homeless man," Nina whined. "I would have liked to come along."

"Would you like to go to St. Anskar's Parish with me later to look for him?" Gretchen's offered consolation prize would serve her own interests, too. She needed transportation.

"Of course," Nina said, perking up.

"In the meantime, let's call Gertie. Maybe my mother went to Michigan to visit."

Gertie Johnson, her father's sister, lived in the Michigan Upper Peninsula. She wasn't related by blood to Nina or Caroline, a fact Nina pointed out every time she heard another story about the aunt-in-law's antics. Gertie had named all three of her children for horses: Blaze, Star, and Heather. Because Blaze was the local sheriff, Gertie fancied herself an expert on police procedure and investigative technique.

"That aunt of yours causes nothing but trouble," Nina said, watching the road with one eye while Gretchen punched in numbers on her cell phone. "She's an odd duck, if you ask me."

Nina and Gertie are exactly alike, Gretchen thought. *Quirky, flamboyant, and always right. That's why they don't get along.*

"Haven't seen her," Gertie said after exchanging the briefest of pleasantries.

Gretchen explained the events of the last few days, and when she finished, Gertie whistled. "That's complicated," she said. "Have they issued a warrant for Caroline yet?"

"No, of course not. She didn't kill Martha."

"Bet my shorts they'll arrest her anyway."

Gretchen shuddered. The thought had crossed her mind as well.

"The answer," Gertie continued. "Is always right under your nose."

Gretchen looked down at Nimrod, who rode on her lap and had a contented smile on his face. At the moment, he was the only thing right under her nose.

She heard a distinctive sniff from the backseat where Tutu rode solo.

"Gretchen, are you listening to me?"

"Yes. But I'm confused."

"Pay attention to everything that's happening around you; watch people's reactions. Add everything up, and remember that nothing unusual that happens will be a coincidence. Trust your instincts."

Gretchen smiled. That's exactly what Nina always said.

"And find the dead woman's bag of clothes."

Gretchen was startled. "What bag of clothes?"

"You said she was homeless, so she doesn't have a home you can search for clues. Normally I'd advise you to break in and have a look around. But this isn't a normal situation. She must have had a few personal things. Where are they, and what are they?"

Gretchen thought about Nacho's garbage bag and Daisy's shopping cart. Even though Martha lost all her worldly possessions, she may have collected personal odds and ends since then.

"I'll check it out. Thanks, Aunt Gertie."

"Have you seen your Aunt Nina lately?" Gertie asked. "That's one goofball. Is she still baby-talking to that spoiled dog of hers and carrying silly miniature dogs in her handbag?"

"Aunt Gert says hi," Gretchen said after disconnecting.

"I heard the whole thing," Nina said, indignant. "The woman's voice carries like a bad virus.

The shuttle squealed to a halt on Michigan Avenue, and Caroline joined the crowd of travelers surging to the sidewalk. The drops of rain had turned into a windy squall but subsided as quickly as it came, and Caroline was grateful for the reprieve. She walked briskly away, ducked under a breezeway, and cut into a department store entryway. Clutching her laptop securely to her, she waited against the wall. No one appeared to be following.

Good. She had taken too many precautions to lose now. They would find her car soon, if they hadn't already. The car, parked far from the Phoenix airport, would buy her more time. Time. Everything depended on her speed and perfect, exquisite timing. She considered calling her sister, but Nina could be unpredictable. A wild card in this game of skill could upset her lead. No. Nina had done enough damage by bringing her daughter to Phoenix.

Thinking of Gretchen drove her back onto the wet sidewalk, and she turned away from Lake Michigan and headed in the direction that would lead her to the doll. The Chicago air hung thick and humid in spite of dark clouds spinning overhead.

She steeled herself for the long walk ahead.

7

*Although an imprint is not always a foolproof indication of au-
thenticity, many antique dolls were marked with a letter or
number to identify the maker and country where the doll origi-
nated. These identifying symbols were incised on the back of the
head, under the wig, or on the back of the shoulder. The early
Bru doll bore a circle and dot on the back of the neck.*

—From *World of Dolls* by Caroline Birch

"No," Nina said, hanging up. "Bonnie says the only thing
Martha had in her possession when she died was the parasol,
the note, and the clothes on her body. And she knows that for
certain, because she identified Martha for the police."

"Okay, we have a starting point. We have to find out
where Martha kept her belongings, if she had any, and we
have to find the man who threatened me." Gretchen said,
watching Nina select two of her mother's Shirley Temple
dolls from a cabinet and arrange them on a bench next to
the front door. She fluffed their costumes and carefully
placed them in position.

"Do you think it's wise to approach someone who recently threatened you?" Nina stood back and admired her
handiwork.

"Do I have a choice?" Gretchen responded. "If you have
a better idea, please share it."

Wobbles made a brief appearance but stalked away
when he spotted Nimrod and Tutu. If he was developing a
friendship with the dogs, Gretchen couldn't detect it.

"What are you doing?" Gretchen asked, staring at the dolls.

"Preparing in case Bonnie's son shows up here again. Detective Albright is in for a little surprise. No more hiding while his backup crew does his dirty work for him. With these dolls as sentinels, he won't dare step foot in here again."

"Like gargoyles? They'll scare him away?"

"Exactly." She rubbed her hands together and checked the watch on her wrist. "Heavens! It's two o'clock. We missed lunch, and I'm starving. Let's see what we can come up with. Come, Tutu and Nimrod, for a leg stretch on the patio."

They bolted off, and Nina returned while Gretchen poked in the refrigerator and pulled out the leftovers from Larry's visit that morning. Nina sliced a papaya. They made bagel sandwiches and a pot of herbal tea and ate in silence.

When Gretchen let the dogs back in the house, she saw that Nimrod was soaking wet. "Nimrod fell in the pool," she called to Nina.

"Oh, no. I forget that poodles are water dogs." Nina thumped her head in exasperation. "I bet he jumped right in. Now I'll have to have him groomed before he goes home."

After towel-drying Nimrod and complaining about the stench of chlorine and other pool chemicals, Nina set off with the promise to return in a few hours for the trip to the Phoenix Rescue Mission. Gretchen checked the answering machine after she noticed its red light flashing. "I'm making progress on these repairs." Larry's voice boomed through the room. "If Caroline turns up, give me a call. Otherwise, I'll keep at it."

Gretchen was grateful for Larry's help, whatever his underlying motives might be. Meeting deadlines was an important part of restoration. Again she went through the motions of checking for messages at her apartment in

Boston, but the effort felt mechanical and wasted. Whatever her mother was up to, it didn't include confiding in her family members.

She changed into her swimming suit and lowered her body slowly into the blue, sparkling water. Wobbles, a true sun lover, basked contentedly on a lounge chair. He lifted his head to the sun's rays with dreamy eyes, and Gretchen envied his relaxed, worry-free existence.

She thought about Steve and their future together. She had lost her job permanently and her mother temporarily, and now she had to face Steve's lack of commitment to her. He didn't seem particularly interested in the events that sent her to Phoenix or the details associated with her mother's disappearance.

For the first time in seven years, she realized that he marginalized her, that he thought his concerns and worries and actions were more important than hers.

If she didn't call him, how long would it take him to call her? Interesting, she thought, to conduct a test.

The doorbell rang, interrupting her calculated decision to outwait Steve. She stepped from the pool, wrapped a beach towel around her waist, and padded through the house, trailing chlorinated water. Matt Albright stood on the porch.

"Come in, Detective," Gretchen said, swinging the door wide after passing the two Shirley Temple dolls. Nina and her pranks. But he deserved it after his cold, callous handling of the search and his false friendliness.

He seemed surprised at Gretchen's warm greeting, took a step forward, and smiled. Once again Gretchen admired the way his face lit up. "I caught you in the pool," he said. "And call me Matt. Our mothers are good friends. No need to be so formal."

When he saw the dolls on the bench, the smile slid from his face, and he stopped in his tracks.

"What's wrong?" Gretchen said with mock concern. "Are you ill? You look feverish." He *did* look pale and slightly unsteady. Panic flickered in his eyes.

How could a buffed-up cop exhibit such fear over a harmless doll? Nina's trick didn't seem so funny after all, and Gretchen felt mean-spirited for going along with it.

"Give me a second," she said, snatching the dolls and quickly transferring them to a shelf in the closet. "Would you like some iced tea?"

He nodded wordlessly and followed her into the kitchen. Gretchen poured two tall glasses. "Lemon?" He nodded again.

Gretchen handed him a glass and led the way to the patio, choosing a table under a wide umbrella. She fluffed her damp hair and sat down, still wearing the towel around her waist. The sun sizzled overhead, instantly sucking the moisture from her skin. The swim a few minutes ago seemed like a distant memory as her body temperature climbed.

Before sitting down next to Gretchen, the detective stopped to stroke Wobbles, running his hand over the cat's long body several times. *At least he doesn't have some feline phobia,* she thought.

"You probably will regret offering me iced tea when you find out why I'm here," he said.

"Try me."

"We've issued a warrant for your mother's arrest," he said. "We want her for questioning in the death of Martha Williams."

"Quit beating around the bush," Gretchen said with exaggerated sarcasm. "Get right to the point. All this small talk is killing me."

"I'm sorry. I couldn't think of an easy way to break it to you."

"You're making a big mistake."

"All the signs point to her."

"Expound on that," Gretchen said tightly, working to dredge up some of that Birch inner strength.

Strength. That was something she and her mother knew about. A malignant tumor like Caroline had encountered inspired courage and resolve in the face of adversity.

She twirled her mother's pink bracelet.

"First, we have the note Martha managed to write before she died. That's damaging. We have the first evidence of a motive. Money. That doll from your mother's workshop was worth three thousand dollars. The entire list could be worth a half million dollars or more."

"The entire collection of dolls on the list, perhaps," Gretchen agreed. "You're forgetting that they no longer belonged to Martha when she died. For all we know, the collection was broken up and the dolls sold as individual pieces. One three thousand dollar doll is hardly a motive for murder."

"That remains to be seen." He studied Gretchen. "Your mother also had means. Martha died on that mountain." He pointed up to the peak. "Practically in Caroline Birch's backyard. And where is she when we want to question her? She's disappeared."

"Circumstantial evidence, Detective." Gretchen followed his gaze upward. The red rocks glowed in the sunlight. "I can't believe you got a warrant on those grounds."

He held up his hand, and with his other hand ticked off each point. "She had means—it happened on her home turf." He tapped a finger. "She had a motive—valuable dolls." Tap. "And she's missing—no alibi." Tap.

"She'll explain everything when she comes home," Gretchen insisted.

"We have witnesses," he said, dropping his hands to the table and spreading his fingers wide. "A man and a woman were hiking together on the mountain at the time it happened."

Gretchen felt light-headed. "They saw it? They saw my mother murder Martha Williams?" Her voice climbed several octaves.

He shook his head. "They didn't see Martha fall. But they saw your mother fleeing. She came from the exact spot where Martha Williams was pushed."

"Martha Williams committed suicide," Gretchen said weakly.

"I'm afraid not. Martha Williams was murdered."

Gretchen stared at the mountain blankly. There had to be a logical explanation. All the strength she had summoned threatened to seep away. Two witnesses saw her mother on the mountain when Martha died. She could no longer dismiss his theory as pure speculation. Something awful occurred on Camelback Mountain, and her mother was there at the time. What explanation would she give for running away? Did innocent people run?

"We have an APB out on her car," he continued. "I'm sorry."

Gretchen's gaze met his, and she almost believed that he truly was sorry.

"You have to tell me where she is. She has to come in and clear this up." He leaned closer. "Where is she?"

"I'm afraid I really don't know."

Maybe, Gretchen thought, *it's time to pool our resources and work with the police. To a degree.* She considered sharing the discovery of the doll shawl and photograph with him, but that might only give the police more reason to suspect her mother. It wouldn't help find her, and it wouldn't help exonerate her. The bag Gretchen found must remain her secret until she understood its significance. Until she located the French fashion doll and the trunk, the shawl would stay hidden with Nina.

"She left without telling anyone where she was going. That's why I came to Phoenix. Nina's worried about her."

"You wouldn't withhold information to protect her, would you?"

Gretchen shook her head. "Believe me, I want to find her more than you do. Tell me who appraised the doll you found in the workshop?" April Lehman knew about the doll shawl, and Gretchen hoped she hadn't shared her knowledge with the police.

"An appraiser over in Glendale. April Lehman wasn't available. Seems she left town for a few days."

The detective drained his glass of iced tea and stood.

Gretchen slipped on a pair of flip-flops and walked with him through the backyard gate and around the side of the house. The home's landscaping matched the wildness of the Sonoran Desert and Camelback Mountain: spiked cacti, red-hued boulders, and spindly, whiplike ocotillos that were leafless in dry July but exploded with red blossoms in April.

A chameleon darted across the walkway in front of them.

"Someone threatened me last night," she said, and related the encounter and the words spoken by the homeless man: "Get out while you still can."

"And you think he has something to do with the Williams murder."

Murder. Gretchen cringed at the word.

"Yes," she said. "I think he knows something important. My plan is to find him."

"Well, my plan is to find Caroline Birch." Matt stopped at his car, a nondescript blue Chevrolet with no official markings. "How about this? You keep me informed, and I'll do the same."

"Aren't you going to threaten me with jail if I withhold information? I am, as you recall, the main suspect's daughter."

Matt smiled. "You watch too many cop shows. This isn't a movie. Besides—"

She interrupted him. "I know. Our mothers are friends."

Gretchen sat on a stool in the workshop and imagined her mother bent over a broken doll, in the process of restoring it to its original splendor. A healer. Her mother's lifework brought renewal, not destruction.

From one of the repair bins marked as sale dolls, she selected a grime-coated wax doll with a damaged nose. Once the doll was cleaned and repaired, her mother would take it to a doll show along with boxes of other dolls collected for that purpose.

Sitting in the shop, she felt closer to her mother.

Using light pressure, she began to clean the doll with cold cream, carefully spreading it around the eyes and ears with a Q-tip.

Gretchen smiled to herself. When she was learning the business, her mother had set her up at a table laden with paraffin wax and candles and supplies, and instructed her to experiment. Carve it, she'd said, mold it into shapes, and color it with crayons. Then melt some in a pot and create something entirely new.

It was one of her most memorable adult play days, and when she had finished, she possessed a working knowledge of wax dolls and their care.

This particular doll's nose had worn away. Gretchen reached for a hair dryer hanging from a peg over the bench, turned it on, and blew the hot air on the area until the wax surrounding the worn nose became malleable. Carefully and patiently, she pushed the wax toward the end of the nose until she had created a new one.

She held the doll up and examined her work.

Caroline approached the luxury condominium without a concrete plan of action. Turning off Michigan Avenue, she found the condo units she sought. Complete with indoor parking and spectacular lake views. A uniformed doorman stood at attention inside the glass doors, a buffer between the building's self-proclaimed elite and the commoners from the street below.

Caroline tucked silver strands of hair under her baseball cap. She brushed her hands across her shorts and top, smoothing out wrinkles caused by sleeping in her clothes. Her right hand clutched her laptop. She knew she would never get past the guard.

She entered a series of numbers on her cell phone, and the same woman picked up on the first ring.

"Please," she said, trying to keep the sound of desperation out of her voice. "I realize that Mr. Timms is away, but

if I could only see the doll for a minute. That's all I need."
It was the truth. One of the first truths in this scheme of deception and lies.

Caroline leaned against the side of the high-rise building and closed her eyes.

When she opened them, the security guard had repositioned, moving closer and eyeing her with distrust.

"Mr. Timms called early this morning," the woman said. "I told him you had arrived. His private plane will land within the hour. His trip was successful, allowing him to return earlier than expected. Call again in a few hours."

"Thank you." Caroline disconnected as large raindrops splattered on the walk around her. *Thank you. Thank you.* She trembled in anticipation. A few hours of waiting would feel like several long, agonizing days. She could hear every lost minute ticking away in her mind.

Rain pelted her, and she ran to the other side of the street, protecting her laptop and cursing Chicago's unpredictable weather: damp, humid, dreary.

With any luck she would be out of this city by nightfall.

8

The key to repairing an antique doll head is to make the repair as inconspicuous as possible. The porcelain must be simulated, and the colors must be exact. Quality fillers and sealers are applied, and colors are perfectly matched. Detecting such work is difficult when expertly done. A dishonest dealer might represent a repaired doll as mint and sell it for much more than it is worth. A beginning collector is wise to seek an appraisal before purchasing an expensive doll.

—From *World of Dolls* by Caroline Birch

Nina sat at the kitchen table, her hands covering her face in horror while Gretchen broke the news. Tutu and Nimrod, temporarily forgotten by their caregiver, ran roughshod over the house. Gretchen heard a warning hiss from the bedroom followed by a yelp, and both dogs bolted back into the kitchen. Tutu sported a fresh claw mark on her nose, and Gretchen measured the extent of Nina's anguish by her failure to even notice.

"This is a nightmare," Nina wailed. "Slap me. Wake me up."

Gretchen would have gladly followed Nina's instructions if she thought a slap would help. Wasn't she the one who should be crying on Nina's shoulder, not the other way around? What had happened to her cool, mystical aunt?

"Call Steve," Nina said through broken sobs. "We need a lawyer."

"Steve's a divorce attorney. He won't be able to help us. Matt said the most important thing is to find her and bring her back."

"Matt who?" Nina asked through a space between her fingers.

"Matt Albright, the detective."

"Oh, suddenly he's Matt. What happened to Detective Albright? You're forgetting who the enemy is."

"No, I'm not." Gretchen handed Nina a box of tissues. "He's right. She has to come back and explain what happened. He isn't the enemy. Martha's killer is the enemy."

"What are we going to do?" Nina blew her nose loudly. "Caroline better have something to say for herself. How could she become involved in anything like this?"

"We need to find out who really killed Martha." Gretchen paused to absorb the scope of what she was proposing. "And we need to find out why my mother was on Camelback Mountain. What happened up there?" She chewed the inside of her cheek while she thought about the possibilities.

Nina slammed her hands on the table. "Let's go. I can't stand just sitting here."

She rounded up her dogs, stuffing Nimrod in his purse and bundling Tutu in her arms.

Gretchen nodded. "Let's go find the elusive Nacho."

Nina drove like her life hung in the balance, and Gretchen realized for the first time how close her mother and her aunt really were. She, too, fought against a growing pressure around her own heart, the physical pain of life gone awry. Losing her job seemed insignificant now. Even her issues with Steve seemed petty.

"Slow down," Gretchen called. "We won't be much help to her if we're dead."

"Where did April go?" Nina asked, easing off the gas a little. "April didn't say anything to me about going away."

"It's to our advantage. I didn't tell Matt about the shawl and picture and was worried that she might."

"I think she knows more than she's letting on. Maybe she wants to beat us to the doll. Remember, it was her idea to keep it a secret."

Gretchen gripped the dashboard as Nina took a sharp right turn. "You might be overreacting. April seemed harmless to me."

"She hated Martha. You saw her reaction. She even admitted it. She could be our killer."

Gretchen considered April—enormous, lumbering April. "How could she have climbed up the mountain to push Martha? She can barely manage a porch step."

"You'd be amazed at how limber large people can be when they want to," Nina said, turning onto Thirty-fifth Avenue and continuing past the Phoenix Rescue Mission.

"There it is." Gretchen pointed, and Nina swung over and found a parking space. She left the car running and cool air continued to circulate.

Gretchen and Nina stayed inside the car and looked at the church.

St. Anskar's Parish was set back from the street. Its whitewashed facade gleamed in the sun, and a large gold cross glistened above a small courtyard leading to the massive front doors.

"We're a little early," Gretchen said, impatiently checking her watch.

Fifteen minutes later people began to arrive at the church. Most of them came alone, shuffling slowly down the street, silent and weary from the heat, motivated by the promise of a free meal. Each turned in to the courtyard and followed a walkway that led around the side of the building. Gretchen and Nina watched from the car.

"Should we wait here until he comes by?" Nina asked. "Or go inside?"

"Let's wait here and confront him on the sidewalk," Gretchen said. "We don't know how he will react, and we don't want to create a scene inside. When he comes, I'll get out and stop him." She glanced at the dogs in the backseat. They panted heavily and smeared saliva on the back windows.

Gretchen watched an old man limp past, wearing more clothes than should be bearable.

"Well," Nina said. "I hope he comes along soon, or the car is going to overheat."

Gretchen turned slightly in her seat and peered down the street in the opposite direction. "We're in luck. Here he comes," she said, clutching Nina's arm.

He wore the same clothes he'd worn last night and carried the same black garbage bag tucked under his arm. As he approached, his gaze fell on Nina's red Impala, and he froze in place.

"What . . . ?" Gretchen began, confused by his response. He was reacting to the car as though he knew it. She jumped out when she saw him running away.

"Stay here," she commanded, slamming the car door and breaking into a run. He turned a corner, and she followed. Gretchen's pulse throbbed as she gave pursuit. She was in excellent condition from hiking and jogging and could keep up with almost anyone. But he had a wide lead that she would have to close.

Her eyes were riveted on the man ahead. He glanced back over his shoulder and increased his pace. Gretchen's legs pumped faster.

Nacho cut across the street against the lights. Horns blew. Someone shouted out a warning.

Gretchen's eyes never left the fleeing man as she raced across the street behind him, even though she realized the danger in crossing a busy street. She heard her name called out and instinctively turned her head.

Nina cruised next to her in the Impala with the window down. "Let him go," she called. "It's not worth it."

Gretchen looked ahead just as he left the sidewalk and disappeared between two commercial buildings. Ignoring

Nina, she gave chase. Nacho was the path to her mother, the key to Martha's murder. She felt sure of it. This might be her only chance, and she wasn't about to blow it.

He ran like a desert coyote, like his life depended on it, his arms pumping hard, his eyes, when he glanced back, frightened.

Gretchen remembered the alcohol on his breath the night before and wondered where his stamina came from. Maybe his fear was greater than hers, and his fear drove his momentum. In spite of having nothing material to show for his life, he might have more to lose than she did. If that was possible.

She began to gain on him. Closer and closer. She could hear her breath, usually controlled when she ran distances, pounding in her ears. Now it came out ragged, and she struggled to establish a rhythm. The sweltering heat beating down from the desert sun was unbearable.

He vanished behind another building, and Gretchen rushed after him. Rounding a corner, something shot out at her from a Dumpster against the wall and struck her below her knees. Gretchen felt herself falling. She lurched forward, trying to recover from the fall, but it was too late. She put her hands out in front of her to break the fall and felt a sharp pain in her left wrist as her body slammed into concrete.

Footsteps thundered past her. Then silence.

She struggled to her feet, holding her wrist.

Nacho, her only lead, had vanished.

When Gretchen emerged from between the buildings, Nina jumped from the car and shouted at her. "Are you crazy?" she screamed. "You could have been killed. You didn't know if he had a gun. What were you going to do if you caught him?" She clasped her hands on top of her head. "He could have had a knife and sliced you to pieces."

Gretchen gasped for breath. She bent over and cradled her wrist.

"What happened to you?" Nina said, noticing Gretchen's protective stance.

"Hurt . . . my . . . wrist." An image of Nacho running flashed through Gretchen's head. His long strides. His arm motions assisting him, increasing his speed. The arms were important.

"Let me see." Nina hurried over to her.

Gretchen shook her head. "He . . ." She gasped. ". . . tripped me."

The arms, she thought. *What am I missing?*

She realized what it was. "He dropped the bag."

Nina scowled. "What are you talking about?"

"The garbage bag. He must have thrown it off somewhere along the way." Gretchen straightened up. "Hurry. We have to find it."

Gretchen ran quickly along the sidewalk, retracing her steps. Nina swung the car around and followed. The dogs, sensing a game afoot, watched side by side out the back window. Tutu yelped encouragement, her excitement spurring Nimrod to join in.

When did she notice that he was swinging both arms? After they crossed the intersection but before Nacho ducked between the buildings. She walked to the intersection and studied her surroundings. Sharp pain shot through her wrist, forcing her to support it with her other hand.

Where was Nacho now? Was he watching from a hiding place? She had to beat him to the garbage bag. Gretchen looked up and down the street but didn't see him. She peeked into a trash receptacle on the corner, then motioned to Nina with her head.

"What?" Nina asked, stepping out of the Impala.

"You'll have to grab it," Gretchen said. "He stuffed the bag in here." She gestured with her hands.

"Do I have to?" Nina said, wrinkling her nose.

"Afraid so."

Nina pulled out the black bag with a grimace of disgust and held it away from her body. "Now what?"

"Let's look through it in the car, then I'll return it," Gretchen suggested. "I don't want to take it away from him. It's all he has."

Nina looked at her sharply. "After what he's put you through, how can you sympathize with him? He threatened you. And look at your wrist. An innocent man doesn't run away like he did. And you don't want to take his bag? Unbelievable!"

Nina continued to grumble as they returned to the car, and her protests grew louder when she realized she'd have to search the bag herself. Gretchen's wrist began to swell and turn a deep purple.

The search produced a single change of clothes, not especially clean, and a thick, tattered notebook held together with two rubber bands. At Gretchen's insistence, Nina found a piece of paper and a pen and Gretchen wrote out a message for Nacho with her good right hand, advising him that she had his notebook. She would return it, she wrote, when he was ready to answer her questions. She included her cell phone number.

"I'm holding it hostage," Gretchen said to Nina. "Maybe he's written something useful in it."

Nina stalked over to the garbage receptacle and stuffed the bag inside. "He'll probably murder us in our sleep," she said on returning to the car. "That's how he'll get his notebook back."

Gretchen wondered why he had run away. What had scared him?

Nina pulled away from the curb. "Where to?"

"That gas station on the corner for ice," Gretchen said, wincing. "Then the hospital."

Caroline's eyes traced the arch of the high ceiling, the original paintings on the walls, and the marble floor beneath her feet. She sat on a high-backed tasseled sofa. Rudolph Timms sat across from her in a broad leather chair—tall and slender, with a pronounced widow's peak and dark, piercing eyes.

"I still don't see the fuss over this particular doll," he said.

"As I explained earlier, I'm researching my next book, and I'd like a photograph of the doll you own," Caroline said, her story believable even to her ears. "For the book."

He chuckled, obviously proud of his latest acquisition. "It *is* a perfect Madame Rohmer from the mid–eighteen-hundreds. Original costume and the blue Rohmer stamp on the leather body. Quite a find."

"Glazed china," Caroline muttered. "Swivel head?"

Rudolph Timms nodded. "And blonde wig."

Caroline held up a small Leica camera. "A shot or two would be appreciated." The day before her frantic race across the country, she had dropped off film for developing and tossed the empty camera in her satchel-like purse. It was proving useful today as a prop, with or without film.

His thick brows met the dark widow's peak. "How did you find me so quickly? I only acquired the doll recently."

"I followed the auction on eBay," Caroline said, feeling chilled in her damp clothes. "I considered bidding myself."

"I would have outbid you, no matter the cost," he said. "I had to have this doll for my very own. Whatever the price."

Caroline arched a brow. "Whatever the price?" she repeated.

"Yes," he agreed. "I would have paid whatever it took."

Rudolph Timms rose. "I'll get her."

Caroline held her breath as he walked away.

• 9 •

Antique bisque, china, and parian doll heads were all made from the same type of clay, but different finishes were given to the porcelain. Each doll maker mixed the ingredients in a unique way, and the recipes were fiercely guarded. Parian dolls retained their white porcelain finish, and bisque dolls had flesh-colored tints added to the clay. China dolls were glazed to a high, shiny gloss.

—From *World of Dolls* by Caroline Birch

When Gretchen emerged from Scottsdale Memorial Hospital at a little after seven o'clock with a cast on her broken left wrist, she found Detective Albright leaning against his car at the curb. He sauntered over to join her.

"I'm looking for Aunt Nina," Gretchen said coolly while she scanned the immediate vicinity for the red Impala. "She isn't in the waiting room."

"Your Aunt Nina tried to hide a mutt in her purse, and the emergency room staff didn't appreciate the humor in it," he said.

"Tutu wouldn't fit in her purse," Gretchen said. "That's absurd."

"That's what the staff said."

Matt glanced at her wrist. "Broken, I see."

"I tripped and fell." Gretchen's eyes searched for Nina. She wasn't in any mood to deal with the police, and the quicker she found her ride home, the better. She hoped the painkiller administered by the nurse would kick in soon.

"Your aunt left," he said, his lips twitching in amusement. "I told her I'd wait for you."

"What?" Gretchen couldn't believe her ears. Nina abandoned her? And left her trapped with the cop who wanted to put her mother behind bars? What was Nina thinking?

"I can see by the look on your face that you aren't happy with the arrangement." He walked around the car and opened the passenger door. "My mother is helping Nina call the Phoenix Dollers club members together for an emergency meeting. I didn't give your aunt a choice."

"Is this a trick?" Gretchen's eyes narrowed. "If I get in the car, will you take me to Nina or . . ."

"Or what?" Matt laughed. "Kidnap you for interrogation and lock you in the bowels of the police station? No. Better than that. I get to hang out with a roomful of people who know Caroline Birch, and I get to listen to them discuss ways to find her."

He still held the door open.

"You can't do that," Gretchen said, sliding into the seat, careful not to jar her arm.

"Yes I can," he said. "I'm an honorary member."

"How did your mother get the club together on such short notice and on a Saturday night?"

"Easy. She tempted them with the promise of food."

As they pulled out of the hospital parking lot into traffic, Gretchen wondered about Nina's mental state. She had always been on the sidelines of rational thought. But leaving Gretchen with a cop, never mind his remote connection to the doll group . . .

The detective must have intimidated her with his badge or threatened her in some way.

Matt rolled up to a stop sign and looked both ways. "Aunt Nina's trunk produced interesting new material in the Williams case. She turned over the items you found on Camelback Mountain—a shawl and doll picture—but she wasn't happy about it."

"You searched her car?" Gretchen said.

"Standard procedure when someone tries to smuggle contraband into a hospital," he said. "Some might call it withholding evidence."

"So, arrest me."

"Can't," Matt said lightly. "I'm using you as a decoy."

"As in hunting for ducks." Gretchen stifled a smile. He did have a certain charm. If you liked arrogant witticism and superficial friends.

Matt nodded. "Just like that. I'm hoping your mother will spot you floating in the water and fly in for a reunion."

Gretchen didn't like being compared to a sitting duck. "She's too smart to think there's any water in Arizona. She'll know it's a mirage."

Bonnie Albright attempted to call the meeting to order with flair. She banged a kitchen mallet on the stovetop. People milled around holding plates heaped with assorted appetizers. Cheeses, crusty bread, fruits, and tiny sandwiches.

All ignored Bonnie.

Bang. Bang. Bang

Tutu coolly surveyed the scene from her throne on the sofa, and Nimrod entertained the club members, who passed him from lap to lap, by being cute and cuddly.

Gretchen counted three purse dogs waiting patiently in their uniquely customized bags. All, Gretchen guessed, graduates of Nina's fine purse school. Nina really knew how to sell a product.

Bang. Bang. Bang.

"Give it up, Bonnie," Nina said, "before you pound a hole in my stove. Pop the cork on that champagne." She pointed to a bottle and a line of flute glasses. "And come and join us."

Bonnie shook her head, and her red lacquered flip moved in sync. "The last time you popped the cork, social hour went on for hours, and by the time we started with actual business, no one could focus on the task at hand."

"This," Nina replied, "isn't a normal, boring meeting filled with hours of tedious planning. The agenda for this evening is Caroline, and she's a worthy reason to stay sober. But I still need a drink. Matt, would you open the bottle, please?"

Nina clapped her hands together. "All purse dogs outside. Rita, please let them out."

Pandemonium reigned while miniature dogs swarmed through the room like greyhounds off to the race.

Nina gestured at the champagne bottle, and Matt moved around her and worked the cork until it exploded like a gunshot. He filled glasses and handed them out. Gretchen, refusing a glass because of the painkiller she'd taken earlier, raised an eyebrow when he held up a glass, met her eyes, and took a sip.

"Aren't you on duty?" she asked.

"Yup," he said. "I'm undercover, remember? I'm blending in. Don't tell anybody, but this is only water."

Gretchen surveyed the group. She counted twelve heads, most of them familiar from past visits. Larry and Julia stood in the far corner in a small group of specialty collectors. Gretchen remembered each of them by their areas of interest. Rita Phyller collected Barbie dolls. Susie Hocker, the youngest member of the club, had an extensive collection of Madame Alexander dolls. Karen Fitz bought as many contemporaries as she could afford on a kindergarten teacher's wages—Lee Middletons and Zawieruszynskis were her favorites, if Gretchen remembered right.

Nina pulled her aside. "How's your wrist?"

"Broken," Gretchen said.

"You're not mad at me, are you?"

"What? For dumping the detective on me? Or for giving him the shawl and doll picture?"

"I tried to resist, but he threatened to call for backup and arrest me. I'm sorry. I really am." Nina sipped from her glass. "He's very charming in a rugged sort of way. He was only doing his job."

"If I remember right, you called him 'the enemy' earlier today."

"I was distraught. I overreacted a little."

"He's a parasite. I can't get away from him. Every time I turn around, he's right behind me. How did he know I was at the hospital? Did you call him?"

"No. When that nasty nurse escorted Tutu and me out of the building, he was parked at the curb like he knew we were inside."

Gretchen thought it over. "He's been following us."

"I never noticed. I'm sure I would have noticed."

Gretchen glanced across the room and met the detective's eyes. He saluted her with his glass. She looked quickly away. "We have to be more careful from now on."

Nina worked her arm through Gretchen's. "Let me introduce you to Joseph Reiner. He's an antique doll dealer from Mesa and is a brand-new member of the Dollers."

Gretchen followed Nina's gaze. She would have remembered if she had met him in the past. Dark and swarthy, with diamond studs in both earlobes and a goatee, he wore a short-sleeved pink button-down shirt tucked into yellow shorts.

"I know," Nina said. "You're wondering if Joseph is gay. No one knows for sure. No hard evidence, and I would be the last one to start a rumor."

Gretchen grinned at Nina. "Of course you wouldn't."

"Just don't offer him a glass of champagne," Nina said.

"Why not?"

"He spent three months in jail. DWI. His fourth one. I hear he hasn't touched a drop since he was released."

Nina pulled Gretchen along and made the introductions. Joseph clutched a can of Diet Coke in his left hand, while he asked about the cast on her wrist.

Bonnie called out. "Yes. Tell us what happened. How did you break your wrist?"

Matt had a smart-aleck grin on his face as Gretchen gave them an abbreviated version, leaving out the part about the footrace. Even if Matt had been following Nina's car, he couldn't know about her encounter with Nacho, which took place behind a building off the street. So there was no accounting for the smirk on his face at the moment.

Then she remembered the chase across the busy street. Had he been there?

"Clumsy of me," she finished, lamely. "I must have fallen on it wrong."

"Speaking of falling wrong," Nina said addressing everyone in the room. "Martha Williams took a serious fall wrong. I called this meeting to discuss Martha's death and to ask for your help in locating Caroline. It's no secret that a note was found with Martha that had Caroline's name on it."

Several heads nodded in agreement. Gretchen saw Matt scowl at his mother. She surmised that Bonnie wouldn't be privy to any more juicy bits of evidence thrown her way by her son.

"And a valuable doll parasol was found in her pocket," Nina continued.

Detective Albright slapped a hand against his head and looked up at the ceiling.

After a whispered consultation with Gretchen, Nina told the club members about the paisley shawl and the photograph of the French fashion doll and trunk, and about April's evaluation of their worth. Gretchen heard the appropriate oohs and ahhs when they learned that the doll was designed by the world-famous Bru.

Gretchen could tell that the detective was disturbed by the direction the discussion was taking. It threatened to expose his shrouded secret evidence, and she planned on making her own contribution.

"Detective Albright," Gretchen said. "Why don't you show the club members the picture you confiscated. Maybe someone will recognize it."

"Good idea," Bonnie said. "Matt, you should have thought of that."

After sending a scathing look at his mother, Matt went out to his car and returned with the bubble-wrapped package. He pulled at the tape until the items inside were exposed to all the club members.

No one from the Phoenix Dollers owned a Bru French fashion doll, nor did they know of anyone in the valley who might possess such a rare find. Murmurs of appreciation filled the room when they saw the photo.

"I heard that Martha owned a French fashion doll years ago," Rita Phyller said.

"That's an old rumor," Joseph said. "I knew her quite well before she took to the streets, and she never said anything to me about owning a Bru."

"What was a Bru parasol doing in her pocket then?" Karen Fitz wanted to know.

"Caroline has some answering to do," Bonnie added, glancing at Nina. "I know she's your sister, and I don't want to say anything bad about her . . ."

"That would be a first, Bonnie," Nina said, glaring at Bonnie then holding up a hand. "I know it doesn't look good. But Gretchen and I are convinced that if we can locate her, she will be able to clear this up. Has anyone seen her since Martha died?"

Gretchen listened in dismay as she realized that no one in the room had any helpful information. They threw around theories, careful not to insult Nina or Gretchen with innuendos, but in the end, nothing new came to light.

"Joseph," Matt said. "You said you knew Martha well?"

Joseph rubbed his fingers on his right ear, a nervous gesture, Gretchen thought.

"She'd come around to see what I had in stock. We'd talk shop."

"Did she ever buy anything?"

"Naw. She didn't have two nickels to rub together. She only came to look."

"When's the last time you saw her?"

"I'd have to think about it." Joseph's fingers twirled a

diamond stud, and Gretchen could see tension etched on his face.

"We can wait," Matt said.

Bonnie tittered nervously. "What is this? The third degree? Next you'll be asking all of us for alibis."

The detective's eyes met Gretchen's. "At the moment," he said. "I'm only interested in one specific alibi."

Caroline's hands trembled as she held the nineteen-inch china doll on her lap. She studied the marking on the doll's body and stroked the cream dress with dainty blue feather wisps in the design. Was this it? The Madame Rohmer she had crossed the country to find?

It had to be. Could there be another exactly like the one she sought? Impossible. But she had to be sure.

Caroline would have examined the inside of the doll's head if the pate had been loose. With the doll's new owner sitting next to her, she couldn't very well rip its head off.

"Do you have a flashlight I can use?" she asked.

Rudolph Timms's piercing eyes searched hers questioningly. "Excuse me? I thought you wanted a picture."

Caroline, remembering her ruse, quickly arranged the doll on the ornate sofa and moved back, camera to her eye. "I hope you don't mind," she said, after snapping several pictures with her filmless camera. "It's not every day that I have the opportunity to examine such a wonderful specimen so closely."

Rudolph preened as though she were complimenting him personally.

"A flashlight would illuminate the doll," Caroline said, desperate to convince him of the truth of her lie. "The picture will be more striking with additional lighting."

"Oh, yes, of course." He hurried across the room and opened a drawer in a desk against the wall. "This should do."

To continue the illusion, Caroline arranged the light and took more pictures. Then with the doll on her lap, she tapped on the doll's head and listened. She tapped again on its cheek. She heard a dull thud. Her excitement grew.

She pulled the wig high and held the flashlight against the back of its head. She examined the face of the doll, moving the light as she worked.

Rudolph Timms cleared his throat.

"Remarkable," Caroline said, without looking up from her work. "Simply remarkable."

The light's rays penetrated the layers of transparent porcelain.

Caroline's gasp of relief caught in her throat.

Yes. Yes. Yes.

She had the doll right in her lap.

Deceptions are practiced wherever money can be made, and the doll world is no exception. Swindlers scour the country buying damaged dolls and sometimes work with an accomplice who repairs the dolls for them. These con artists represent the dolls to avid buyers as something they are not, sell them at inflated prices, then quickly disappear from sight.

—From *World of Dolls* by Caroline Birch

As Gretchen stood outside of Nina's house, she heard a coyote howl in the distance. Larry and Julia were the last to leave. Larry wandered out to join her while Julia and Nina worked in the kitchen. Julia, apparently allergy-free tonight, had offered to help clean up in the spirit of renewed camaraderie. More likely, she hoped for an earful of tantalizing new gossip.

"Where did you and Julia originally live?" Gretchen asked. "Everyone in the Phoenix area seems to be a transplant from another state, mainly from the Midwest. I have yet to meet a native Arizonian in Phoenix or Scottsdale."

"We're both from Cleveland," he said, laughing. He wore sunglasses to hide his facial tic, and Gretchen wondered how he could see through them in the dark of night. If she didn't remove her sunglasses before entering any type of building, she couldn't see a thing.

"Ah, you started out here as snowbirds." Permanent Arizonians, Gretchen knew, weren't particularly fond of Northerners who fled their home states every winter to bask for a few months in the sun. When the cherry and apple trees began to blossom, the snowbirds returned home.

"Didn't we all?" he asked.

The coyote's howl was joined by other howls, and a choir of yipp yipp calls sounded across the desert.

"Thank you for your help with the repair projects," Gretchen said.

"My pleasure. Julia doesn't let me work on restorations much anymore. She wants me out buying and selling. I forgot how much I enjoy it."

"It's relaxing," Gretchen acknowledged, recalling the many times she had assisted her mother, immersing herself in a doll project, forgetting about the passage of time and life's pressing responsibilities. "Repairing a doll is one of the few times I actually live in the moment," she said. "There's something very Zen about it."

Larry agreed. "I'm making a wig for one of Caroline's customers. It's time-consuming but gratifying. Working on it gives me that same sense of timelessness."

"Really? You're making a wig?" Gretchen was surprised. Her mother saved wigs from dolls that were beyond repair and used them to replace damaged wigs. "That's well beyond the call of duty. The workshop has bins brimming with supplies. You could look there for a wig that would work."

"I enjoy the challenge. Wig making is one of my specialties."

"What material are you using? Mohair? A kit?"

"Kits are for amateurs, you know that. I'm using human hair. It's going to be an extraordinary wig when I'm finished."

"Is a local salon saving hair for you?" Gretchen had found several human hairpieces stored in the repair shop, but she knew her mother avoided making them unless a customer couldn't be satisfied in any other way and if the price was right.

"I can't give out my secrets," Larry said crisply. "Your mother might move into my territory."

Gretchen eyed him. "I think it's the other way around. But seriously, I appreciate your help, and I'm sure she will, too, when she gets back." She didn't add that her mother would have more problems than she could deal with when she resurfaced without worrying about her customers' needs.

"Maybe I can pitch in soon and help you out," she added.

"No rush."

Julia, her bulldog jaw leading the way, whirled out in a flurry of activity, and the Gerneys waved from the car windows as they drove off.

"He's still out there?" Nina asked, joining her and peering into the night.

Gretchen nodded and glanced down the street where the detective sat in his car. "Does he really think I'm going to lead him to my mother?"

"That tells me he's out of ideas. He's hoping you come up with something."

"He and I are in agreement on that," Gretchen said wearily. "But I don't know what to do next."

"We can start with that disgusting dirty journal you swiped from Nacho."

"I completely forgot about it." The painkiller seemed to be affecting her mental alertness, but at the moment she didn't care. The pill had done its magic, and her wrist didn't hurt.

With one last look at the detective's car, Gretchen returned to the house, fished through her purse, and extracted the worn notebook. Nina carefully drew the curtains, and the two of them settled at the kitchen table.

"He wouldn't creep around and look in the windows, would he?" Gretchen asked, carefully removing the rubber bands encircling the notebook.

Nina shrugged. "Who knows what he will do? We should have brought a few of Caroline's dolls over to post at the windows and doors as guards." She watched Gretchen open the thick wad of paper with disgust. "What a mess."

Without the rubber bands to hold the notebook together, bits and pieces of paper slipped out onto the table. A few fell to the floor. Gretchen bent down and retrieved them. "He must have saved every receipt he ever received." She picked through a variety of purchase receipts from fast-food restaurants and liquor stores. "He drinks a lot of wine," she noted.

"I'm not at all surprised." Nina gingerly sorted through a stack on the table. "Here's a gas receipt."

Gretchen glanced over at the paper in Nina's hand. "A gas receipt? He has a car?"

"Of course not. He must have picked it up from the street." Nina squinted at the fine print.

Gretchen took the receipt. "The gas was purchased yesterday with a credit card."

"Who knows why he has it," Nina said, dismissing it. "Keep going."

Gretchen put it aside and unfolded a piece of paper that had been folded multiple times, one of many stuffed into the notebook. "Phone numbers, random scribbles, pages ripped out and stuffed back in. I can barely make out his handwriting. Sorting through this mess is going to take time."

"Spend the night here," Nina suggested. "I'll make some herbal tea, and we'll get it done, however long it takes. Every hour counts."

"Let's get to it then," Gretchen said. "And make us something stronger than herbal tea. Give me something with caffeine. Coffee, if you have it."

Several hours later and after multiple cups of coffee, Gretchen and Nina were nearing the back of the notebook and the last few pages.

Gretchen turned a page and almost spewed coffee across the scattered papers on the table. "Look at this."

She held up a crumpled sheet of paper.

Nina gasped.

It was a copy of the picture of the French fashion doll reposing serenely in her wooden trunk. The exact same photograph Gretchen had found on the mountain that now was held as evidence by the Phoenix police. "We should have started at the back of the notebook. Doesn't it figure?"

Gretchen stared at the copy of the valuable doll, then turned the paper over. "There's a message on the back," she said, reading aloud. " 'I have the doll, but the trunk is too large. Hide it for me.' " She glanced quickly up and handed it to Nina. "The handwriting is different from the rest of this notebook. It's not Nacho's, but I know that handwriting from somewhere."

"You should know it," Nina said. "It's Caroline's."

Caroline studied Rudolph Timms and wondered about the best approach.

"Were you aware when you purchased the doll," she said, "that it had been extensively repaired."

Timms uncrossed his long legs and stood up. "Impossible," he said. "This doll is in mint condition."

"I'm afraid it isn't." Caroline shone the light on the doll's head. "Porcelain is translucent. Repair materials are not. See the streaks?"

Timms leaned forward. "Yes. I see them."

"The streaks indicate repaired cracks. If we removed the doll's head, I could demonstrate more effectively."

"That won't be necessary," Timms said weakly. "I'll have to see about a refund, I suppose. I don't mind purchasing a repaired doll, but the price must be right. What I paid for this particular doll was obscene."

Obscene by his standards? Caroline's eyes scanned her opulent surroundings.

If Timms had been an experienced collector he would have thoroughly examined the doll before agreeing to the price. Caroline wondered, in the end, if Timms's pride would prevent him from pursuing the dishonest seller.

Perhaps the seller, in a hurry to unload the doll, hadn't known that the doll had been restored. Caroline wasn't about to admit that she, herself, performed the repairs. It hadn't been her intention at the time to deceive a potential buyer.

"Please tell me who sold you the doll." Caroline contained her anticipation. The name. She needed the name of the seller. "The doll community is very tightly knit. We dislike those who give our industry a bad name."

Timms looked embarrassed, a tinge of pink spreading from his neck and creeping toward his widow's peak. "My secretary arranged the transaction for me. I believe an escrow service was involved."

"She must have a name. At the very least she should have the name of the service."

"Of course. She handles all my affairs very efficiently. There's a small problem, however."

"Yes?" Caroline asked, impatiently. "A name shouldn't be complicated."

"My secretary is away at the moment. Somewhere in the Amazon on a small boat or something equally remote. I'm afraid I'm helpless without her."

He gazed longingly at the doll. "Such a waste. Perhaps I'll keep the doll after all but at a reduced price, of course. My secretary will return next week, and she will handle the transaction."

Caroline stared at Rudolph Timms in dismay. A week would be too late. The muffled voice on the phone had been clear about that. She'd be dead by then.

· II ·

The Internet has revolutionized the doll industry. eBay and other online auction services connect doll collectors and doll dealers around the world. Rare and sought-after items appear for sale on a daily basis, and it is the wise doll connoisseur who follows the auctions. Remember the old adage—the early bird gets the worm? In doll-collecting lingo that translates in a meaningful way. The earliest buyer always wins the prize.

—From *World of Dolls* by Caroline Birch

Gretchen greeted Sunday morning with a moan. It took her a good minute to realize she was in Nina's extra bedroom. She hated mornings, and she hated energetic, bubbly morning people who thought watching the sunrise gave them special powers. At the moment, she hated Nina.

"It's already nine o'clock, sleepyhead." Nina sat down on the bed with a bounce. "Two things. First, you left your cell phone in the kitchen, and Steve called this morning. I told him you'd return his call when you got up."

Gretchen managed to sit up with the support of her one good arm behind her. She cracked an eye.

"I'm going to my meditation center," Nina said. "If I clear my head of all this stuff floating around, maybe I'll get a reading on your mother."

Nina's methods of handling emergency situations differed drastically from Gretchen's.

"Take the dogs with you. Please," Gretchen said.

"I can't very well take Tutu along. How would I watch her? Nimrod could stay in his purse, but he'd be a distraction. Anyway, he'd much rather stay here with you." Nina patted Gretchen's leg. "I'll stop at Caroline's and check on Wobbles."

"Feed him."

"I will. I won't be gone long. Have some coffee, it's fresh, and call Steve back. What's the plan for the day?"

Gretchen managed to remain sitting upright without the leverage of her arm. She rubbed her eyes. "I can't think straight. I need coffee first."

"I'm off then." Nina fluttered around, gathering her things, kissed Tutu good-bye, and left.

Gretchen slipped into a borrowed robe, pink with green satin trim at the knee-length hem, and shuffled into the kitchen. She poured a cup of coffee and leaned against the counter, sipping it. Everything seemed to move in slow motion without the use of her left hand, but she was grateful that it didn't hurt this morning.

After she poured the second cup, she returned Steve's call and related the events of the past two days. For once, Steve heard her all the way through without interrupting.

"You need to come home," he said when she finished. "This is nuts. You don't want to involve yourself in something illegal. This is murder we're talking about."

"I can't leave now. Nina needs me."

"I need you, too. Doesn't that factor in at all?"

"Of course it does." Gretchen felt a flash of guilt. She really hadn't given much thought to Steve recently. But why should she? Couldn't Steve get by for a few days without her? "But I have to find my mother," she insisted.

"And what have been the results of your search so far?" he demanded.

Gretchen didn't say anything.

"She'll show up when she shows up," Steve continued. "It doesn't matter if you're in Arizona or Massachusetts. I have my career to think about. We can't have any scandal, especially right now when the firm's partners are deciding my future. The timing couldn't be worse."

Ah, Gretchen thought, *the truth comes out.* He wasn't concerned about her well-being at all. His request that she come home was a precautionary career move.

"I'm going to see what happens today," she said. "I'll call you tonight."

"I'll expect to hear from you by eight. Boston time. You'd think one broken bone would be enough for you."

Gretchen closed the phone and threw it in her purse. For seven years she had hoped her relationship with Steve would evolve into something permanent. That dream was fading as fast as a drop of moisture in the desert.

Would she end up in spinsterhood like Nina? She already had the stereotypical cat.

Was the cost of marriage to Steve worth the price she'd have to pay? She had already lost the ability to refuse his increasing demands, her inability to say *no* more pronounced when dealing with him. She rarely crossed him for any reason. Had she subconsciously dimmed her own personality to accommodate his?

Could she move past his recent indiscretion and forget, as well as forgive?

Worry about that later, she scolded. *Focus on today and the task at hand.*

Tutu caught Gretchen's attention when she trotted down the hall and whined at the front door. Nimrod trailed at a distance.

"Okay," Gretchen said in a surly tone. "I'm coming. But be quick about it."

She opened the door, and Tutu ran out. The dog didn't stop in the yard to sniff around and find the perfect spot, and if Gretchen had been more awake, she would have remembered that Tutu preferred wee-wee pads and indoor plumbing over normal dog outhouses.

Tutu lowered her body close to the ground and ran full-out down the street without a single glance back, like an escaped convict with the irresistible taste of freedom in her mouth.

Gretchen stood in the doorway with her mouth open in shock. Recovering somewhat, she slammed the door before Nimrod had the chance to join in the escape. Running barefoot into the street, she shouted Tutu's name. The spoiled schnoodle was nowhere in sight.

Gretchen had managed to lose Nina's dog mere moments after beginning her dog-sitting assignment.

She had a decision to make. Follow the demented dog immediately in bare feet, wearing Nina's pink and lime green robe, or quickly change into her own clothes and pull on her sandals. Tutu already had a wide lead, and Gretchen's only hope of catching up with her would be if the roving rascal encountered a distraction. A cute boy dog would do the trick.

Gretchen gasped. What if Tutu was in heat?

An image of Nina's reaction to the loss of her prized pet trotted through Gretchen's head, replaced quickly by an image of Tutu giving birth to schnoodle mutts.

She took off running.

The desert morning heat was already oppressive. The pavement under her feet felt hot and sticky. A bird perching on an overhead electrical wire panted through its small, open beak, and the sound of sprinklers laboring to water the lush tropical yards filled the air.

And sun, sun, blazing sun everywhere.

"Wait up," she heard someone call out behind her. She whirled to see Matt Albright loping toward her, wearing running shoes, cargo shorts, and a yellow T-shirt. He looked fresh and scrubbed, and he wore that dazzling yet deceptive smile.

Gretchen turned back to the task at hand and continued running, squinting against the sun's intense rays and wishing for a good pair of sunglasses more than a pair of shoes.

"I heard you were an avid runner, but your commitment

astounds me," he said, catching up. "Me? I would have changed out of the robe and probably worn shoes."

"There are vast differences between the two of us, Albright." Gretchen ignored the pain in her tender soles. "For example, if it was my investigation, I'd be out questioning Martha's acquaintances, and I'd be compiling a list of suspects."

"My henchmen take care of that," he said, jogging easily. "Can I get a picture of this?"

"Of what?" Gretchen peered between houses as they ran side by side. If she had shoes on, she could leave him in her desert dust.

"A picture of you jogging in your cute robe."

"Go away," Gretchen said, huffing slightly.

Matt stopped running and fell behind. "If you step on a scorpion, you'll be back at the hospital," he called after her. "I spent enough time waiting around there for you yesterday."

Gretchen slowed and stopped, staring at the ground with growing panic. "I hadn't thought of that." Scorpion stings were excruciatingly painful, according to reports by several Arizonians who had been stung and lived to tell about it. Their venom wasn't deadly, but death seemed preferable to the pain they inflicted.

"They have clear bodies and that makes them hard to see." He stood with both hands on his hips. "Anyway, that isn't what you're looking for? What's up?"

"Tutu escaped."

"The yappy mutt?" he said. "I thought she seemed in a rush when she blasted out of the yard." Matt looked down the block. "But are you sure you want to find her?"

"Tempting thought, but I have to. Nina would kill me."

"I'll help then. I wouldn't want to be partially responsible for your demise."

After a brief consultation on the best search tactics, they returned to the house, Gretchen walking gingerly, alert to the threat of stinging monsters. Matt walked another half block to get his car. He waited outside while Gretchen changed into the same clothes she had worn yesterday: green capris, a white tee, and sandals.

They cruised slowly down the street in Matt's unmarked police car. Gretchen decided to make the most of this opportunity to pump the cop for information, forgetting momentarily that she could count her future health by mere minutes if she didn't find Tutu.

"Who tipped you off about the doll in my mother's workshop?" she said.

"What makes you think someone tipped me off?"

"Why do you answer every question with another question?"

"Do I?"

Gretchen sighed heavily and continued to scan for Tutu. She rolled down the window and called Tutu's name. The more Gretchen thought about the police search at her mother's house, the more certain she became that the police had known not only what they were looking for, but also where they were looking for it. "Did it ever occur to you," she said, "that your tipster might have planted the evidence?"

"Vivid imagination," Matt said. "You must be some sort of artistic type. What do you do for a living?"

"Nothing at the moment. I'm unemployed. I have another question for you."

"Of course."

"Who claimed Martha's body?"

Matt stopped the car and studied her, his brows furrowed. Eventually he said, "I guess telling you won't hurt the case. Her body and personal effects haven't been released yet, but Joseph Reiner is making arrangements."

Gretchen was surprised. "The same Joseph Reiner I met at Nina's house yesterday?"

Matt nodded. "He's Martha's nephew."

"Why didn't he mention that?"

"I didn't know myself until late last night when he called me. He seemed embarrassed by the family connection.

That explained all the nervous twitching I observed at the meeting."

In Gretchen's mind, that didn't explain anything. It only led to more questions.

"Okay," Matt said. "I shared information with you. What do you have for me?"

"Nothing yet," Gretchen said, thinking of the photocopy in Nacho's notebook and the note on the back in her mother's handwriting. *"I have the doll. Hide the trunk."*

Gretchen felt a confusing mix of anger and fear for her mother. What in the world had her mother gotten herself into? Sitting in the car next to Matt, she realized she was clenching her fists, and she forced herself to relax.

She saw movement out of the corner of her eye, and Tutu appeared from the side of a house, her tongue hanging out so far it almost scraped the ground.

"There she is," Matt said. "We've got her."

"How was I supposed to know she couldn't be trusted outside alone?"

"The backyard is fenced for a reason," Nina said, alternating between sending Gretchen piercing glares and rubbing her face in the schnoodle's fur. "Poor baby, lost alone in the big world."

"How's Wobbles?" Gretchen asked.

"Obviously he enjoyed more care and attention than Tutu."

Gretchen stuffed her purse with the contents of Nacho's notebook, slipping the picture of the French fashion doll into her wallet.

"I can't bear sitting around doing nothing," Gretchen said. "I'm taking your car for a few hours. You start calling everyone my mother knows, including relatives you might not like."

She realized the chances of proving her mother's innocence were evaporating with every piece of new evidence.

Instead of uncovering information that would lead to a new suspect, she was cementing the case against her. She could see the headlines now: "Daughter Leads Police to Prove Mother Is Killer."

At the moment, unsubstantiated evidence pointed to a conspiracy between Caroline and Nacho to steal the French fashion doll from someone. Why else would they discuss hiding the doll and the trunk?

"We have to find out who owns the doll," Gretchen said.

"How are we going to do that?"

"We'll find Nacho and make him tell us. He's the link. And we are going to pay a visit to Martha's nephew and ask him why he's creeping around the doll club and concealing his identity."

"Who? Who?" Nina said, sounding exactly like a great horned owl. "Who is Martha's nephew? I think I missed something."

"Joseph Reiner."

"No," Nina said in disbelief. "Martha was his aunt? He never said a word." She plunked the car keys into Gretchen's outstretched hand. "I should come along to protect you," she said in a small voice.

"I won't be gone long. Start making phone calls."

Caroline stood in the incessant rain staring at Rudolph Timms's condominium complex, a small figure lost in the early morning mass of humanity swarming around her. She clutched the case containing her laptop close to her body. It was her last hope.

She had spent the night in the Amtrak train station, acutely aware of the indigents attempting to blend with legitimate travelers, seeking dry benches to pass the night. She had become one of them, her remaining dollars slipping through her fingers as her body demanded nourishment. Soon, out of desperation, she would take a chance and use a credit card.

Her Phoenix source had apprised her of the latest developments, and she knew that a warrant had been issued for her arrest. A wanted woman. Also wanted by a more dangerous force than the local authorities.

She turned off Michigan Avenue and sought cover under the canopy of the entrance to the Holiday Inn. Glancing back once more toward the opulent Timms home, she realized there wasn't anything more she could do in the center of downtown Chicago. She had to keep moving.

"Dead," the voice had whispered. "You are next unless you give me what I want."

Caroline understood the message perfectly.

She was dead either way.

Searching for dolls to add to your collection is fun and challenging. Dolls can be found in the most unlikely places. Garage sales, block rummage sales, local estate auctions, flea markets, even nestled among other antiques in a friend's attic. The possibilities are endless. Keep your eyes open, and happy hunting.

—From *World of Dolls* by Caroline Birch

Gretchen sped along Lincoln Avenue toward downtown Phoenix, feeling released from the claustrophobia she always experienced when she spent too much time around other people. The only personal space she'd managed to find in the past three days was on a rocky mountain in arid summer heat where risking death by bugs or reptiles seemed more desirable than one more minute with Nina and her cast of loony fuzz balls.

In honor of the moment, she purchased lunch at a convenience store—a large bag of potato chips and a sugar-laden soda—and vowed to eat until the chips were history. The challenge was eating, drinking, and driving with only one good arm, but she smiled smugly at her ability to adapt to adverse conditions. She popped another chip into her mouth.

As long as her cell phone didn't ring or Detective Albright didn't appear in her rearview mirror, she could handle this level of multitasking. So far, there was no sign of the dogged detective who seemed to have no social life. When did the guy take a day off?

Gretchen chomped chips and admired the scenery. Luxury homes dotted the hillside along Lincoln like embedded jewels, and palm trees lined the boulevards. The weatherman reported the current pollen count.

Phoenix reminded Gretchen of the setting for a fantasy novel or science fiction movie. It even smelled foreign and exotic. As she descended from the hills into the base of the city's valley, a brown cloud of pollution rose to greet her, the consequence of building a city's hub in a protected basin. A strong rain or high winds would clean up the air, but Gretchen doubted that it rained much in July.

She maneuvered into a parking space near the Phoenix Rescue Mission and, after studying the outside of the building, she walked inside and approached a wizened woman behind a desk.

"Everybody gone. Eight o'clock," she replied in broken English. "Back to street. Find work or go church or what."

"Thank you," Gretchen said, noticing a sign at the desk reminded all guests to vacate the premises by eight in the morning.

Gretchen had missed him, thanks partly to pesky, runaway Tutu. Reluctantly she admitted her own share of blame. She should have set an alarm.

She attempted to describe Nacho to the woman, but based on the confused expression on her face, the woman simply didn't understand what Gretchen wanted to convey. Nacho's name and an animated description of the knob on his head drew a blank, uncomprehending stare.

As she left the Rescue Mission, she chastised herself for never learning Spanish.

Central Avenue seemed oddly familiar after she'd spent several hours driving it the day before. Gretchen glanced at her broken wrist, the only thing she had to show for yesterday's efforts. That and Nacho's notebook, stowed safely in her purse. She had been mistaken to think he would call, that she could force him to respond.

As always, driving helped clear Gretchen's mind, and

she sorted out the connections among those involved in Martha's life. Nothing made sense.

Her mother obviously knew Martha better than Nina thought, based on the parian doll and the inventory list found in her workshop. The picture in Nacho's notebook connected him to Caroline as well.

Joseph Reiner had failed to let the doll club know of his relationship with Martha, quite an omission, considering she had just died.

And April, who openly disliked Martha, had abruptly left town after appraising articles found on the dead woman's body. Gretchen wondered what that was all about.

She drove around the block and headed back down Central Avenue without a plan. Morning traffic clogged the street, giving her time to continue with her mental exercise and attempt to understand what was happening.

Her mother had hidden a parian doll in her workshop that had once belonged to Martha and she had also hidden a French fashion doll that, according to the inventory list, had never belonged to Martha. Martha had a picture with her when she died of the same French fashion doll.

The note found with Martha implied that Caroline had killed her. But would Martha have had enough time to write out a message to the police?

The message scrawled by Caroline on the back of the photocopy of the picture of the French fashion doll and trunk upset Gretchen the most. She could think of multiple reasons for her mother's disappearance and for the note found in Martha's hand. But the picture she found last night in Nacho's notebook wasn't ambiguous. It stated the facts boldly.

Caroline was hiding a doll, and not just any doll, but a doll worth a lot of money, and it didn't belong to her.

The parian found in the police search hadn't belonged to Caroline.

The French fashion doll—whereabouts unknown— didn't belong to Caroline, either.

If she didn't know her mother as well as she did, she might agree with the authority's decision to issue an arrest warrant.

Gretchen glanced at the two pink bracelets on her right wrist. She would never lose faith in her mother. There had to be another explanation, and she would find it.

As soon as Gretchen turned onto First Avenue she spotted Nacho pushing a shopping cart. He saw the car at the same time and looked desperately around for an escape route.

Gretchen slid the Impala along the curb and slammed on the brakes. She jumped out, sure that she had Nacho trapped this time. If he took off, he'd have to abandon the cart, which he gripped possessively.

"That's Daisy's cart," Gretchen said to him as she approached, noting a few familiar items under Nacho's black garbage bag, which sat on the top of the heap. She lifted a corner of the bag, and Nacho slapped her hand away.

"Hey," she said. "Keep your hands off me."

She smelled unwashed body odor and sour alcohol.

"Yo no entiendo inglés," he said. *"Tú debes irte."*

"I know you can understand me," Gretchen said. "You spoke perfect English when you threatened me at the restaurant."

Nacho glared at her and kept his hands firmly locked on the cart. He tried to move past her, but Gretchen ran to the front of the cart and pushed back.

A crowd of people walked by, and several turned to look.

"Leave the poor guy alone," someone shouted.

Gretchen scanned them with a weak smile but stood firm.

"You are going to answer a few questions first," she demanded. "Where is my mother?"

"Yo te dije antes que te fueras. Tú solo eres un problema."

Gretchen stared at him. Somehow she had to force him to speak English. "Police," she said, bluffing. "I will call the police."

That did the trick. Nacho's eyes widened in fear. "No police," he said. "That would be foolish."

"I need some answers from you."

"You stole something from me. I want it back first."

"Wait here." Gretchen went to the car, keeping a watchful eye on Nacho, and returned with the notebook. She handed it to him, and he wedged it into the plastic bag.

"You should be more afraid," he said. "Aren't you scared?"

Heavy traffic streamed by them, music blared from open windows, and the ground shook from amplified bass settings. Sunday strollers ambled by. At the moment, Gretchen felt reasonably protected from a violent assault.

"What would you do to me? Would you kill me like you killed Martha?"

Nacho's response was quick but wary. "Martha was my friend. You're talking nonsense."

"Tell me about the French fashion doll and the trunk."

"You're snooping where you aren't welcome."

Gretchen was angry. "My mother is missing, and she is accused of killing your supposed friend. I plan on snooping into your life until you give me answers. Now tell me what I want to know."

Nacho's eyes flicked briefly to the shopping cart before answering. "I know nothing about any doll."

Gretchen leaned her body into the cart, one hand resting on top of the plastic bag. Nacho's eyes shifted nervously from the cart to Gretchen.

"Where is Daisy?" Gretchen said evenly. "This is her cart."

"Daisy asked me to watch it for her," Nacho said, finally answering a question. "She had business."

"What's inside the cart, Nacho?"

His knuckles were white, and sweat slid down the side of his face.

"Hide the trunk," Caroline had written. Where would a homeless man hide a large doll trunk? Certainly not on the street or in the Rescue Mission. Finding a safe hiding place would be a complex task for a man without a home.

Gretchen reached into the cart and tossed his garbage bag onto the pavement. Before he could resist, she pulled the top layer of junk aside.

"Well, well," she said. "If it isn't a doll trunk."

The antique wooden trunk was wedged in the cart between layers of clothing. Gretchen glanced up at Nacho. He backed away.

Gretchen held up a hand in warning. "Don't go," she demanded. "You have to help me."

"Yo traté de ayudarte," he said, forgetting to speak English in his haste. *"Tú debes irte."*

And Nacho grabbed his plastic bag and broke into a run. Gretchen refused to abandon the trunk to pursue him. She watched helplessly as he disappeared around a corner.

Great, she thought, *now what do I do?*

She wheeled the cart the few feet to Nina's car and gingerly lifted the doll trunk from the cart and placed it in the passenger seat. She flipped through the other items in the shopping cart without finding anything else of significance. Two shabbily dressed women sat on a park bench watching pigeons compete for bakery scraps. One of the women tossed a torn piece of bread onto the sidewalk and scrutinized Gretchen as she approached.

"Do you know how to find the Rescue Mission?" Gretchen asked them.

After some thought, one woman said, "Yes."

"Will you take this cart there?" Gretchen said.

"No," the same woman responded.

"I will pay you five dollars."

"Yes," said the other woman. "I will take it."

"Walk slowly, and if a man asks for the cart or tries to take it from you before you get to the mission, give it to him. If not, leave it with the people there."

Gretchen handed over the five dollar bill, and both women rose and shuffled down the street, guiding the cart in the direction of the mission.

She sat in the car with the air-conditioning turned all

the way up and the doors locked, and studied her remarkable find. Approximately twenty inches long, as April had
predicted, the outside of the trunk was in excellent condition. No major flaws in the wood. The brass-headed tacks
and brass handle shone as though recently polished. She
carefully opened the trunk, and even though she knew
from the message found in Nacho's notebook that the doll
had been hidden someplace else, she half expected to see
it inside.

The upper tray, designed to hold the doll, was empty.

The interior of the trunk was lined with finely striped
beige and blue fabric. When Gretchen removed the tray,
her eyes lit up with delight at the wealth of accessories.
She gingerly picked up each one, elegantly hand-stitched
dresses, little ankle boots, a tortoiseshell comb, corset,
bonnet, fan, and a full-length brown kid leather raincoat.

She carefully replaced the accessories, closed the trunk,
and pulled out into the early afternoon traffic.

Gretchen racked her brain for her long-dormant knowledge of doll collecting. This was an unbelievable trunk,
worth a slew of money. *Think, Gretchen. Think back to
your mother's book and the chapter on French fashion
dolls. What can you learn from examining this trunk?*

The size of the doll, Gretchen thought. Based on the
length of the trunk and the size of the clothing, the doll
must be about seventeen inches tall. Was that information
helpful? Not at the moment, but she filed it away for future
reference.

Why did her mother think the trunk was too large to
hide? Granted, it wasn't a tiny, slip-in-your-pocket trunk,
but her mother had plenty of rooms in the house in which
to tuck away the trunk. Unless she thought someone would
search her house for it. Which they had.

Where had Caroline hidden the French fashion doll?

And, more importantly, why?

At this point, Gretchen knew of two dolls her mother had

concealed in her game of intrigue. It had all the elements of a conspiracy if she counted Nacho as an accomplice.

Were there more dolls hidden away somewhere?

Her third day in Chicago stretched out before her in slow motion, painfully slow.

Caroline chose Paneras for the café's high-speed Internet access. She sat at a small table in the back of the restaurant, watching the Sunday crowd of diners and sipping black coffee. After a pause, she opened her laptop again. How many times had she logged on? How many times had she keyed in the online auction Web address and watched the green computer light flicker as it completed her search?

Her fingers flew on the keyboard. "Antique dolls." Click.

She scanned the listings for a familiar doll without success.

Caroline wanted to slam her fist into the table next to her laptop.

Sell something, she screamed silently. *Sell something, you miserable animal!*

· 13 ·

*Patience is the doll collector's most valuable quality. All serious
collectors dream of owning one special doll. Chasing the dream
can be exhilarating. That doll, once found, will represent the
culmination of a lifetime of marvelous memories, remarkable
dolls, and wonderful friendships. With that in mind, remember
that one must not let emotions overrule common sense. Take
time to smell the flowers, as the saying goes. Or, in the case of
collectors, take time to enjoy the quest.*

—From *World of Dolls* by Caroline Birch

"April's back," Nina said while fondling the doll costumes.
"Well, not exactly back. She never left."

"What?" Gretchen said.

"She had valley fever. It was awful, April said. A fever,
aches and pains, a bad cough. She's recovering at home
and ignored her phone calls until she felt better."

Valley fever. A lung infection, Gretchen remembered,
caused by an airborne fungus. Not uncommon in the
Phoenix area.

"She was out four-wheeling," Nina explained. "And got
caught in a dust storm."

Gretchen tried to picture enormous April on an all-
terrain vehicle.

"She should have worn a mask," Nina finished.

"Somehow," Gretchen said, "I never thought of April as
the rugged, outdoors type."

"I hope she didn't give it to Tutu."

"I don't think valley fever is contagious, Aunt Nina."

"You can't be too careful."

Gretchen and Nina sat at the workbench in Caroline's repair shop, admiring the doll trunk. Wobbles, exhibiting new-found confidence around Tutu and Nimrod, perched lazily on a shelf overhead and cleaned his face with his paws. The dogs had learned to tread lightly around him ever since he had won his first boxing match with a well-placed left claw to Tutu's inquisitive nose.

"Wobbles has a superiority complex," Nina observed.

Gretchen tried in vain to concentrate on the doll trunk and her missing mother. Nina whirled through a room like one of those dust storms April claimed she four-wheeled into, and the animals weren't helping matters. The yapping and clicking of toenails on the tiled floor irritated Gretchen's already strained nerves.

A cool shower would put everything back into perspective.

Leaving Nina to fend for herself, Gretchen stood in the shower under the lukewarm water while holding her broken wrist out of the stream. It was more of a trick than she thought it would be. She raised it higher and attempted to wash her hair with one hand.

Drying it proved impossible. She draped a towel over her head and struggled into white capris and a short red halter top, intending to ask Nina for help with her hair. But when she returned to the workshop, Nina sat crying at the table.

"I can see Caroline's aura in my mind's eye," Nina said through sobs.

Gretchen, well-versed in Nina's alleged ability to see energy fields in the form of colors emanating from objects, sighed heavily. According to Nina, all matter has auras, including Boston mosquitoes, Phoenix cockroaches, and Tutu poop. However, Nina hadn't figured out what all the colors meant or how to interpret them.

Much like her dreams.

"I didn't know you could see auras in your mind's eye," Gretchen said.

Nina sniffed. "I didn't either until now."

"And?" Gretchen was reluctant to ask but knew it was inevitable. "What did you see?"

The question sent Nina off into another bout of hysteria.

Gretchen ran the towel through her wet hair and waited. She made a mental note to buy a pair of aura glasses as soon as possible. The woman in the New Age shop had assured her that anyone could see auras with the proper glasses.

Nina sniffed. "Her aura is black. I don't know how to tell you this, but I think it means your mother killed Martha. And I can't bear it."

"That's ridiculous."

"Intrigue, conspiracy, death," Nina said in a stage whisper. "The writing is on the wall."

"The writing isn't on the wall," Gretchen said. "It's on a piece of paper. In Martha's cold hand. In Nacho's notebook. I have to admit, it looks bad. But looks are deceiving. You know that."

Gretchen leaned over and gave her aunt a strong hug. "We have to fight, Aunt Nina. We can't give up hope."

As the two pink bracelets on Gretchen's wrist said, Share Beauty Spread Hope.

"Every time we discover new clues," Nina pointed out, "they incriminate Caroline. Maybe we should stop helping."

"Our luck has to turn soon." Gretchen sat down and cupped her chin in her good hand. "Where would my mother hide a French fashion doll?"

"It can't be here. The police searched the house."

"Did she have a storage unit someplace?" Gretchen asked. "Or a large safe-deposit box?"

Nina shook her head. "Nothing that I know of. That Nacho character is creepy. I can't believe you went to see him alone."

Gretchen didn't respond. She gazed out the window at the rugged beauty of the mountain. "She must have the doll with her."

"It's not important," Nina said. "Finding the doll won't help your mother. We have the trunk." Nina gestured at the wooden doll trunk and the scattered costumes. "And what good is it? With our current streak of bad luck, we'll find the doll, remove its head, and we'll find a note. The note will say, 'Caroline Birch murdered Martha Williams.'"

"No need for sarcasm, dear aunt. Your pessimism is getting to me."

Gretchen gathered up the doll clothes and accessories and replaced them in the trunk. She opened a cabinet, rearranged the shelves to make room, and slid the trunk inside. A stack of folded fabric placed in front of it concealed the trunk from the casual observer.

"I have to keep moving," she said. "Every minute at this house feels like wasted time."

"I'm coming along." Nina's voice held a hint of stubbornness.

Gretchen watched Nimrod tackle Tutu. Playful snarls filled the room. Having Nina along meant having Nimrod and Tutu as well. The term *comes with baggage* took on a whole new meaning.

"Someone has to look out for you," Nina said, stuffing Nimrod in his traveling purse.

April Lehman lived in Tempe, close to Arizona State University. Nina drove quickly along a newly opened expressway. Gretchen couldn't believe how many new routes were available in Maricopa County making access easy to surrounding cities such as Tempe, which was situated a few miles southeast of Phoenix. It had a small-town college atmosphere that Gretchen appreciated.

As they approached Tempe, Nina raised the subject of Steve.

"How's it going with you two?"

"Fine," Gretchen replied, looking out the side window.

"Your life doesn't seem too exciting," Nina continued. "Where's the action?"

"What do you mean? Are you saying I don't have a life?"

"All I'm saying is it could be more exciting."

"It's more exciting than I care for, right now."

"Humpf."

Maybe Nina is right, Gretchen thought. *My life hasn't been exactly movie material. The same boyfriend for seven years, the same job, which never quite materialized into an established career before it unceremoniously terminated, and numerous torturous business-related events in the name of Steve's rapid rise in the law firm.*

Gretchen thought about friends her own age, or rather her lack of friends. A few college buddies seen occasionally to relive the past, happy hour with coworkers before the long drive home in the early evening, a book club group once a month. She thought of the stray voice messages left on her cell phone. Casual acquaintances. No true friends. Not one person particularly concerned over her whereabouts.

Looking back, she realized that she hadn't taken the time to develop friendships because her relationship with Steve required constant care and attention, even as Steve spent less and less time with her. She had allowed some friendships to lapse, and as a result she was intensely lonely.

Her small and quirky family had been a steady ship for her, a cast of strong females who colored Gretchen's life with animation. Ten years ago she couldn't imagine herself thinking this, because at that time she was emotionally geared for independence. But at twenty-nine she didn't hesitate to list her missing mother as her best friend.

Martha's murder and her mother's disappearance certainly verged on cliff-hanging entertainment, excuse the pun, but those events weren't about her life. They were about other people's lives.

Gretchen vowed to work on spicing up her own life in more positive ways just as soon as this family crisis was resolved.

Nina turned onto Apache Boulevard and parked.

The temperature registered one hundred and five degrees according to a large display sign above a local bank. The time was a few minutes after three. The heat hit Gretchen with something like physical force when she left the car. She could have been strapped to a stake in the middle of a blazing fire. Nina adjusted a cardboard windshield shade along the dashboard and began assembling her canine clan.

Gretchen studied April's dilapidated home. Peeling paint and a green AstroTurf lawn that effectively eliminated the need for watering and weeding. The house sat on a tiny lot without benefit of a swimming pool or exotic tropical landscaping. As she followed Nina along the crumbling sidewalk, Gretchen hoped April had air-conditioning.

"Come on in," April called out from inside, her voice muffled but audible through the front door. The fact that the door was closed indicated the presence of cool air. "You got here fast."

Gretchen and Nina found April's massive form sprawled across a sagging sofa. She wore a muumuu with green and purple stripes and had hiked it up around her thighs, exposing treelike legs snaked with varicose veins.

A window air conditioner droned loudly, the motor struggling to lower the temperature of the small room, with limited success.

"You look awful," Nina said. "I wish you had called me when you were diagnosed with valley fever. I would have helped you out."

"I didn't want to bother anybody," April said. "I'm feeling pretty good now. Gretchen, what happened to your arm?"

"I tripped and fell yesterday." Gretchen caught Nina's eye, hoping Nina would follow her lead and refrain from sharing the details of the encounter with Nacho.

"That's too bad," April said.

Nina sat down in a torn and faded cloth chair with Tutu leashed at her feet. The top of Nimrod's purse was vacant, indicating a napping puppy inside. Gretchen remained standing and couldn't resist scrutinizing the room.

Piles of doll magazines littered the floor, and every inch of table space was covered with dolls.

Gretchen stifled an involuntary giggle. Enormous April collected miniature dolls, all types and styles. The table next to Gretchen held several dolls, an eight-inch Lee Middleton, a Strawberry Shortcake riding her trike with Custard Cat in the basket, a five-inch cloth doll with an embroidered face, and an antique German bisque with jointed arms, wearing a blue dress.

"I have almost all of the original boxes and packing," April said proudly, looking at Gretchen with a schoolgirl's beam. "You didn't know I was a miniaturist, did ya?"

"These are marvelous," Gretchen said. *And inexpensive,* she thought. None of the dolls in April's collection were worth much more than twenty dollars. Based on April's lifestyle, that was all she probably could afford. Her appraisal service might be the backbone of the collecting business, but it didn't pay well.

"I always wanted to get into collecting doll houses and furniture," April said. "But the time hasn't been right. For my thirtieth birthday I'm going to treat myself to my very first doll house."

Thirty! Gretchen had assumed April was well into her fifties, but she was the same age as Gretchen.

Nina piped up. "Caroline is still missing, April, and it's turning ugly. We have to ask you a few questions about Martha."

April stiffened noticeably, and her warm smile froze. "I never liked that woman."

"You need to tell us why," Nina said encouragingly. "It might help."

April shifted on the couch, and her muumuu rode higher. "Eight years ago, Martha's husband died, and she came into some money through a life insurance policy. She went on a buying spree, buying the most fabulous dolls you could imagine. And the prices she paid." April slapped her forehead. "But she couldn't control herself. She bought dolls instead of paying off her mortgage, like she should of. She went wild.

"Then the whole thing collapsed around her. She started drinking because she couldn't face the financial problems. Three years ago the bank called her loan and repossessed her house."

"What happened after the bank foreclosed?" Gretchen asked. "What happened to the dolls?"

"I knew she was going to lose the dolls right along with the house, and I could hardly stand to watch it happen, but look around you," April said, sweeping her arms across the room. "I couldn't afford to buy them from her either. She wouldn't have sold anyway. She was in denial and probably drunk most of the time and didn't believe anything could happen to them. She adored her dolls."

Nina frowned. "But what made you so mad at her?"

"A lot of the Dollers tried to help her out by offering to buy her dolls. But part of the problem was that she wouldn't even let us *see* her collection. Over the years, she'd talk about a doll here and there, or we'd see one of them, but no one knew the actual extent of the collection."

"She certainly was an odd one," Nina said.

"She had one miniature doll that she showed me about a year before all this happened. It was only three and a half inches high." April spread her fingers to show how small three and a half inches really was. "It was a German bisque miniature, hand-painted with inset blue glass eyes. The prettiest thing you'd ever see. I loved that doll at first sight."

"She wouldn't sell it to you, would she?" Gretchen asked.

April nodded. "As it turned out, the bank or somebody acting for the bank took the whole thing away from her. What would it have hurt to give me that tiny little doll?"

"Did anyone ever find out for sure what happened to the collection?" Gretchen anticipated April's answer, but had to ask anyway.

"No. It vanished without a trace."

"There are a lot of things around here that seem to vanish without a trace," Nina observed.

April struggled into a sitting position, and a fine line of sweat dripped down the side of her face. She wiped it away. "I better head out," she said. "I'm late to work out. I missed my exercises all week because I was sick. I can't miss again today, or I'll fall behind on my new health program."

Nina shot a warning glance at Gretchen, and Gretchen composed her face.

"April has lost fifty pounds," Nina said to Gretchen. "She's working out at Curves."

Gretchen hadn't noticed any poundage loss, but she had spotted April's purse on the side table by the door and a set of keys beside it. She'd also noticed an overnight travel bag tossed carelessly on its side by the bedroom door. A cosmetic bag and a hairbrush had slid out onto the floor.

It looked like the woman stricken with valley fever had been away from home.

"Maybe she's packing for a trip," Nina said, when they returned to the car. They opened all the car doors, Nina turned on the ignition and the air-conditioning, and they waited on the sidewalk while the car cooled down. April lumbered to her crumpled Buick and waved as she drove off. Nina opened the back door and helped Tutu onto the seat. Nimrod squirmed out of his purse and ran back and forth in the rear as Nina took the driver's seat and belted up. "Maybe she's leaving today."

"I think she lied about the valley fever," Gretchen said, digging a folded piece of paper from her shorts and scanning the copy of Martha's inventory list. She found the doll April had once coveted: "German miniature, all bisque, jointed, marked German 10 on back of head, original handmade dress, three and a half inches high." She glanced up at the street ahead. "Can you catch up to her? Let's see if she's going where she said she's going."

"Fun. My first tail."

Nina stepped on the gas, and Gretchen's head snapped back. "Take it easy. I don't want any more trips to the hospital."

Several lights ahead, the back of April's car came into view, and Gretchen watched it turn onto University Drive and head for Phoenix. Fifteen minutes later April pulled over in front of a building bearing a small overhead sign, Curves. Curves, a popular fitness center exclusively for women, was sweeping the country, and Gretchen had considered paying a visit to one. This was her chance.

"Now we'll go in and ask her if she's leaving town," Nina said.

"We can't say it just like that." Gretchen watched April enter the building. "I'll go in and think of some reason for following her, something we forgot to ask her before she took off. You stay here with the dogs."

"We can all go in."

"I'm sure they don't allow dogs," Gretchen said. "Let's not cause a scene." She walked into Curves.

April was waiting for her.

"I thought I saw Nina's car following me," she said, eyeing Gretchen up and down. "You could stand to lose a few pounds, and there's no better way to do it. You want to give it a try, don't you?"

Gretchen gave April a weak smile. "That's why we decided to follow you. What do I do?"

April looked over at the front desk. "That okay with you?" she said to the woman sitting behind the desk. "That's Ora, the manager."

"Hey," Ora said to Gretchen. "April will take good care of you."

"You can be my guest today," April said, pride in her voice. "Follow behind me, and I'll show you how to use the machines. But watch that bad arm. You'll have to skip some of the arm weights. Our workout usually takes thirty minutes, but we'll cut it short since we're both on the mend."

April jumped onto a piece of equipment as an energetic
voice called from a CD overhead, "Change stations now."
Gretchen peered out the window and caught Nina's eye.
She sent a telepathic message to let Nina know that she'd
be back in twenty minutes and hoped Nina's invisible antenna was operating at peak performance.

A circle of women on various machines and platforms
moved in unison, performing simple stretching exercises.
Gretchen joined in next to April and spotted Bonnie Albright and Rita Phyller at the opposite end of the circuit.
She waved. They waved back.

Jogging in place on a platform, Gretchen said, "Is this
the local hangout for the doll club members? I see Bonnie
and Rita."

"It is," April said, rowing away on a machine, her elbows flapping like chicken wings. "Usually we have more
than this. Where's Nina?"

"She didn't want to leave the dogs alone in the car. It's
too hot without the air-conditioning running."

With each "Change stations now," April and Gretchen
rotated on the equipment circling the room. Gretchen had
to skip at least half of the machines because of her broken
wrist. She jogged in place instead.

"Did you hear from your mother yet?" Bonnie shouted
over the beat of disco music.

Gretchen shook her head, noting the glances exchanged
between the two doll collectors on the other side of the
room. She wondered what they said when she wasn't present, and whether they thought her mother had killed Martha.
It made for good gossip regardless of the final outcome, and
Bonnie could squeeze juicy tidbits out of a barrel cactus.

"Now move away from your station and find your heart
rate." Every woman in the room raised her hand to the side
of her neck as the prerecorded instructor called off the
count.

Gretchen heard April breathing in sharp, jagged gasps.
The front of April's shirt was soaked as though she had

taken a dip in a swimming pool with all her clothes on. As a few women cleared the workout stations around April and Gretchen, Bonnie and Rita skipped ahead and joined them.

After one time around the circuit, April sat down on a chair by the door. "I need a breather. Ten minutes is about all I have in me all at one time," she said thickly. "You go on around again. I'll catch up."

"I'm going over to South Phoenix to look at a Barbie," Rita said. "It's a Ponytail with a black-and-white-striped swimsuit, and in its original box. I looked at it yesterday and can't decide if I should buy it."

"What's holding you back?" Bonnie said.

"The price," Rita said. "They want twelve hundred dollars, and I really can't afford it."

"That's a lot of dough," April called out from the chair.

"That's why I'm looking at it again," Rita said, bending over and touching her toes. "I'm hoping they'll come way down on the price."

"I haven't been able to touch my toes since high school," April observed wistfully.

"Keep losing weight the way you have," Gretchen said encouragingly, treading steadily on a machine labeled the stepper, "and you'll be touching your toes in no time."

"Change stations now."

Everyone rotated.

"When I went to look at the Barbie yesterday," Rita said to Bonnie, "I saw you going into the Rescue Mission. Are you volunteering there?"

Bonnie looked startled. "You must be mistaken," she said. "I wasn't anywhere near the Rescue Mission."

"That's funny. I was certain it was you."

"No," Bonnie said, shaking her red shellacked flip. "It wasn't me."

Gretchen studied Bonnie. Flaming red hair and makeup painted on in exaggerated colors. It would be hard to mistake someone else for her.

"Anyway, what else is new?" April rejoined the group with renewed vigor and put everything she had into the shoulder press machine.

Gretchen, dancing on a platform, couldn't believe how easily the conversation turned in the right direction. Without missing a beat, she asked, "Anyone planning any trips?"

Death.

Caroline had felt its presence ever since that horrible moment when the doctor spoke the chilling words: "Breast cancer." The disease she had feared the most had invaded without a warning battle cry, its army of killer cells waging a war for supremacy within her chest.

She had felt death accompanying her through the ensuing surgery and the inescapable chemotherapy treatments. Death continued to whisper an incessant promise of eventual victory, and she had been on a quest ever since to find meaning in her life.

The answer to her existence continued to elude her in the same way that the doll she sought continued to slip away.

She had cheated death once before.

She could do it again.

· 14 ·

*A successful doll dealer must learn the fine art of subtle persua-
sion. He must present himself as a valuable asset to the collector, learning what the collector seeks and dissuading her from
negotiating with his rivals. At the very least, he must have good
relationships with established customers and offer a fair return
policy if he wishes to survive in his trade. To thrive rather than
simply survive, he must be a gifted performer.*

—From *World of Dolls* by Caroline Birch

"No, April isn't planning a trip," Gretchen informed Nina
when she returned to the car. "Not a short one or a long
one, nothing in the future, nothing in the past. If she can be
believed."

"I still think she had valley fever," Nina said.

"The newest development concerns Bonnie. Rita says
she saw her go into the Rescue Mission yesterday, but Bonnie denies it. Why would she be hanging around that area?"

"You've been there twice looking for Nacho. Maybe she
is, too."

"That's what bothers me."

"Where next?" Nina asked.

Gretchen unfolded a piece of paper with names and addresses she'd copied from the telephone directory. "Let's
visit Martha's relative," she said. "I really want to know
why he hid their family connection."

It was a short hop from the city of Tempe over to Mesa,
which was known as a Mormon town. With more than

twenty golf courses, it touted itself as an affordable and ideal retirement community.

They pulled into a drive-through restaurant, ordered at the window, and sat in the car eating green chile burgers and French fries. Nina hand-fed pieces of hamburger to Tutu and Nimrod after picking off most of the green chiles. A wee-wee stop afterwards completed the fine dining experience for the two dogs.

Exhibiting extreme willpower, Gretchen refused an order of fries, remembering April's comment about Gretchen's weight at Curves.

"Do you think I need to lose a few pounds, Aunt Nina?"

"No," Nina said, laughing. "You need to develop a life."

"You're terrible. Cruel and inhuman."

"I have an idea for you."

"I can't wait."

"Why don't you come and work for me? We can train purse dogs together." Nina nibbled on a French fry, and Gretchen watched with envy. "I've been turning away clients because I don't have enough time. You'd be good."

Gretchen rolled her eyeballs to the ceiling of the car, then glanced at Tutu and Nimrod in the backseat. Nimrod had mustard on his face from the hamburger. The canine profession suited Nina perfectly, as did doll restoration for her mother.

Gretchen, alas, still searched for her own niche. Dog training was decidedly not it.

"I don't think I have the patience," Gretchen said. "And Wobbles wouldn't approve. Besides, I'm going back to Boston soon, back to Steve and back to the search for a 'real' job."

"Are you implying that purse dog training isn't a real job?" Nina said.

Gretchen gave in to temptation and snitched one of Nina's fries while she searched for a quick response to cover having blurted out the truth. "It demands a certain amount of connection with different energy sources, uh . . . a special ability to read auras must be important in training puppies. I bet only a few people have what it takes."

"You could be a cat trainer." Nina's eyes lit up at the idea. "Are cats trainable?"

Gretchen chuckled at the thought of any cat taking orders from a human being. She tried to picture Wobbles traveling in a purse and snorted out loud. "No," she said. "They really aren't."

"What about that guy in Key West? The Catman," Nina said. "He makes cats jump through hoops."

"I'd love to see that sometime. But right now, let's go talk to Joseph Reiner."

Joseph's Dream Dolls was located on Southern Avenue and was appropriately named. The shop cabinets and countertops brimmed with fabulous dolls arranged in groupings. Rare collectibles were locked into a large cabinet where Gretchen stood admiring a Kestner boy doll through the glass. Joseph rushed to the front of the store to greet them.

"Hey, you two," he said, noticing the dogs for the first time. "I'm closing up. It's five o'clock. I'll just lock the door. You two stay put." He rolled a finger across the top of Nimrod's head, then bent to give Tutu equal attention.

"I'm showing Gretchen around town," Nina said. "We thought we'd stop by."

"Look around. Enjoy yourself, but keep a good eye on your dogs. The teacup poodle in the purse is priceless." He breezed away to lock up.

What a delight, Gretchen thought, reveling in the combination of old and new—a Door of Hope Mission doll from China, several Queen Annes, and a large selection of contemporary artist dolls. She admired a Dy-Dee Baby and two celebrity dolls, Marie Osmond and Annette Funicello. The collection of dolls was endless, and for a time, as she wandered through the shop, she escaped into a make-believe world of color and glamour and beauty.

Joseph cleared his throat and brought her back from her

welcome escape from reality. "I didn't mean to startle you," he said, pulling at the diamond stud in his left ear.

"I'm okay." Gretchen laughed lightly. "We came by for several reasons, to see your shop, of course, but I wanted to show you this picture again when all the club members weren't present."

"I thought that detective took this picture as evidence," Joseph said when she handed it to him.

"This is a copy." Gretchen wasn't about to tell him of the second picture or about her mother's message on the back of it. She had stashed that one safely away after making a copy of the picture of the doll. "I know you saw the picture yesterday at Bonnie's, but take another look. Have you ever seen this French fashion doll before?"

"No," he said. "But I want to. It's amazing." He handed the copy back to Gretchen and rubbed his goatee with two fingers. "Why do you ask?"

"You know my mother is missing. And you have to know that the police suspect her in Martha's death." Gretchen watched Joseph carefully. He seemed unnaturally nervous, as he had at the meeting at Nina's house.

Joseph nodded. "I'm not passing judgment on Caroline. She's innocent until proven guilty as far as I'm concerned."

"Thank you. I appreciate that. This doll might have something to do with her disappearance, or it might not. I think the picture is worth showing around in case someone recognizes it."

"Sorry I can't help you."

"Maybe you still can," Gretchen said. "It's my understanding that Martha was your aunt. Am I correct?"

"Who told you that?" Joseph spoke a little too loudly, a little too defensively.

"Was she your aunt?"

Joseph rubbed his face with his hands as though he were rubbing away a bad dream. "Embarrassing to admit, but yes, she was my aunt. I'm related to that pathetic, homeless drunk. Or was. We weren't close, and I didn't mention it to the club members because I had no desire to share my ancestry with them."

"She apparently didn't go out of her way to cultivate alliances," Gretchen said.

Joseph nodded. "She led a self-absorbed life, at least after the alcohol took control. The ability to look beyond her personal self-interests drowned in a pool of stale booze, a common symptom of alcoholism."

Gretchen remembered what Nina had said about Joseph's own problems with alcohol and his resolve to beat the disease.

"Did she have any family other than you?"

"A sister in Florida, but they hadn't spoken for years. She's in a nursing home in the final stages of Alzheimer's. She wouldn't understand that Martha is dead or that she even had a sister."

"How about friends?"

Joseph laughed bitterly. "Aunt Martha didn't have any real friends left. I suppose you could count those down-and-out characters she roamed the streets with as friends."

Gretchen heard Nina's cell phone from somewhere in the shop playing the *Star Wars* theme. "Hello," she heard Nina say.

"Martha had an expensive collection of dolls at one time," Gretchen said to Joseph. "Can you tell me what happened to it?"

"I've had this shop for seventeen years," Joseph said. "She bought her first doll from me, at a discount, of course. After that, she became very secretive about what she purchased and where she bought it. She hid the dolls around her house, worrying constantly that someone would steal them. She became distrustful of everyone. What's the point of having a collection if you can't have fun with it?"

"Then?" Gretchen said, encouraging him to continue. She heard Nina's voice drifting from across the room.

"I offered to take the collection on consignment when I found out she faced bankruptcy, but she refused. She had a pernicious personality. Her fingers were caustic, destroying everything she touched. And she never let go. I don't know what happened to her collection. I have to assume that she acted with her typical irrational behavior, and the collection is lost forever."

"You hesitated before answering. You don't believe it, do you?"

Joseph shrugged. "She cared about those dolls in a way she never cared about any living person. She would have died for them before she'd let anyone take them."

Maybe she did die for them.

"Last I saw her, she was hopelessly lost in one of many bouts of what I called schizophrenic paranoia. She showed up here at the shop. Someone was always out to get her. Nations plotted to overthrow her. This time the secret agent stalking her was someone she called 'the Inspector.' I assumed she meant the state of Arizona was finally going to force her into a rehab program. Too bad they didn't move a little quicker."

Nina came around the corner, her face as white as unpainted china.

"What's wrong?" Gretchen asked, afraid to hear the answer.

"They found your mother's car," Nina said, her voice thick and shaky, "in northern Scottsdale."

"And?"

Gretchen watched Nina's mouth slowly form the words. "The car left the road and ran into a drainage ditch. It must have rolled several times, because it landed upside down."

Gretchen's hands flew to her mouth. "No," she said in disbelief. "Is she . . . ?"

"Caroline's in critical condition at Scottsdale Memorial. She's in surgery right now."

· 15 ·

When restoring an antique doll head, the aim is to make the re-pair as inconspicuous as possible by simulating the original glazes and colors. A successful repair depends on a perfect blend between the surface and the cracked area and on successfully matching colors. Flesh is the color used most often, and it can be mixed by adding small amounts of red, yellow, and brown to white paint until the desired skin tone is produced.

—From *World of Dolls* by Caroline Birch

While Gretchen drove to the hospital, Nina dialed several phone numbers before reaching someone who could help. Larry Gerney agreed to meet them in the visitor's parking lot and arrived at the same time they did. Hurrying, they transferred Tutu and Nimrod to Larry's car. Gretchen handed over the key to her mother's house. "It's much closer for you than driving them all the way to Nina's," she said. "Leave the dogs there."

"I'll take care of it," Larry said and pulled away as they ran into the hospital.

Nina's ability to think in a linear path under duress amazed Gretchen. By the time they arrived at the hospital, Nina had notified most of the Birch family members across the country, arranged for pet care with Larry, and had even left a message for Steve to return her call. Gretchen, on the other hand, had driven in silence, almost paralyzed by fear and shock.

Now she wanted to stand up and scream at everyone—at the dispassionate receptionist attending the waiting room desk, at the nurses strolling through in their impenetrable groups, quietly murmuring among themselves and consulting clipboards. She wanted to scream at Nina for her endless chatter.

This couldn't be happening. She stared out a hospital window at pavement and parked cars and at nothing at all. Nina forced her to take a cup of coffee, but her one good arm felt too weak to lift it to her lips. Instead of drinking the coffee, she clutched it like a lifeline.

Hospital sounds whirled around her. An overhead paging system called for Dr. Kay. Mechanical noises created by massive generators churned, and carts creaked down harshly lighted halls that smelled faintly of chemicals and sanitizers.

Someone walked by and stopped. Gretchen turned her head.

"She suffered a subdural hematoma," a woman in scrubs said. "A severe head injury. She's in surgery now to relieve the pressure and control the bleeding. We won't know anything for several hours."

"Did anyone speak to her?" Nina asked.

"She was unconscious when she arrived."

"Is the bleeding in her brain?" Nina said while Gretchen remained speechless.

"No," the woman explained. "It's the area external to the brain, below the inner layer of the dura."

Nina nodded and gripped Gretchen's fingers below her cast.

"Thank you," Gretchen murmured and the woman walked through doors clearly labeled No Admittance.

In novels, the heroine never cries, Gretchen thought, watching Nina dab her eyes with a balled-up tissue. Gretchen looked away, wondering who the heroine could be in this real-life drama. She didn't know why, but the sight of other people crying always brought tears to her own eyes.

Two uniformed police, stationed at the end of the hall,

stood guard. Because of Caroline's arrest warrant status, they would remain at the hospital until she awoke and was able to be questioned.

If she awoke.

If. If. If . . .

Larry returned from taking the dogs home and sat down beside them, visibly agitated. Detective Albright appeared and strode purposefully across the waiting room toward them.

"I headed here as soon as I heard," he said. "I don't have much information. We don't have any witnesses to the accident, at least not yet. A passing motorist observed the car lying upside down in the ditch on Pima Road and called nine-one-one. It took quite a while to extricate her from the vehicle, and she lost consciousness during transport in the paramedic unit." He looked at Gretchen. "Have you heard anything yet?"

"She has a head injury," Gretchen said faintly. "She's in surgery. Were you at the scene?"

"Of the accident? No. I didn't hear about it until they had time to run the plates. She was on her way to the hospital by then."

"Did anyone talk to her?" Larry asked, blinking wildly.

"She was in shock," Matt said. "She didn't make much sense."

"Nina asked the hospital staff the same thing," Gretchen said. "But no one had an opportunity to ask her about the accident. She was unconscious when she arrived."

"Why don't you take a break," Matt said. "Go home for awhile. I'll call you when she comes out of surgery."

"I'll stay, too," Larry said.

Gretchen shook her head. "I couldn't possibly leave."

"We had to turn off our cell phones when we entered the hospital," Nina said. "Let's go outside and try to get through to Steve again, and I'll update the family."

"Who's Steve?" Matt asked.

"Her fiancé," Nina replied, stretching the truth even in

time of crisis. "He's an attorney, so you better watch your-self. No more illegal moves while he's round. I think I might have a lawsuit against you for searching my car."

"I'll be on my best behavior," Matt said, displaying the palms of his hands. "Promise."

Gretchen had lost all feeling. Her body and mind were numb. Nina took the coffee cup from her hand, placed it on the table, and led her outside. She didn't feel the heat. She shuffled along like a woman without hope, like the home-less men and women wandering the streets.

"Turn on your phone," Nina said harshly. "Snap out of it."

Gretchen numbly dialed Steve's office number. "No one's answering at the office."

"It's Sunday," Nina said. "Call his cell phone."

She gazed into Nina's frightened eyes and listened to the third ring. She chewed her lip.

"Gretchen," Steve said when he answered. "What's go-ing on?"

Mechanically, she related the events surrounding her mother's accident as they had been told to her.

"I don't know what to say," Steve said. "This is awful. Are you okay?"

Gretchen wanted to say *No, I'm not okay. Nothing is okay. How could I be okay?* Instead she said, "I'm with Nina. We'll be at Scottsdale Memorial until we know the outcome of the surgery and I get a chance to see her. I can't use my phone inside. You'll have to call the hospital if you want me."

"Just do whatever you need to do. And call me as soon as you know anything."

Gretchen signed off. She wanted to scream at him, too. Why hadn't he offered to come? Didn't he know she needed his support, needed him at her side? *Calm down,* she scolded. *Stay cool. You're overreacting. It's the stress that's making you feel crazy.*

"I have your aunt Gertie on the line," Nina said with dis-taste, covering her cell phone with her hand. "She's willing to catch a flight today if you want her to. She said your mother has to be exonerated and needs help now more than ever because she can't defend herself."

Gretchen took the phone from Nina. "Hey, Aunt Gertie. I can't worry about the murder investigation right now. All I care about is whether or not she's going to live."

"Quality of life counts, too, you know," Gertie said. "She isn't going to be happy in prison. She needs you to keep working for her because she can't do it herself."

"Don't come yet. I'll let you know if I need you."

"We're a crusty line of women," Gertie said. "You have what it takes. Keep me posted, and stay strong."

Gretchen heard her disconnect.

Stay strong. Good advice from Aunt Gertie.

Larry continued to make himself useful. At eight o'clock, he drove back to Caroline's house to check on Tutu and Nimrod and feed Wobbles. "I confined them to the kitchen. Not Wobbles," he said quickly when he saw Gretchen's expression. "The two dogs. I had to. They were behaving like a bunch of teenagers who discovered the parents were away. What a mess."

He caught Nina's look. "Don't worry. I cleaned it up."

Matt paced the hall, drinking coffee and occasionally huddling with the officers on duty in the hall. At some point, he thrust a tuna sandwich into Gretchen's hand and forced her to take small bites.

Three eternal hours after they had arrived at the hospital, the doctor appeared.

"She's in recovery," he said. "The surgery went well. She's not out of danger yet, though. The next twenty-four hours are critical."

Gretchen and Nina fell into each other's arms and let the emotions that had been boiling under the surface escape. Damp-eyed, Gretchen asked to see her mother.

"She'll be in recovery for a while. Go home, and we'll call you when she wakes up. That won't be any time soon."

Gretchen glanced at Matt. At least he had the good sense

to refrain from requesting an interrogation. She wondered how soon the attending physician would allow police officials to question his patient. When Matt sat down next to the coffeepot and crossed one leg over his knee, Gretchen knew he was in for the long haul. So was she.

"I'm staying," she said to the doctor, with a piercing glance at Matt. She sat down hard in a chair and crossed her arms. "And I expect to be the first one notified when she is able to have a visitor."

The doctor approached the detective. "It'll be some time before you will be able to interview her. Her family will be the only ones allowed in initally."

Matt looked over at Gretchen. "I understand. I'm staying anyway. After all, I'm almost like family."

How quickly he went from family friend to family member. A charlatan, our craggy detective.

"I'm staying, too," Larry said.

Another round of waiting began. Gretchen watched the sun go down from a chair next to the window. The officers standing guard resorted to playing cards. Nina left to monitor her pets with Larry in tow, and Gretchen found herself alone with Matt. He glanced up from a magazine.

"What did she say?" Gretchen asked.

"Excuse me?"

"You said she was in shock at the scene of the accident."

"Schmidt," he said, calling to one of the officers. "You talked to Caroline Birch?"

The taller of the two officers looked up from his card hand. "Yah, but she talked gibberish."

"What did she say?" Gretchen said.

Officer Schmidt lowered his cards and folded them into his beefy palm and frowned in concentration. "Let's see. She musta thought she was auditioning for a part in a movie or something. She said she was waiting forever to be discovered, and this was her big break." He fanned the cards and threw one down. "What do you expect? She was in shock."

Gretchen sat up straight in her chair. She felt a wave of dizziness and clutched the side of the chair. "How did you identify her?" she asked slowly. The answer was important, more important than they knew. "How did you know she was Caroline Birch?" she demanded, rephrasing the question.

The officer continued to scowl. "We ran the plates."

Matt leaned forward and abruptly dropped the magazine on a side table. "What?"

"She wasn't carrying identification," the officer said defensively, sensing he'd said something wrong.

"No purse?" Matt asked.

Officer Schmidt shook his head. "Not a scrap of paper anywhere. No purse. No wallet. Just a paper bag with a few dirty clothes wadded up inside."

Gretchen jumped up. She wanted to scream at the top of her lungs. Instead she shouted to no one in particular, "That isn't my mother in recovery. She didn't have a car accident."

"What are you saying?" Matt said.

"The car accident. It wasn't my mother in the car. It was Daisy, the homeless woman."

Gretchen and Matt stood beside her bed. The nurse in charge of the recovery room watched to make sure they obeyed the rules. Their instructions had been clear. No speaking to the patient. One minute, no more, to make the identification.

This was highly irregular. Frowned on by administration. But under the circumstances . . .

She seemed small and helpless wrapped in hospital linens and gown, and her eyes were closed. Her head was wrapped in white bandages, and tubes snaked from beneath the bedding and traveled up into a maze of equipment and monitors.

The woman who was her mother. But wasn't.

If Daisy were conscious, she would be pleased at the attention, the part she unwittingly played. She had finally received top billing to a sold-out audience.

Gretchen struggled between feelings of intense relief that she wasn't viewing her injured mother and overwhelming guilt because of that relief. A woman lay before her, struggling for life. Whatever distance Gretchen had felt from Daisy and her way of life was now shortened. Her possession of Caroline's car had established a connection, and Gretchen vowed to do whatever she could to help Daisy. If only she would live.

Where was her mother? Gretchen's search led her in a circuitous path, and with each loop she found herself traveling closer to Nacho and Daisy. How did a ragged collection of indigents get to occupy center stage?

Gretchen felt a gentle nudge and looked up into Matt's questioning eyes.

She nodded.

· 16 ·

Modern baby dolls have soft bodies and natural hair that can be brushed and styled. Some even have that wonderful baby smell. The need to nurture plays a key role in our love of baby dolls. We all need to give love and reach out for companionship, and we learn it at a young age. You have only to watch young children feed, dress, and cuddle their own baby dolls to understand the complex emotions of maternal joy.

—From *World of Dolls* by Caroline Birch

Gretchen opened one eye. She was lying in her mother's bed. Sunlight beamed through the slatted blinds, and Wobbles rose from the bed covers and stretched luxuriantly.

Images from the night before flashed through her mind. Nina's expression when she learned that Daisy, not her cherished older sister, lay beyond the waiting room doors. Endless phone calls, correcting false information dispersed earlier to frightened relatives. The reaction that remained central in Gretchen's mind was Aunt Gertie's unique analysis: "The woman who fell from your mountain obviously wasn't murdered for love, so it had to be about money," she had said late last night. "She hid her dolls, and everyone's scrambling around hoping to cash in. It appears you and your airhead Aunt Nina and, of course, the cops, who never know anything anyway, are the only ones who don't know what's going on."

"What about my mother?" Gretchen had asked.

"Your mother knows more than anybody," Aunt Gertie insisted. "That's why she's holed up."

Holed up? Gretchen hadn't heard that expression since the days she watched old westerns with her father. The Hole-in-the-Wall Gang and Bonnie and Clyde. *Holed up* invoked images of outlaw behavior, albeit romantic, glorified criminals who died young.

Gretchen forced the image of Bonnie and Clyde's last moments from her mind. Riddled with bullets.

Aunt Gertie's down-home attitude appealed to Gretchen in spite of her phrase turning. She said what she meant and did what she had to do and didn't care what others thought of her. You always knew where you stood with Aunt Gertie. She epitomized their family of mostly strong women.

Gretchen couldn't say the same for herself. She was the exception.

She made her second vow in the last twenty-four hours. The first was to Daisy and their future relationship. The second was to herself. She would, in military terms, muster up, find those strength genes running renegade inside her, and harness them together.

Today she would wear her new attitude like a gun holster on her hip.

"Let's go," she called to Nina, buried under a pile of blankets on Caroline's sofa where she had collapsed in exhaustion. Tutu's head popped out at the bottom of the blankets next to one purple-lacquered toe. When Gretchen pulled back the covers she found Nimrod sleeping in Nina's armpit. "Rise and shine. We're on a mission today, and you'll have to start out at a run to keep up with me."

Wobbles wound through her legs while she made coffee. She dumped two extra tablespoons into the filter to symbolize her new strength and fortitude and then fed all the animals. "The dogs are staying home today, Nina. We have to stay flexible because . . ." She leaned into Nina's blanketed form as it rose and moved toward her like a zombie from beyond. ". . . today we will either find my mother or find out what really happened, or both."

Nina, slumped in a kitchen chair while Gretchen toasted sourdough bread and sliced a thick wedge of Vermont cheddar. "Eat," Gretchen ordered.

She checked her array of voice machines: apartment in Boston, cell phone voice mail, and her mother's personal answering machine. A few acquaintances in Boston wondered when she would be back, a message from Steve sounding annoyed and wanting to know what was going on "since yesterday's fiasco," and a message from Larry.

"I've put all Caroline's projects on hold," Larry said. "Except a few of the most pressing jobs. When I let the dogs out yesterday I also reprogrammed the voice message on Caroline's business machine, directing all calls to my number until further notice. I hope you don't mind. If you find that you have to do something with your hands because waiting is driving you mad, I left a few simple restringing jobs behind. There's no hurry on those, though. Keep me posted."

Briefly Gretchen wondered if Larry's intentions were as unmotivated as he pretended. Reprogramming her mother's machine seemed like a bold thing to do, considering the competitive nature of the doll business. Well, Gretchen reasoned, her mother would have lost customers with unmet deadlines anyway.

She decided to ignore Steve's message and his petulant remark. This was the new Gretchen Birch.

She drove away from the house with a grumbling, pet-free Nina riding shotgun. Detective Albright pulled out from the curb behind them. "Doesn't he have anything better to do?" Gretchen said. "He knows by now that I don't have a clue where she is. Is he waiting for me to solve the case for him? Tagging along to claim the prize and win a promotion?"

"He's probably looking out for you," Nina said. "I think he's cute."

When they turned onto Lincoln, Gretchen dialed 911. "I'm being followed," she said into the phone. "The driver is shaking a tire iron at me in a threatening way and displaying obscene gestures. In fact, he tried to run me off the road. Please help."

Nina stared at Gretchen.

"No, he's too close to read his license number." Gretchen gave the dispatcher her location. "He's driving a blue Chevrolet. Me . . . ?" Gretchen hesitated, searching the cars ahead of her and spotting a likely candidate. "I'm driving a yellow Mercedes convertible. We'll be passing Twenty-fourth Street soon."

A few minutes later, Gretchen heard sirens in the distance. Without signaling, she abruptly pulled over on the shoulder of the street, startling Matt, who had no recourse other than to continue on ahead of her. He slowed, then pulled over when he heard the siren and saw the lights looming behind him.

"Imagine his surprise," Nina said, watching the police vehicle slide in behind Matt's car.

Gretchen pulled back onto Lincoln and drove past the startled detective, who was already out of his vehicle flashing his badge at the responding police officer. "We don't have much time to make our getaway," she said, adapting a choice word from Aunt Gertie's repertoire. "He'll be after us as soon as the police officer realizes who he is."

"I didn't know you had it in you," Nina said, incredulous.

Gretchen smiled wordlessly.

Nacho streaked down the street with Gretchen in hot pursuit and Nina somewhere behind in the Impala. She wore her favorite running shoes in anticipation of this exact scenario. Best of all she had surprised *him* instead of the other way around. She had seized the advantage and was right on his heels.

But she had yet to figure out how to stop him, short of a

full-body tackle, because she really didn't want another broken bone.

She was so close behind him that his smell filled her nostrils, ripe body odor and dirty clothes. And fear. She smelled his fear. Even though she had never smelled fear before, she knew this was it, the same way any predator knows the smell. She'd had her share of fear last night. It was his turn.

Passersby looked on in astonishment as the two darted down the sidewalk clogged with people heading for work. A dog barked. Gretchen reached ahead with her good hand and tried to get a grip on the back of his shirt. He squealed and wrenched away.

How to stop him? She might have an uncanny new inner strength, but her dull mental processing could use some sharpening. Suddenly the answer came to her.

"Daisy's hurt," she managed to call out through bursting lungs. "She had . . ." Gretchen puffed. ". . . a car accident. She's in the hospital."

She sensed him wavering, an almost imperceptible change in his speed.

"She needs you."

Nacho slowed to a trot, and Gretchen forced herself to be patient. Don't grab at him. Let him come to you now.

He twirled, still moving, backwards. "You're lying."

"No, she was driving my mother's car." Gretchen saw a flicker of recognition in his eyes. *He knows,* she thought. *He knows about the car but not about the accident.*

"She's hurt badly. I can take you to her."

She pulled her cell phone from a clip on her belt. She had planned ahead to keep her hands free from the burden of a purse. The clip was Nina's idea to allow her freedom to move. Gretchen wished she'd thought of it sooner.

"We're ready," she whispered into the phone.

From the corner of her eye she saw Nina's Impala pull up to the curb, and Nacho warily slid into the backseat, tensed to make a run for it if necessary.

Gretchen slid in right behind him, leaving Nina alone

up front to taxi them to the hospital. "You're traveling light today," she said, "Where's your bag and Daisy's shopping cart?"

"At my place," he said. "Like it's any of your business." *"My place?" He had a place?*

"Take Sixteenth Street," Gretchen advised Nina. "We don't want to run into our persistent detective friend."

They drove the rest of the way to the hospital in silence, a dubious expression on Nina's face. The windows were rolled down to disburse the rank air. Nacho stayed alert, one hand on the door handle. Gretchen sat on an angle, eyeing Nacho in case he decided to make a swift exit.

The critical care receptionist scrunched her nose and gaped at Nacho. Her eyes flicked up and down his body suspiciously, taking in the protrusion on the side of his head, but her expression lightened when she recognized Gretchen.

"Your mother's feeling better today," she said, still operating under mistaken identities. "She's awake."

"We'd like to see her," Gretchen said, well aware of the family-only rule and seizing the opportunity to bypass it without having to explain that Daisy's next of kin was an imaginary movie producer.

"Only for a few minutes. The doctor will be in soon." She studied Nacho. "Is he family?"

"Uncle Nacho," Gretchen said. "And this is Aunt Nina."

"You have quite a family," the receptionist said, unaware of the hostile glare Nina shot at Gretchen. "Room three twelve. Only one of you in the room at a time. We don't want to tire the patient."

The critical care unit was a formidable place, capable of intimidating the most resilient visitor. The air buzzed with activity in spite of the hushed atmosphere.

After finding the right room, Gretchen cast a look down the hall and, after making sure they weren't watched, motioned to Nina and Nacho to follow her in.

Daisy, encased in white bedding and bandages, looked like an octopus, tentacles of plastic tubing rising in the air.

She opened one eye and smiled when she saw Nacho standing in the doorway.

"Look at this," she said. "The show is sold out on opening night. Hello, fans."

"You gave me a scare," Nacho said, moving close and taking her hand. "I worried about you when you didn't come back."

"We all worried about you," Nina said.

"This is like a fancy resort for me," Daisy said. "Three squares a day and a button for room service. I might learn to like it here."

Nacho continued to hold her hand.

"Did you tell them?" Daisy asked him.

"Not yet." Nacho's face softened.

"It's time to tell them. They're her family," Daisy said.

Nacho blew out a sigh and turned to Gretchen and Nina.

"Caroline flew out on a plane right after Martha died," he said. "She didn't want to leave a trail, so I moved her car away from the airport. She gave me a credit card, and I drove it to Cave Creek and used the card to fill up the gas tank. I did it just like she said."

"Where did she go?" Gretchen asked.

"She said she had to take care of something important that involved Martha. She wouldn't tell me anything more than that."

"How do you know my mother?" Gretchen asked. "And why would she ask you to help her?" She didn't say the obvious, that Nacho had little to give in the way of support.

"Martha trusted her. That was good enough for me. You'll have to ask her yourself why she came to me."

Gretchen eyed Nacho. Unkempt, a knob on his head sprouting up like a cactus through the dry desert earth, defiance in his stance. "Do you know there's a warrant for her arrest? The police think she may have killed Martha."

"That's not true."

"What about the doll trunk?" Nina said.

"She left a bag in the backseat of her car. She told me to

open it and follow the directions she had written on the picture."

"The same bag I found in the shopping cart? With the doll trunk?"

Nacho nodded.

"Where's the doll?"

"I never saw a doll."

"Okay," Gretchen said. "You went to the airport with her, she gave you a credit card and her car, and asked you to take care of the doll trunk. And all this time she didn't tell you where she was going or why she was going there. Do I have that right?"

"You got it," Daisy said, her voice like a dove feather, soft and lilting. "Only I love to drive around. Haven't had a car since the late eighties. Whee, it was fun."

"That's why you had Daisy's shopping cart?" Gretchen said to Nacho. "Because she wanted to drive around?"

"She was supposed to park it over by McDowell," Nacho said. "That was the plan. Instead, Daisy was gone overnight."

The unemployed actress put on an appropriately chastised expression, as if to say that the bandages wrapped around her head proved that her punishment outweighed her crime.

Gretchen studied Daisy, and it struck her that the homeless woman would have viewed the car as more than a simple pleasure ride. She would have thought of it as shelter. "Instead of abandoning the car you were sleeping in it, weren't you?" Gretchen said.

"I know I shouldn't have," Daisy said. "I wanted to take one last ride, then I planned to park it right where Nacho said."

Nacho scowled at her, eyebrows meeting in one bushy line, tufts of stubble sprouting from unlikely pores in his face. Concern, rather than anger, apparent in his eyes. An obvious bond existed between them.

"And I would have, too, if someone hadn't rammed into the back of the car. I lost control and flew right off the road."

Detective Albright waited in the lobby. Gretchen could feel his anger saturating the climate-controlled hospital air, his face tight, the space around him crackling with static tension.

"Who are you?" he said to Nacho, his voice as controlled as the air-conditioning. He made a point of ignoring her.

"My brother?" Nina managed to croak.

"You need to say that with more conviction. If I didn't know you so well, I might think you made it up," Matt said to Nina. He grabbed Gretchen by the arm and steered her away from the others. "I need to speak with you.

"I could charge you with obstruction of justice," he hissed when they were out of earshot.

"I could charge you with police brutality." Gretchen wrenched away from his grasp.

"I can't believe you called the cops on me."

"It was a case of mistaken identity. I didn't know it was you."

"We seem to have a lot of mistaken identities as well as disappearing acts going on." Matt ran his fingers through his hair. "Who's the colorful character?"

"A friend of Daisy's."

"We had an agreement to share information, remember?"

"That was your idea, not mine. As far as I'm concerned, we're on opposing sides."

Matt leaned in. "We both want the same thing. We want to see this case closed."

"We differ in the end results. I care about the outcome." Gretchen glanced over at Nina and Nacho. What could she tell him that would help her mother? Nothing. What could she say? *Excuse me, but the latest facts are a little puzzling. You see, my mother conspired with these nice homeless*

*people to conceal her movements in an effort to throw off
pursuers and evade capture.*

She glanced at Nacho. What other bits of useful information could she share?

*Then there's the note I found scribbled on a photocopy of a doll. My mother hid a French fashion doll and
asked her coconspirators to hide a valuable doll trunk,
which they did. Oh, and by the way, I stole the trunk from
them.*

The situation kept getting better and better and her involvement deeper and deeper.

Gretchen thought of one thing she could tell him that
might help. She wondered how much information Daisy
would willingly offer the authorities. Based on her lifestyle,
probably not much.

"Daisy had the car accident because someone rammed
into the back of my mother's car," Gretchen said. "Since the
Birch women don't believe in coincidence, let's assume it
was intentional. This means that someone was trying to kill
Daisy or someone was trying to kill my mother."

With one last scathing look, Matt headed for the elevator.

Caroline stood inside a Western Union on the south side of
Chicago and counted out the money in her hands. Thanks
to her sister-in-law's generosity and her amazing ability to
stifle her ususal runaway curiosity, Caroline would buy a
change of clothes, splurge on a hot meal, and check into a
modest hotel room for a much-needed shower.

She had had no choice but to appeal to someone for
help, and her late husband's somewhat cantankerous sister,
Gertie, had been the right choice after all. No questions
asked. Beyond the limited information Gertie was offered,
she had a certain innate understanding of the complex circumstances that controlled Caroline's actions.

Of course, she'd wire the money.

Caroline left Western Union and hastened along, her

laptop an extension of her arm, anxious to find a private place to search the Internet once again.

Hurry up. And wait. Hurry up. And wait.

This whole unpleasant business was taking much longer than she anticipated. Without a strike soon, she was doomed. Like a broken doll consigned to the waste heap.

She fervently hoped she was right and that his greed would compel him to sell another one. It could as easily be a woman, she reminded herself. She had no idea who her antagonist was. Male or female, it didn't matter at all.

The time had come, she decided, to call her daughter.

17

Collectors have as many ways of displaying their collections as their unique and creative personalities allow. Some like to be surrounded by their dolls, in the kitchen, halls, and covering every available space throughout their homes. Some collectors dedicate one room to their dolls, practicing strict temperature control and avoiding humidity fluctuations. Some use cabinets to keep the dolls free from dust and other airborne particles. Some hide their dolls in locked rooms, guard them jealously, and live in constant fear of break-ins.

—From *World of Dolls* by Caroline Birch

Gretchen had many questions for Nacho, but he became withdrawn and uncommunicative without Daisy to prompt him along. His eyes grew fearful, his glance darting, searching for an escape route like a trapped animal.

It was the thunder that did it.

They stood in front of the hospital and watched the sky. The wind had picked up speed, roaring to the south. Rain clouds were visible on the horizon and moving toward them.

"I thought it didn't rain in Phoenix in July," Gretchen said to Nina. "Maybe the storm will bring cooler weather."

Nina snorted. "Don't count on it. This isn't the East Coast. Arizona is a planet of its own, like Mars or Jupiter, and it'll stay stifling hot with or without rain."

Lightning speared into the desert floor somewhere in the distance, and Gretchen could feel static electricity snapping through the air.

"The monsoon," Nacho muttered, with increased agitation.

"Flashflooding," Nina said.

Nacho turned to Gretchen. "You have to take me home. Quickly."

"Lead the way," she said, feeling she was finally breaking through a barrier.

The storm moved in behind the Impala as they traveled from Scottsdale into Phoenix's central city. Nacho led Gretchen past the Southern Pacific Rail Yard and the freight trains that brought lumber and building materials into the construction-crazed city. They drove along the Black Canyon Highway on an elevated viaduct and exited with the first drops of rain beginning to splatter on the windshield.

The monsoon, Nina explained as they drove, started in July and ended sometime in August. It brought torrential rains and damaging hail, water that the hard-packed earth couldn't absorb and the inadequate drainage system couldn't transport.

Streets could become rapidly moving rivers, tearing out trees and destroying buildings.

"Surely, you're exaggerating," Gretchen said, her eyes wide.

Nina shook her head. "Six inches of fast-moving water can knock you right off your feet. I've seen cars swept away."

Gretchen glanced back and saw black sky outdistancing them and swirling clouds approaching fast. Ahead, in the boulevards, palm trees bowed under the increasing force of the wind.

Nacho directed them to pull off beneath a freeway viaduct. As soon as the car stopped, he bolted out the door and ran down into a shallow wash. Nina and Gretchen followed, stumbling on the rough ground. Nina, who thought shopping at the mall qualified as strenuous exercise, scrambled to keep up, and Gretchen slowed to wait for her.

"How do we know he isn't dangerous?" Nina puffed. "He could have killed Martha and lied about helping your mother."

"I'm willing to take that risk if it means finding her."

The sky gave way, and rain pounded down, hammering the car and everything else in its path. The bridge overhead saved them from the deluge.

"This isn't too bad," Gretchen said. "We can wait out the rain right here."

"You have a lot to learn," Nina said, tripping along. "It's a good thing I'm around to protect you. This dry wash will be underwater in no time at all. You're standing in the worst possible place."

Gretchen looked back at the rain, then turned in time to see Nacho disappear into the side of a large beam that supported the viaduct. One minute he was running toward the support beam, the next minute he was gone. She opened her mouth in surprise and started running. Rain trickled past her feet. Over the roar of the wind, she thought she heard her cell phone ringing on her belt clip. She let it ring and kept running in the direction she had last seen Nacho.

On closer inspection, his shelter under the cover of the bridge was a work of genius. Nacho had created a facade around the beam, a false wall of cardboard made from several refrigerator boxes. He had painted the cardboard a slate gray to match the color of the beam and brought the pieces together with gray duct tape, effectively concealing his makeshift home from prying eyes.

Gretchen found the opening and pushed through. Inside, Nacho leaned against Daisy's shopping cart and took a long draw from a cheap bottle of wine. He offered her the bottle, and she shook her head. He raised it to his lips and drained what was left. The shopping cart, filled to overflowing, took up most of the room in his hand-made shelter. An old piece of outdoor carpeting covered the ground.

Gretchen knew enough about the plight of the homeless to feel a deep empathy for Nacho and Daisy. Through the years the homeless had been herded from a visible presence in tent cities to old warehouses where they huddled conveniently out of sight. The few social programs still operating couldn't support the growing numbers, and now jails were becoming the new shelters of the future. Nacho had found an alternative to living on the street and an alternative to abiding by the rules of the government-funded shelters.

The gale-strength wind threatened his newfound home. The cardboard rattled violently, and Gretchen wondered how much longer the duct tape would hold.

Nina slid through behind her. "We have to get out of here," she said, an edge of panic in her voice. "This wash is a death trap."

"I can't leave without my stuff." Nacho's arms swept to encompass the tiny room. "And Daisy's cart."

"The cart won't fit in the car," Gretchen said. "We'll wheel it up to the top of the wash and unload the contents into Nina's car. Maybe we can tie the cart to a girder so the wind won't blow it away."

"This entire wash is going to be a running river before you get done talking about it," Nina screamed into the wind as they pulled the cart along. A large black lawn bag filled with Nacho's possessions bounced behind him as he half carried it, half dragged it along.

Water rose over their shoes.

The rain pelted Gretchen's arms and face as they hurriedly stuffed the contents of Daisy's shopping cart into the trunk. Nacho tossed his bag into the backseat and ran back down into the growing water swell. He called out, but the wind lifted the sound away from her. Gretchen watched him splash through the growing swell, then he disappeared inside the corrugated board.

When she moved to follow him, Nina grabbed her arm. "Stay here. He's a fool."

"What's he doing?" Gretchen wiped her wet face with her good hand. So much for staying dry. Her clothes were soaked. Ignoring Nina's advice, she decided to follow him. What if he refused to abandon ship? She would drag him out if necessary.

She slipped into his shelter and he seized her from behind, pining her arms against her side, his breath foul on her neck. She realized how isolated she was. Nina couldn't help her from the top of the wash. If he had killed Martha, he would kill her without hesitation. Then what? Would he go after Nina? No one knew where they were; it might be days before someone discovered their bodies. Victims of flashflooding. Who would guess the truth?

His hold was strong, and she bent forward, twisting and pushing up to free her arms. When she began to struggle, he released her and backed up. "You shouldn't have followed me," he said with dark, emotionless eyes.

"I came to help," she said, breathing hard.

He shoved her. "Get out while you still can."

The same words he had spoken to her outside of the restaurant. At the time, she assumed he was threatening her, but now she wasn't so sure. Maybe, then as now, he was warning her away from a dangerous situation. He was a strange man with abrupt and edgy mannerisms. Not quite right by society's standards, a little off.

Gretchen burst through the opening and glanced back to see him following. Nacho kicked through the flowing water, carrying another bag.

Six inches of water, Nina had warned. Strong enough to bowl you over and sweep you away. They struggled through the water, not running now. Walking thickly, off-balance with each step.

"Follow the flow," Nacho said, close to her ear. "And angle toward the embankment."

They had no choice but to turn away from Nina and the car. Gretchen felt the calf-deep water pulling her along. She quit fighting against it, accepting it instead, but edging slowly at an angle toward the embankment. She glanced back and saw Nina waving her arms frantically.

Gretchen felt firm footing below, less pull from the current, as Nacho rose ahead of her on the hill, clutching the bag. She looked back at the swelling river then loped all the way back to the car.

"Martha's," Nacho said, peering intensely at Gretchen and pushing the bag at her. She took the bag from him and threw it in the backseat.

"We don't have anything to secure the shopping cart," she said with rain pouring down her face. "We'll have to abandon it."

"It's not like she can't get another one," Nina shouted.

Nacho wedged it between the face of the concrete ramp and a metal pole, and Nina pulled away just as the whirling water ripped apart Nacho's home.

Lightning struck, closer this time, and Gretchen envied Wobbles and the canines for their dry and protected home. Water from her soaking clothes pooled on the floor around her, and the seat felt squishy and wet.

Nina ground the car to an abrupt halt.

A sign loomed ahead. Do Not Cross When Flooded. The street ahead looked like the inside of a whirlpool with all the jets at full blast.

"I can show you a way out," Nacho said, pointing to the right. "Go that way." And Nina swung the wheel.

Ten minutes later, at Nacho's insistence, they dropped him at the Rescue Mission. He heaved his own large bag out behind him, and after another piercing look at Gretchen, he ran for cover.

"I feel like I'm letting him get away," Gretchen said. "I have so many questions, and he's the only one who might be able to answer them."

"We know how to find him," Nina said.

"He knows so much more than he's telling us. I can feel it."

"That's the Birch psychic intuition finally coming out in you." Nina grinned. "It's about time. That's a good thing."

"At least he left all this other stuff in the car."

Nina wrinkled her face. "That's the bad thing."

They passed a car caught in flooding in a wash along the side of the street. Two men sat on the roof of the car, and rescue vehicles were parked at the curb on higher ground. Firemen attended to the men and directed traffic away from the area. Gretchen saw a helicopter overhead, scouting for stranded motorists and dangerous situations.

"We'll get home eventually," Nina said. "The long way. Those two unlucky men will be ticketed under the dumb motorist law." She laughed wryly. "Phoenix has a campaign called 'Turn around, don't drown.' That could have been us if we hadn't obeyed the signs."

Gretchen was mesmerized by the freak of nature she was witnessing. Actually, everything about Phoenix seemed otherworldly. First the intense heat that scorched the land creating a crisp, brown, leafless environment hostile to most life-forms. Then the sky opened up and torrential rains flooded the entire city, virtually drowning the parched land.

She remembered the call that she had ignored while pursuing Nacho under the freeway bridge, and she reached for her phone. The clip was empty.

"Pull over," Gretchen said. "My phone's missing."

"I'm sure it's in here someplace," Nina said. "Wait until we get home, and you can look around without getting soaked." Nina slid a glance at Gretchen. "Too late for that, I guess."

"I don't think it's in the car. I might have lost it while pushing Daisy's cart up to the car. We have to go back."

"Sorry, dear. Anything left behind is gone by now, and I wouldn't risk going all the way back anyway."

Gretchen searched the seat and floor around her then crawled in the backseat and rummaged around under the bag Nacho had said belonged to Martha.

No cell phone.

As soon as they stopped in her mother's driveway under the carport, she dug through the trunk.

No cell phone.

How, she wondered, could she live for even one day without her phone?

Caroline stared at the bleak motel walls. Close enough to O'Hare for a fast flight out, far enough away to escape the steep prices associated with instant airport accessibility.

Twenty-six calls from her daughter in the past few days, mostly from Gretchen's cell phone, a few made from Caroline's house. At least the same number of calls from Nina, received and also ignored. Now, when she needed so desperately to warn her daughter away from Phoenix, she couldn't locate her.

All her calls to Gretchen had gone unanswered.

She sat alone in a musty room with a foul odor clinging to it, the smell of too many years of cigarette smoke and too many untrained pets. The first thing she did on entering the room was to yank the bedspread off the bed and toss it into a corner.

Planes continuously roared overhead, drowning out the television, turned on but unwatched.

Caroline considered leaving a message on Gretchen's voice mail, but what would she say? Explain too much or too little, and she couldn't predict the extent of the damage to herself or to Gretchen.

She had failed. She could tell Gretchen that. Her laptop hummed on the scarred dresser top, but it hummed off-key, the music Caroline had hoped to hear never played.

Wireless Internet, even in this dilapidated sorry excuse for a motel.

She tried calling her house. No answer.

With any luck, Gretchen was back in Boston and wouldn't need a warning.

Nacho should have called by now. Hah, he should have called a long time ago. He was her only link to the events taking place in Phoenix, and he was as unreliable as always. Self-medicating inside a wine bottle to numb the pain or to calm his nerves, or to render inactive the voices only he could hear. Who knew what really went on inside that misshapen head?

Reluctantly, she speed-dialed Gretchen's cell phone number again, left a terse, uninformative message, and hung up, feeling regret for avoiding her daughter these past few days.

Why didn't Gretchen answer?

18

A professional doll restorer spends as much time searching for doll parts as she spends performing the actual repairs. Without a well-stocked inventory, her ability to replace parts damaged beyond repair can become severely limited. Anyone hoping to break into the business should start a collection of at least the basics: heads, legs, arms, eyes, wigs, clothes, hats, and shoes, keeping everything organized in separately marked bins. A replacement doll part must complement the doll it is joining. No mixing and matching. Attaching a vinyl leg to a hard plastic doll is a faux pas not tolerated in the doll community. And the doll community is smaller than one might think.

—From *World of Dolls* by Caroline Birch

Tutu and Nimrod greeted them with enthusiasm. Gretchen was enormously relieved to find they had behaved themselves without leaving the whirlwind mess in Caroline's house she'd feared. One natural disaster for the day was enough.

Wobbles, a fairly large tomcat, stalked between the two dogs, towering over Nimrod and standing almost eye to eye with Tutu. A formidable trio, but Wobbles was clearly the ruler.

Ever since Tutu had suffered a scratched nose, she watched Wobbles with a healthy respect.

The respect wasn't reciprocated.

Wobbles feigned indifference, but Gretchen suspected that he knew exactly where the dogs were at all times. He even tolerated Nimrod's puppy playfulness. As for Tutu, he didn't allow her much leeway after cutting her down to size with one swift swoop of his armed paw.

"Six o'clock, and it's dark outside already," Nina said. "Monsoon season is the only time of year that we have such short days. If the sun never set at all, I'd be perfectly happy."

Nina ordered a delivery of Chinese from a nearby restaurant, and they changed into dry clothes, Nina selecting a loose sundress from Caroline's closet.

"Watch what I'm teaching Nimrod," Nina said to Gretchen, crouching and holding open his personalized purse. Nimrod ran right in, turned around, and peeked out joyfully. Holding the handbag, Nina stood and adjusted it on her shoulder.

Gretchen said, "Rumor has it you tried to sneak Tutu into the hospital in a purse."

"I would have pulled it off if I had a larger purse. I used to carry Tutu around all the time, but she weighs about twelve pounds, and my back isn't as strong as it used to be. Nimrod, when he's grown, will be only four or five pounds, the perfect weight for a purse. Now watch this."

Nina strolled across the bedroom with Nimrod and purse, past the dresser filled with Shirley Temple dolls. She pivoted at the closet, started back, and stopped before she reached Gretchen. "Nimrod, hide," she whispered, turning her head toward Nimrod.

He instantly ducked inside the purse.

Nina grinned with pleasure. "Okay, good boy." Nimrod peeked out again.

Gretchen laughed out loud, a deep, throaty, full-bodied laugh. The first one since she arrived in Phoenix. Once she started, she couldn't stop. She laughed until tears streamed down her face.

"It's so easy to train a puppy," Nina said wistfully. "I wish I had taught Tutu that trick before she grew up. The old adage is true. Teaching old dogs new tricks isn't easy."

"Let me guess," Gretchen said, wiping her eyes. "You're

teaching Nimrod to hide so you can take him into stores where he wouldn't be welcome."

"Exactly. And he loves it. He burrows down and takes a catnap. Or rather a puppy nap."

Nina hung Nimrod and purse on the doorknob and sat down on the side of the bed. "Nimrod's family has had an unexpected delay, and they won't be home today. Nimrod needs a place to stay for a few days, a temporary home."

Gretchen stopped laughing. "He seems perfectly happy staying with you."

"We've had a great time."

"But?"

"But I have another client coming," Nina said. "I love Nimrod. He took to a purse with the same instinct he takes to water. But I can't possibly train another puppy with so many other dogs around. The distraction would be counter-productive."

"Can't you reschedule your next client?" Gretchen felt a case of can't-say-no-itis coming on.

"That wouldn't be very professional."

Gretchen glanced at Nimrod. His ears quivered. "Okay, but only for a few days." She lifted his purse from the door-knob and slung him over her shoulder. "Let's see what's inside the bag Nacho gave me. Maybe it holds all the answers to Martha's death."

"You're a dreamer," Nina said.

"Nothing of value at all," Nina said, slapping her hands together and rubbing them as though shedding dirt and grime, a look of distaste on her face. The clothes spread out on the table reeked of cigarette smoke. "This is it? All she owned? And we actually toyed with the idea that she still had her dolls?"

Gretchen studied the paltry collection. Aside from a few pieces of clothing, the bag contained a toothbrush, a near-empty tube of toothpaste, and a stick of roll-on deodorant.

Not much to show for a well-worn life, for years of collecting personal effects.

"Let's throw the whole mess in the trash," Nina said.

"No, this belongs to Joseph now. He can decide whether to dispose of it or not." Gretchen picked up the stick of deodorant and idly lifted the cover. Something made of metal fell and clinked on the floor. She bent down and picked it up.

"A key," she said.

Gretchen handed it to Nina. "Is it a safe-deposit key?" she asked.

"Doesn't seem to be. It isn't a car key, either." Nina turned it over and shrugged. "House key maybe."

"Let's see if it fits one of these doors."

They tried the key in the front and back door locks. It didn't fit.

"That's a relief," Nina said. "We don't need additional evidence pointing to Caroline."

Gretchen couldn't agree more.

The Chinese food arrived, and they ate in silence. Afterwards, Nina gathered her wet clothes together and kissed Nimrod good-bye. "I left Nimrod's food on the counter." She ducked out quickly, leaving a considerable amount of baggage behind in one small, wiggly package.

Gretchen sat and stared at the key for a long time.

Then, with Nimrod at her heels, she went into her mother's workshop and sat at the worktable. Equipment hung haphazardly from hooks on the wall: clamps, scissors, elastic in different weights for stringing, and a curling iron the size of a pinky finger for creating ringlets on her mother's favorites, the Shirley Temple dolls.

Next to the workbench, a library of collector's books, price lists, and identification guides. Guides for hard plastic dolls, vinyl dolls, every conceivable specialty doll—American Characters, Mattel, Nancy Ann Storybook dolls.

Gretchen removed a volume devoted to Sweet Sue dolls and idly paged through it, noting the pages were worn from research.

Sighing heavily, she checked to make sure the doll trunk was still safely stowed in its hiding place on the lower shelf of one of the cabinets. She removed the cloth and peered at the trunk, then stood up.

The bin where the police found the hidden parian doll and inventory list was still ajar. The two assigned officers had come directly into the workshop and searched it meticulously. A superficial, indifferent search of the rest of the house. There was no question in Gretchen's mind that someone had given them information. *But who? Nacho?* He seemed the likeliest.

What was the point of alerting the police? To shift suspicion away from the real killer? An old doll list and a doll of disputable ownership hardly seemed damaging. But that, combined with eyewitnesses on Camelback Mountain, destroyed any credibility her mother might have had, her innocence now questioned by all except her immediate family.

Why did she hide those things in the first place?

Gretchen recalled her mother's expertise at hiding her Easter basket. Caroline had an uncanny knack for concealing surprises in creative places, a game they both enjoyed playing. Every year her mother grew more inventive. Gretchen smiled as she thought of her mother's devious tactics and some of her more creative hiding places. Suspended up the chimney, in nooks and crannies that Gretchen never knew existed in the Boston home she had lived in her entire life, wrapped in towels in the laundry basket, under a half-filled garbage bag in the trash can. That had been one of her best. It took Gretchen hours to discover it.

If her mother really wanted to hide something, no one would be able to find it.

A new idea sent a chill along Gretchen's spine. What if someone else hid the doll and the inventory in her mother's workshop, then called the police to report it? That had to be it.

She picked up the phone and called Nina. "Someone's been in the house," she said.

"What? Right this minute? Did you call nine-one-one?"

"No. Not right now. Before." Gretchen explained her analysis of her mother's ability to hide an elephant, about how convenient the police search had been.

"The second day I was here," Gretchen said, "one of the sliding doors was unlocked, and I was sure I had locked it. And some of my things were rearranged, not quite where I left them. I think someone searched the house and planted the doll and Martha's doll list."

"Gretchen, you want to prove your mother's innocence, that's understandable, but nothing you can say or do will change the fact that Caroline was seen on Camelback Mountain when Martha died."

Gretchen let out a rush of air. "That is a tough one."

"And why did she run away? Innocent people don't run away. She abandoned her business and used two disadvantaged homeless people to conceal her movements."

Apparently, Nina had joined the growing list of disbelievers. Caroline's own sister had abandoned her.

"She's innocent until proven guilty in a court of law, Aunt Nina. People tend to forget our basic rights and judge on hearsay and innuendo. Don't join that narrow-minded mob."

"You're right. I'm trying to keep an open mind." Gretchen could hear the hurt in her voice as Nina continued. "But it's hard. If only she would call."

"She had a reason to run. We have to find out what scared her so much that she thought she had to flee. And what was so awful she couldn't confide in her family?" Gretchen paused, hearing the familiar click of call waiting. "I have another call coming in. I'll see you tomorrow."

"Night, dear."

"Hi, this is Courtney," a young voice said, childlike, waiflike.

"Courtney?" *Wrong number,* Gretchen thought. "You must have . . ."

"No, no, this is the right number. I'm sure of it. This is Courtney."

Dim bulb, Gretchen chided herself. *How many Courtneys do you know? None? Think again. You've heard of one, Steve's Courtney, the intern.*

"Ah," Gretchen said. "Courtney."

"Yes, well, how are you Ms. Birch?"

Ms. Birch? Immediately establishing an age barrier, manipulative, catty. Gretchen had a bad feeling, a Nina moment.

"Gretchen. Please call me Gretchen, and is something wrong?"

"No, nothing's wrong."

"Is Steve all right?"

"Oh, he's fine."

Courtney's voice was vaguely familiar. More than vaguely. It matched the voice of the anonymous caller who had first informed her of Steve's cheating ways.

Silence on both ends. Gretchen waited her out, palms damp, feeling disoriented, a sense of foreboding causing her heart to beat a little too fast.

"Steve told me that you know about our thing," Courtney said.

Our thing? Such small, innocuous words. A certain lack of literary excellence. Like the words *nice* or *good.* But what a punch they pack when used in this context.

Several times in the last several years she'd suspected Steve of being unfaithful. Even before the indisputable proof, she used to have to convince herself that it was her imagination, an uncontrollable jealousy from childhood that caused her to be suspicious over every little occurrence. A flaw in her character, not his. Every time his eyes stayed with a passing woman longer than Gretchen thought they should. Every time his hand brushed gently across another woman's hand. Accidental or intentional?

Steve was a hugger, she'd rationalize. He enjoyed women. Gregarious. Loquacious after a drink or two. And his career mandated proximity to females. Divorce law. Women constantly in and out of his office, seeking solace in his legal strength, projecting hope on their attorney after betrayal, failed love.

Natural, Steve said, to have admirers. After all, his job is to take care of them, like a big brother or uncle or family friend.

Gretchen closed her eyes.

Courtney plowed forward. "Steve has no clue that I'm calling. It was my idea. I wanted you to know that we're still together, in spite of what Steve tells you."

Of course, Steve wouldn't approve of honesty; he'd already become proficient at practicing deceit as well as law.

"I wanted you to know because I can't stand lying to you."

Touching, isn't it? Courtney taking the high road.

"And I want you gone," Courtney said, steering for the low road. "He's mine now."

Gretchen hung up the phone without another word. She wanted to slam the phone, break it, wrench its traitorous cord from the phone jack and wrap it tightly around Steve's cheating neck.

Instead she picked up a broken doll from an overflowing bin heaped with dolls and steadied her shaking hands.

Standing at the padded workbench, she cut a length of elastic in the proper weight and with clamps and hooks spread out before her, she went to work, looping the elastic through a hook in the arm socket, carefully drawing it through and attaching it to the body. Rifling in a parts bin to find a replacement for a missing leg. Finishing one doll and starting another.

What would her life have been like if she had joined her mother's business? Made dolls her life's work? There was something appealing about working at home, dropping out of the nine-to-five rat race. Working in pajamas. Forgetting about snarled rush-hour traffic, appropriate work apparel, the proper business demeanor, fighting for raises, dodging a coworker's efforts to sabotage your chances for promotion.

Gretchen gave a bath to a soft vinyl doll, found underpants, a hat, shoes. The right clothes for the right doll. Worked a bow into her hair.

What would life have been like?

The list of exquisite and valuable dolls was seared into Caroline's memory bank, her human cerebral memory bank, not that of the artificial random access memory lying on the cheap pine dresser. Close to two hundred dolls, each rare and unique, a haphazard, eclectic collection.

A rare George II wooden doll with painted, gessoed face in silk polonaise gown. Two French shoulder papier-mâché dolls with bamboo teeth. A German waxed composition lady with inset blue glass eyes. Parians, chinas, bisques representing the finest from France and Germany. A group of Italian Lenci cloth dolls. A finite list with infinite worth.

Now a collector's dream turned into a freakish nightmare.

Excessive greed had dimmed the glow, dampened the glory of the fine collection.

Caroline could recite all the particulars of the inventory, could describe every photograph in detail, although her hope of recovering any of the collection diminished with every passing hour.

Her lips curled in momentary satisfaction.

At least she had the prize.

The French fashion doll.

· 19 ·

A doll's book value is an arbitrary guide to its actual worth. Most dolls sell for much less than their book price, and many dealers are happy to receive even half of the stated value. Some dolls, however, are so rare, so exquisite, so one-of-a-kind, that they command prices far beyond any written value. For these dolls, collectors with unlimited funds might offer exorbitant prices. Bidding wars are not uncommon.

—From *World of Dolls* by Caroline Birch

Gretchen turned over onto her back and rearranged the beach towel to cover her torso without opening her eyes. Her arms dangled over the sides of the lounge chair and brushed against the tile. The summer storm had passed, and the sun beat down on her face, searing and hot. She didn't care.

A door banged in the front of the house, and the patio doors slid open. She heard Nimrod's tiny nails clicking on the Mexican tile surrounding the pool and a small rush of air as he ran by. Another rush of air. Tutu. Gretchen refused to open her eyes.

"What the . . . !" Nina's voice. "It's a hundred and sixteen degrees outside. How long have you been lying here?"

Gretchen didn't respond.

She poked Gretchen's arm through the towel. "I've been calling you all morning. Your face is as red as a Roma tomato. Can you open your eyes, or are they burned shut?"

Gretchen pried one eye open and squinted at her aunt. "Go away and let me die."

Nina yanked the towel away, ran around to the back of the chair, and pushed Gretchen up by her shoulders. "Come on. Into the shade with you. At least you had the sense to cover the rest of your body with a towel. Otherwise we'd be on the way to the hospital again."

Gretchen slowly rose to her feet and let Nina lead her under an expansive table umbrella. She sagged into a chair and studied her feet. Too tall to be completely covered with the towel, the top of her feet had fried in the sun. Her face felt swollen, and her lips were starting to crack and blister.

Nina, face pinched and ashen next to Gretchen's, plopped into a chair and leaned forward. "Is Caroline dead?" she said, shaky, awaiting bad news.

Gretchen slowly looked up and shook her head. Nina clutched her heart. "That's a relief. When I saw you lying there, that's the first thing I thought of."

It was time to confide in Nina.

"Courtney, the intern, called last night. She and Steve are having a thing."

"A thing?"

"Those were her words."

Gretchen realized how badly she needed a sympathetic ear as the whole story spilled out of her.

Nina leaned back when she was finished and crossed her legs. "That rat. I always suspected as much."

"You did not. You're the one who thought I should give him an ultimatum." Gretchen lifted an arm and tapped her head with the cast. "Is it my imagination, or is that idea a very bad one?"

"You can still offer him a choice. Death by fire or death by shark. I've always thought those would be the two worst possible ways to go, a fitting end for Steve."

"He was continually working, always preparing for a case or meeting with clients or attending company-sponsored events. How did he find the time?"

"He wasn't always working," Nina said. "She turned out

to be the special event he was working. I'm sorry it happened."

"I shouldn't have left Boston."

Nina snorted. "You think if you had stayed, it would have ended between them? Right. Sure. Once a cheater always a cheater, I say."

Gretchen's new perception of her relationship seemed as clear as fog dissipating over the Boston Harbor. Thick, whirling haze had clouded her vision, but now she could see past the horizon. "I can't believe he'd risk our relationship for a quick fling with a summer intern. He's almost twice as old as she is."

"Midlife crisis," Nina suggested.

"He's thirty-two. Too young."

"The rat," Nina said again.

Nina forced Gretchen into the bathroom and turned on the shower. "Keep the water cold," she demanded. "That should snap you out of it. Take your time, and afterwards, I'll work on your face. What a burn."

"What's that?" Gretchen said, noticing a purse hanging from Nina's shoulder for the first time.

"That," Nina said, "is today's purse trainee. He's sound asleep down on the bottom. You gave me such a scare, I forgot he was there."

Twenty minutes later, Gretchen felt almost human again. Nina dabbed aloe vera lotion on her niece's sunburned face and feet, and Gretchen slid into flip-flops.

"Bring a pair of athletic shoes along," Nina said.

"Why?"

"We're headed for Curves. I called April to find out what time the Dollers would be working out." She glanced at her watch. "They'll show up soon, and we don't want to miss them."

"But why are we going to Curves?" Gretchen felt a whine in her voice. "We can see them later. Call a meeting if you miss them so much. I'm really not in the mood to socialize."

Nina smiled. "We're going to sign up. We could both

use some cardiovascular work. Exercise and research at the same time. Maybe we'll find out if Rita really saw Bonnie at the Rescue Mission. That can be your job. Find out. And exercise is good for your mind. Let's leave the dogs in the kitchen." Nina glanced at the purse on her shoulder. "I'll put Enrico in the bathroom."

"Enrico needs his own room?"

"Enrico needs his own world."

"Give my name when you sign up," April said. "I'm working on a free T-shirt. Five enrollments, and I get my very own Curves shirt in orange, pink, blue, or black."

Curves bustled with activity, every station occupied, conversations swelling over workout music. April, Bonnie, and Rita crowded around while Nina and Gretchen signed up for a trial week.

"You should sign up for a whole year," April said, disappointment in her voice. "That's the only way it counts toward my shirt."

"Change stations now," the recording announced.

Nina laid the pen on the counter. "Gretchen might go back to Boston in a few days. She can't sign up for a year."

"She can transfer her membership to Boston. That's the beauty of Curves. They're everywhere," April said, checking Nina out. "You could use a year, too."

Nina narrowed her eyes while Olivia Newton John belted "Let's Get Physical" from a boom box on an overhead shelf. She opened her mouth to respond, but she caught Gretchen's eye and the slight shake of her head. She closed her mouth.

"Stations are opening up," Bonnie called out, her red flip shellacked stiffly around her face.

Gretchen leaped onto the stepper, jostling for a position next to Bonnie, her prey of the moment. She ignored the pain radiating from within her running shoes.

"You sure did burn your face," April said. "Fall asleep in the sun?"

"No," Nina said. "Her boyfriend cheated on her with a coworker, and I found her wallowing in self-pity by the pool."

Everyone gasped, and Gretchen sent Nina a menacing glance. So much for personal privacy. Wallowing in self-pity? Well, Nina was right. She had too much on her mind right now to worry about Steve and Courtney.

She worked harder, running in place faster, increasing her concentration. Focusing on the workout.

"Men are all alike," April said, huffing through the shoulder press. "Bad behavior runs in their genes."

"Not my Matt," Bonnie said, running in place. "Matty's wife was the one who cheated on him. He's going through a nasty divorce right now. Faithful as they come, my Matty."

Probably married to his job more than to his wife, Gretchen thought. *Although the job didn't stop Steve.*

"At least they didn't have children," Rita said. "Children complicate divorce."

"What's nasty about the divorce?" Nina asked. "Without children and child support or a custody battle, the divorce should be smooth sailing."

"She stalks him. She wants him back, and she's not above making scenes," Bonnie said. "The closer they get to the divorce hearing, the more desperate she becomes. Poor Matty's hiding in the streets. Lucky for him, he has a mobile job."

Gretchen, preoccupied earlier with her own problems, wondered what had happened to her shadow. For all she knew, he was outside right this minute, waiting to follow her.

"Radio says more rain later today," April said. "Just what we need."

Nina bent over and placed her palms on the floor.

"Show-off," April said.

"That's amazing, Aunt Nina," Gretchen said, skipping the shoulder press. Working out with a broken wrist proved a unique challenge.

"It's the yoga," Nina said. "I'm limber as a tree monkey,

but my cardiovascular activity is limited to walking back and forth from the car. I guess you can't have everything."

"Run in place on the platforms," April advised. "That'll get your heart rate up. Mine's always at the top end of what's safe." She pulled a hanky from her pocket and mopped her forehead.

"Gretchen's cheating boyfriend is a divorce attorney," Nina said. Gretchen thought about a direct frontal tackle. She could take Aunt Nina down in two moves.

"That makes it worse," April said. "He should know better."

"What are you going to do about it?" Rita said.

Get ready for a ten-second count.

Gretchen's pulse rate went off the chart hanging on the wall. "I don't know," she said, after the count, when she noticed Rita still looking at her and waiting for her answer. "I really don't know."

And she didn't know. That had been the recurring question in her mind since Courtney's call last night. How to handle it. What to say. How to react.

Steve had assured her that it would never happen again, and she had wanted so badly to believe him. What if Courtney was lying?

After two circuits, Nina's face turned the same color as Gretchen's burned face.

"I need to take a break," Nina said.

"Me, too," huffed April.

The two women moved away from the workout area, and Gretchen glanced at Bonnie. The hydraulic machines hissed around her. Rita turned and said something to the woman ahead of her.

"I saw you, too," Gretchen leaned over and whispered to Bonnie, taking a wild shot.

Bonnie smiled at Gretchen, bending to the side, stretching, one arm high and wide overhead. "You saw me?"

"At the Rescue Mission."

"Change stations now."

Bonnie's smile died, and her face closed up.

"Look," Gretchen said, "your hair is hard to miss."

Bonnie's hand jumped to her red hair.

"Your hair is beautiful, don't get me wrong," Gretchen said hastily. "It's unique; that's why I know it was you."

Bonnie smiled with her teeth, gums showing. "Sorry to disappoint, but you are mistaken." She nudged Rita. "We must be almost done."

Rita turned back. "Done," she agreed.

"Never trust a woman whose gums show when she smiles," Gretchen said to Nina as they zipped through traffic on the way back to her mother's house. "Who said that?"

"You just did."

"No, I've heard that expression someplace before."

"Interesting about your friend, Matt. Don't you think?"

"That he's going through a divorce?"

"He's available," Nina said, honking at a passing car that strayed into her lane. "Never ignore opportunity."

"That," Gretchen said, emphatically, "is the last thing on my mind."

"Good. At least it's on the list."

"I can't help but think that she's hidden the French fashion doll right here in the house," Gretchen said over loud, aggressive snarls. Enrico, the Chihuahua, raised his upper lip and growled at Gretchen. "He's going to attack me."

"Chihuahuas," Nina said in an instructional voice, "are as old as the Mayan civilization. We've actually discovered their images carved in stone in the Mexican jungle. The Mayans believed Chihuahuas guided the dead through the underworld."

"This particular one doesn't have *guide dog* written all over him. He should come with a *vicious attack dog* warning."

"Chihuahuas don't like strangers. They don't like other people or other dogs, but they bond with one or two people and are devoted for life."

Enrico continued to snarl at Gretchen.

"Give him a treat," Nina advised, handing Gretchen a liver snap.

"I'm not going near him. And look at Tutu and Nimrod. They're terrified."

Both dogs had backed into a corner, watching the action from a safe distance. Wobbles, on the other hand, strutted past the purse hanging from the doorknob without acknowledging the rabid beast within its confines. He stopped at Gretchen's feet and gazed at the liver snap. Gretchen bent down and handed it over.

"They take a little getting used to," Nina admitted. "Although Chihuahua owners just love them to death. And speaking of death. They can live for twenty years."

"Isn't that nice. Can we get back to my mother and where she may have hidden the doll? According to the note we found written on the back of Nacho's French fashion doll picture, my mother has the doll."

"We've been over this before," Nina said. "The police searched the house. Wouldn't they have found the doll if Caroline had it here?"

Gretchen frowned, and the movement caused burning pain to shoot through her face. What a mess. Broken wrist, second-degree burns on her face and feet. Or was it third-degree? Second, third, or fourth, who cared? All Gretchen knew was that it really hurt.

"They did a poor job of searching. They didn't seem concerned about anything other than the parian doll and the inventory list."

"What do you suggest?"

"Follow me." Gretchen opened the doors to the patio. She walked past the swimming pool into the living area of the cabana. It was exactly as she remembered it. Large, welcoming fireplace, cozy sitting area, wide bed with a locally made

Indian blanket spread across it, more blankets draped on the walls, pottery scattered in nooks and crannies. An Arcosanti bell hanging from the outside eave chimed in the breeze.

She pointed to a stack of boxes pushed against the wall. Unless company arrived, the cabana served as a storage area rather than a guest room, housing the dolls her mother sold at shows.

"Let's start here," Gretchen said. "The police didn't even come out to the cabana. Maybe she hid the doll with her other dolls."

"Seems too obvious." Nina squatted and pried a box open.

"I agree, but we have to start somewhere. I have a copy of the list itemizing all of Martha's collection. Let's see if any of the dolls in these boxes matches any on the list. Keep your eyes out for the French fashion doll. And unwrap them gently; they're fragile."

Gretchen opened a box and carefully unwrapped each doll: closed mouth, open mouth, mohair wigs. Dolls dressed in sailing outfits, gingham jumper dresses, drop-waist dresses in pink polka dot and cotton sateen, marked dolls, sleepy eyes, molded teeth.

"Look at this one," Nina said, holding up a blonde-headed doll dressed in a knit suit with sapphire glass beads. "And this." She picked up a dark-haired doll dressed in a sarong.

"She told me about these," Gretchen said. "They're Mary Hoyer dolls she found at an auction. This one is Dorothy Lamour, and that one . . ." she gestured at the doll Nina held. ". . . is Marilyn Monroe. There should be a Katharine Hepburn and a Lana Turner somewhere in the box."

"Here they are," Nina giggled. "They're cute, too."

A sharp bark sounded from the house.

"I better check on the pooches," Nina said and scurried off.

Gretchen immersed herself in the boxes, unwrapping each doll and checking it against the photocopied list. The contents of the boxes matched her mother's personality: wild and randomly packaged. Dolls from all eras scattered among the boxes. A doll from the forties in this box, another from the same period in that one. No labels on any of the boxes. Disorganized but meticulously cared for. A contradiction of life. Order within disorder.

Gretchen glanced at her watch and realized that an hour had passed since Nina left the cabana. She finished packing up the last box and stood. Nothing. Not one doll from the list. No French fashion doll. She felt disappointed. It should be easier than this.

"I've been playing secretary," Nina said, hanging up the phone when Gretchen arrived in the kitchen. "Larry called for an update and to say he's delivering the doll with the new hand-made wig directly to the customer. He's giving him a bill but will tell the customer to send payment to Caroline. Larry said he'll work out the fee with her later."

"That's nice of him," Gretchen said absently, opening the refrigerator and peering inside.

"April called to say she's decided to work out at Curves every day instead of every other, so we can join her if we want to."

"That's nice," Gretchen muttered.

"And Steve called and left a message."

Gretchen closed the refrigerator. "What did the message say?"

"That he's been trying to reach you on your cell phone. That Courtney told him what she did, and he can explain." Nina snorted. "I'd like to hear him explain that one."

Gretchen took a chocolate croissant from a bag on the counter and bit into it. "I can have this," she said, defensively. "I worked out this morning."

"Are you going to call him back?" Nina wanted to know.

Before Gretchen could answer with her very first firm and resounding no, a snarl erupted from the purse lying on the chair next to Nina.

"Enrico's up from his nap," Nina said.

* * *

Gretchen and Nina walked side by side through the Biltmore Fashion Park. Nimrod rode on Gretchen's shoulder in a white cotton purse embroidered with miniature black poodles. The poodles attached to the purse wore red hair bows, which complemented Gretchen's burned face. The savage demon, Enrico, poked out from Mexican tapestry, a gravelly hum resounding from his throat that threatened to grow into a growl.

After a disagreement with Nina, which Gretchen won, Tutu had stayed at home with Wobbles. The purse dogs traveling by shoulder bag represented Gretchen's reluctant compromises.

"Okay," Nina said. "We made two copies of Martha's key, one for you and one for me."

"I know that, Nina. I was with you."

"It helps to verbalize. Keeps it orderly."

"Right." Gretchen could feel Nimrod's tail thumping against her ribs in perpetual puppy happiness.

"We left the original key right where we found it in that smelly old bag."

"As bait."

"That's the part I don't get."

Gretchen pursed her lips and winced. "I have to buy another tube of lip balm." She brushed her fingers across a blister forming on her lip. "We'll let everyone know that we found Martha's belongings. We'll call all the Phoenix Dollers and—"

"There must be over one hundred members. Most aren't even active."

"We'll call the active members. We'll make the discovery sound exciting and tell them where it is. Then we'll wait and see what happens."

"Maybe nothing will happen."

Gretchen shrugged. "Maybe you're right, but do you have a better idea?"

"Yes, we should find the door that it opens. We'll try it in locks until we find a fit."

"That's also part of the plan."

Nina stopped walking and looked at a storefront. "I'm going into Chico's. Enrico, hide." She tossed a liver treat into the purse, and Enrico dove out of sight. Nina grinned and strode into the shop. Gretchen wandered into the Flip Flop Shop and purchased two new pairs of shoes, one gold, the other silver. With the tops of her feet burnt the color of Tutu's red lace collar, flip-flops were the only shoe she could wear for awhile.

Nina appeared behind Gretchen as she paid at the cash register. Gretchen glanced at her watch. "Let the games begin," she said.

Caroline tapped into the eBay site and keyed in the words *antique dolls*. She heard the computer churning and watched the list of auction dolls appear on her screen. Her eyes were red-rimmed from countless hours spent monitoring the site.

She scrolled down. Closed the site. Keyed in the Mc-Masters Harris Auction Company site and scrolled through the auction lot listings. Then Theriault's. She scanned every online doll auction house. The Internet sites had highly specialized bidding technology, some with audio and video of the live auctions, offering customers the ability to participate with the touch of a keystroke.

Caroline sank into the center of the lumpy motel bed and closed her eyes. An hour later she awoke, startled. A door slammed in the hall, and she could hear muffled voices in the next room through the paper-thin walls.

She struggled up, unaware of the time or the day. She bent over, stretching the taut muscles in the small of her back.

Caroline went back to work, the computer startup display glowing green.

An audible gasp. She rubbed her eyes and looked again.

"French Jumeau Bébé, 1910, paperweight eyes, holding a Steiff monkey."

Caroline knew the inventory list by heart. She clicked on a tiny photograph, and the image opened up. Large and bold. Worth the long wait.

Another of Martha's dolls.

· 20 ·

Little French girls eventually tired of playing with miniature copies of their mothers. Instead they wanted to play with versions of themselves. The Bébé doll, created in the image of young girls, was born in the late eighteen hundreds. Emile Jumeau took credit as the original designer. While some may dispute his claim, no one can challenge the beauty of his dolls' faces or the exquisite detail of the costumes they wore.

—From *World of Dolls* by Caroline Birch

Bonnie Albright worked part-time in the lingerie department at Saks Fifth Avenue. They found her in a back room, opening a box of bras. She had a box cutter in her hand and red lipstick smeared above her lip. Bonnie had been selected by Gretchen and Nina for several reasons; she was the club's president, and she was the most indefatigable gossip of the bunch. She would help them with the legwork. Or in this case, the lipwork.

"Here's the list you asked for," Bonnie said, opening a locker and removing a sheet of paper from her purse. "I've highlighted the active members. Now tell me what this is all about?"

A snarl filled the room, and one of Bonnie's penciled eyebrows shot up. "What's that?" she asked.

"Shhh," Nina said into the purse. "That's just Enrico. Ignore him."

"I'd like to call each of the club members," Gretchen explained, "and ask them about Martha and my mother. It's been six days since Martha died and my mother disappeared, and we still don't know what happened."

"Matty's working on it," Bonnie said with exaggerated pride. "You don't need to get involved. He'll solve it."

"I need to keep busy."

"Should we tell her?" Nina said to Gretchen, and both of Bonnie's penciled eyebrows quivered.

Gretchen nodded on cue.

"We found a bag of Martha's belongings," Nina said. "One of her friends gave it to us, and it has a few very interesting items inside."

"What?" Bonnie said, wringing her hands in anticipation. "What?"

"I don't think we should say until we know more," Gretchen said. "It wouldn't be right."

Nina nodded. "We'll keep the bag in Caroline's workshop for now."

"We should probably notify the police," Gretchen said.

"Soon," Nina agreed.

"Well, my, my," Bonnie said, running her hand over her stiff hair. "Isn't this a new wrinkle."

Afterwards they strolled through the open-air mall.

"I bet she's on the phone right this minute," Nina said, handing her cell phone to Gretchen.

"I have to get another phone," Gretchen said, dialing. "Hey, April, how are you?"

"Tired, achy, I think I need to rest more. This valley fever has me down in bed. I shouldn't have worked out so soon."

Gretchen repeated the same story she had told Bonnie, with the same response.

"Well, isn't that something?" April said. "I'll call around for you and see if any of the club members have any information. There weren't any dolls in that bag, were there?"

"I really can't say right now. Police orders."

"Ahhhhh," April said.

After several more calls, Nina nudged Gretchen. "Don't look behind you, but we've picked up a tail."

Gretchen stopped at a shop window beside a garden courtyard and slowly turned her head.

Their eyes met. Matt smiled, bright and warmly, wearing casual, Southwestern garb as usual. No hint in his attire of his real occupation. Tan. A certain scrappiness about his walk as he approached them.

"Are you always undercover?" Gretchen said.

"Usually," he replied. "I'm coming from a visit with Daisy at the hospital, on my way to Saks to see my mother. I'm off-duty." His eyes traveled over the purses, noting their contents, gazing at Gretchen. "There's something new about you since I saw you last." He ran one finger along his jawline. "I know, new makeup, a slightly pinker shade than before."

"You should never comment on a woman's cosmetics," Nina advised. "You aren't supposed to notice that we wear anything."

"It goes well with the cast on your wrist; sharp contrast. And it matches the color of your feet. Nice."

"She's a pro at accessorizing," Nina said.

"Now that you've had your fun," Gretchen said, "maybe you can tell us how Daisy's doing?"

"I'll tell you over coffee," he said, guiding them toward the Cheesecake Factory.

It was just after five o'clock, and Gretchen realized how hungry she was. With Nimrod and Enrico in hide mode, they slid into a corner booth and kept a careful eye out for waitresses and management staff while stowing the pups in the purses on their laps. Matt seemed amused at their efforts but refrained from comment.

They ordered a large pizza and two cheesecakes to share—White Chocolate Chunk Macadamia Nut and Tiramisu—both selected by Nina.

"Daisy's fine," Matt said. "She's settled right in and isn't in any hurry to be released, but the doctors say she's ready to go if she can find a quiet place to recover." He wrapped his hands around a cup of coffee. "The investigation into her accident didn't reveal any conclusive evidence, but the team found inconsistent paint chips on the back bumper."

"Inconsistent?" Gretchen said.

"They didn't match the car paint," Nina said.

"We aren't taking Daisy's word for it. She isn't a very reliable witness," Matt said.

"Why? Because she doesn't have a mailing address?"

"No," Matt said carefully. "Because she's the driver and there weren't any other witnesses."

"She seemed confident of the facts when I talked to her."

Matt shrugged. The waitress brought the pizza, and the pups stayed out of sight. Nina plucked sausage from the pizza, and her hand disappeared under the table. The waitress returned with the cheesecakes and a pot of coffee. She refilled Matt's cup. A growl grew under the table.

"What's that?" the waitress said, glancing quickly at Nina.

Nina rubbed her hand on her stomach. "I must be really hungry."

"We won't need any more coffee refills," Matt said. "In fact, we won't need anything else."

"Smart thinking," Nina said to him when the waitress walked away. "I don't mind getting kicked out, but I'd like to finish eating first."

"Good thing I'm off-duty, Nina, or I'd have to arrest you."

Nina laughed.

"Why would someone run Daisy off the road?" Gretchen said. "Unless they thought she was my mother."

"If we can believe her account," Matt said, "that would be a logical assumption. But why? Where's the motive? I think she's covering for herself, making excuses for her own inattentive driving."

"I don't think Caroline ran away from the police," Nina said. "I think she's hiding from someone. The attack on Daisy proves she's in danger."

"Sounds melodramatic," Matt said, biting into a piece of pizza.

"Is Daisy being charged with anything?" Gretchen asked.

"No. She had a valid driver's license and cooperated with the investigation. We could find something to charge her with, but why bother? There's an issue of whether she had permission to drive the car, but until we locate Caroline, we have to assume she drove it with the proper approval. Unless you know something we don't."

Gretchen shook her head distractedly. She was surprised that Daisy had a driver's license. She sliced into the macadamia nut cheesecake with the side of her fork.

"Do either of you know someone named the Inspector?" Matt asked.

"I've heard that name before," Nina said, frowning in concentration.

Gretchen remembered exactly where she'd heard the name. Martha had complained to Joseph about someone called the Inspector. "Why do you ask?" she said.

"Martha mentioned him to Daisy. According to Daisy, she was extremely upset over something he had done. Daisy said she never saw Martha so angry. I want to find him."

"Or her," Nina said. "This Inspector could be a woman. Right?"

"I suppose," Matt said, reluctantly. "I just assumed it was a man."

"What kind of inspector? A building inspector?" Gretchen asked. "Housing inspector?" Gretchen thought about Nacho's makeshift home and wondered if the state had laws against cardboard construction on public land. Probably.

* * *

They rearranged the puppies in their respective purses, and
Gretchen wandered ahead while Nina and Matt traded
witty repartees. Their laughter floated on the breeze. The
palm trees in the mall's courtyard swayed, and the sun vanished in a darkening sky. The monsoon and another rain
squall were moving in.

Gretchen felt useless here. She seriously considered going back to Boston to deal with her own crumbling personal life, which was spiraling out of control.

She needed a steady job and income, and she needed to
decide what to do about Steve. In a brief interlude of self-
pity she listed her current problems. A mother wanted for
questioning in a murder, clearly the most pressing problem
at the moment. A cheating long-term boyfriend who was
afraid of commitment, another monumental problem. Her
lack of employment and a dwindling savings account.
Right this minute she didn't even own a phone.

Anything else? Oh yes, let's add a few physical problems. A broken wrist and second-degree burns on her face
and feet.

And she had absolutely nothing to show for her efforts
to save her mother except a key of unknown origin. Instead of clearing her mother's name, she'd implicated her
further. If she stayed longer, who knew how much more
physical harm she could inflict on herself, how much
more physical evidence she could dredge up against her
mother.

She decided to call Steve from the house, then catch
the next flight home before Courtney permanently dis-
placed her.

She lifted Nimrod out of his purse and held him on her
shoulder. He licked her ear. "Right now," Gretchen said to
him, "you're the best thing I've got going for me, and
you're only a temporary visitor. Sad, isn't it?"

* * *

"You can't go home!" Nina wailed. "I can't handle this by myself. What about the key? It's going to open the right door. You'll see. If you don't stay and fight for Caroline, who will?"

"Why isn't she here fighting for herself?" Gretchen threw clothes into her open suitcase lying on the bed. Wobbles watched the action with a steady gaze, his ears flatter on his head than usual.

"What about a flight? You can't go to the airport without a ticket."

"I'll wait on standby. Nina, I'm desperate. I can't let my whole life pass before my eyes."

"What are you talking about?"

"Name one thing that's going right in my life."

"Let me make you a cup of green tea." Nina pulled several pairs of shorts out of the suitcase and returned them to the dresser. "This is impulsive. Let's talk about it. I know, call Steve. Work it out on the phone."

Gretchen tossed her hiking boots into the suitcase and stomped into the kitchen to retrieve the cordless phone. "I'll call and let him know I'm on my way," she said, carrying the phone into the bedroom and closing the door.

"Explain," she said to him after waiting an inordinate amount of time while his secretary located him, annoyed that she still wasn't on the interruptible list, that special group of coddled clients that commanded instant attention. Instead she had to resort to intimidating an overworked secretary.

"This is bad timing, Gretchen." Steve said, sounding rushed. "I'm in the middle of sensitive negotiations. Why didn't you return my call earlier?"

In a meeting at 9:30 in the evening, Boston time? "I needed time to think."

"I don't know what to say for myself. I love you, you know. Sometimes, I admit, I'm a bit misguided."

"That's it?" Gretchen said. "That's all you have to say?"

"It's over with Courtney. It hadn't really even started. She got carried away."

"Does she understand that? That you were a little misguided and she expected more than you were willing to deliver?"

Steve hesitated, and Gretchen could hear his breath, labored and anxious. "Yes. She understands clearly."

"Maybe I should give her a call," Gretchen suggested lightly. "After all, she's practically a child. She must be devastated."

"Ah. That wouldn't be wise. Might even make the situation worse. Besides, she's on vacation. Someplace in South Carolina."

How convenient, Gretchen thought. She watched Wobbles snuggle into the suitcase surrounded by her clothes. "You haven't asked about me or my mother, about what's happening in Phoenix."

"I really don't have time right now, but I want to ask. I've been thinking about you. Later. I'll call later after my meetings."

Later, Gretchen thought wearily, wait till later. Wasn't that always the response? Maybe later. Gretchen had waited all these years for a later that never arrived.

She saw a flash of lightning out the window and heard the immediate crash of thunder. Rain pounded hard against the roof, and she thought about flipping on the bedroom light. Instead she sat in the gathering gloom and watched nature's dramatic interpretation of fireworks.

"What about us, Steve? I'm coming home so we can figure out where to go from here."

"I love you, Gretchen. We can work this out. We can't throw away the last seven years."

"I'll come then." ·

"I have to go to Hilton Head for a few days. Business. A conference, and I'm the keynote speaker. Right after that we can get together. I know I've disappointed you, but I'll make it up to you. Promise."

Gretchen stared in the mirror, her eyes pale and pained. Courtney vacationing in South Carolina, Steve on his way to Hilton Head. Gretchen hoped Steve was more convincing when he went to trial with his court cases. Was it a nervous slip of the tongue or merely coincidental these two people would be traveling to the same state?

No, Gretchen thought, *I'm becoming exactly like Nina. I no longer believe in coincidence.*

"Call me later," Steve said, hanging up and leaving her holding a dead phone.

When Gretchen opened the bedroom door, she gave a loud start.

"You scared me, Nina," she said, peering at her motionless aunt who stood in the hall. "We need to turn on lights. Who'd guess it's only four o'clock in the afternoon. It feels more like midnight."

Nina remained rigid in front of her.

"What's wrong?" Gretchen asked.

Nina, moving woodenly, took her hand and led her to the workshop doorway. "Martha's bag is gone," she said, her voice leaden. "Someone must have been here when we went to see Bonnie."

"We should have hurried right home," Gretchen said in shock. "What were we thinking when we stopped to eat? Are you sure it's gone?"

"It's gone, all right. And there's more."

Nina flipped a switch by the door, and a fluorescent light hanging over the worktable illuminated the room.

Gretchen saw it hanging over the padded table and moved closer. She drew in her breath, sharp and quick.

Someone had hung one of her mother's Shirley Temple dolls from the overhead light with a piece of restringing elastic. Blood dripped from its face and pooled on the floor. The doll swayed gently from the noose around its neck, eyes wide and sightless.

The screen glowed, casting an eerie light over Caroline's intent features. She quickly registered as a member and hesitated briefly at the password prompt. She keyed in an appropriate password: counterattack. If this were a game of chess, she would be planning multiple moves into the future, but she hadn't studied openings for this particular game. Besides, she couldn't have anticipated her opponent's deadly first move.

All that mattered now was the endgame. A draw wasn't an acceptable finish. There could be only one winner.

Caroline's hands trembled in anticipation as she worked her way through the red tape associated with Internet bidding. She clicked on the French Jumeau Bébé listing and frowned. The seller had set up a private auction, effectively cloaking his or her identity until after the final accepted bid. Only the highest bidder would be allowed full contact information about the seller.

She entered her first bid, determined to win.

Someone else's bid immediately canceled hers out.

She keyed in a higher amount, determined to avoid the other bidder's strategy of proxy bidding. Allowing the online service to bid for her until her maximum dollar amount was reached would have stripped Caroline of her feeling of power. She wouldn't relinquish control.

Besides, she had no maximum level at which she would withdraw.

She had to win, and she had to win her way.

21

*The operative word when discussing the value of a doll is
original. Just as real estate depends on location, location,
location, doll collectors insist on original, original, original.*

*An antique doll is in excellent condition if the following
qualifications are met: the doll has all its original parts, no
marks or blemishes mar the skin, original eyes are intact, the wig
has not been soiled or restyled, and it is wearing the original
clothing, including the original dress, underclothing, shoes, and
socks. Mint in box (MIB) means the doll has all of the above
and is in its original box, preferably with original tags and labels.*

—From *World of Dolls* by Caroline Birch

Gretchen stared at the hanging doll, cold fear jettisoning
through her body. Was the intruder still in the house?
She quickly closed the workshop door and locked it. She
picked up a pair of scissors lying on the table, and, with
Nina as backup, she opened the closet door and peered in.
Nothing inside but more bins. She sighed with relief. "It's
empty," she said.

Nina dropped the repair hook she had grabbed as a
weapon, and it clattered to the floor. "I almost died of fright."

Gretchen retrieved the hook and placed it on the workbench with the scissors. "I'm calling the police. Let's stay
in here until they arrive."

"What about the animals?" Nina asked shrilly.

"I'm sure whoever did this is gone by now," Gretchen
said, dialing 911. "But let's stay smart. If it was me, if I was

the bad guy, all I'd care about would be a safe way out of the house."

"What if we came home while he was here," Nina said, "and he's trapped inside with us?"

"Then staying in the workshop will give him time to escape." Gretchen wasn't sure she liked the idea of hiding, but after another glance at the swinging doll, she decided not to risk a confrontation.

She gave the dispatcher the necessary information, alerting him to the remote possibility that the intruder might still be in the house, and hung up.

"Red paint," she said after touching the pooled liquid on the floor and noting an open jar of paint on the table.

"Don't contaminate the crime scene," Nina advised. "I hope they dust for prints."

"How many people knew Martha's bag was here?" Gretchen asked.

"Bonnie, April, Rita, Larry and Julia, Karen Fitz." Nina ticked them off on her fingers. "And anyone they might have told. We weren't trying to keep it a secret."

"We really botched this one," Gretchen said, thinking, *What else is new?* "Who had a key to the house?"

Nina shrugged. "I don't know." Then she widened her eyes. "We gave the key to Larry at the hospital when we thought Daisy was Caroline. He checked on the animals, and I suppose he could have had a copy made."

Gretchen shook her head. "The sliding door was unlocked before I gave Larry the key. I think whoever did this was also in the house earlier. Who else?"

"Clients and friends were in and out of here all the time, but I never knew Caroline to give out her keys."

Gretchen heard sirens in the distance, growing louder and stopping outside. With all the noise only a bungling fool would still be inside the house.

After a thorough search, a police officer with a perky ponytail and a cautious stance discovered the point of entry. "Jimmied the lock," she said, studying the patio doors leading to the pool. "Probably came over the fence and forced the lock."

"Anything else gone?" another officer said, holding a notepad and pen. "Other than the bag?"

"I don't see anything else missing," Gretchen said.

"Me either," Nina said, plopping on the living room sofa surrounded by canines, a firm hand on Enrico, his incisors bared. "I should take him home. He isn't handling all the excitement very well," she said to Gretchen. "I'll come right back."

"You have to fill out this report first," the woman said handing a clipboard to Nina, a wary eye on Enrico. "Why would anyone break in to steal a bag of old clothes?"

"Someone wanted the key," Gretchen said. "Someone knew what the key would open."

"And what does it open?"

"We don't know."

The officers observed Gretchen and Nina with steady stares. "And you don't know why anyone would hang the doll and smear red paint all over it," the officer with the notepad said.

"Right," Gretchen and Nina said simultaneously.

"Looks like a warning to me," perky ponytail said. "Or a threat. There's a warrant out for Caroline Birch. Could she have done this?"

Gretchen gaped at the police officer. "Why would my mother break into her own home? Wouldn't she let herself in through the front door?"

"That's right," Nina said, the pen in her hand poised midair, jabbing at the officers. "She wouldn't try to scare her own sister and daughter." She shook her head, and Gretchen smiled. She could hear the wheels turning in Nina's head, berating the cops for what she considered total ineptness.

Their eyes met. *We'll have to take care of this on our own, won't we?* Gretchen thought.

Nina nodded slowly, and Gretchen blinked. Nina's psychic thing was getting scary.

* * *

"Most of it is simply intuition," Nina said, explaining what Gretchen referred to as her psychic abilities. The police officers had departed, and Nina had returned the cheeky Chihuahua to his owner. "Nothing magical about it. And it usually runs in families, so you probably have it, too, but you haven't figured out how to channel your powers."

"Did you hear what I was thinking when that officer suggested that my mother had broken into her own house?" Gretchen asked, dishing up food concoctions for Tutu, Nimrod, and Wobbles. All thoughts of finding a flight to Boston vanished from her mind.

"Not exactly. I caught the gist of it, though."

"Well that isn't so hard. You probably could tell from my expression that I didn't have any faith in their ability to solve the burglary."

"That could be true." Nina placed two bowls on the floor and watched Wobbles jump onto the counter to eat his.

"Cats on the countertop are disgusting," she said, making a face.

"Wobbles knows he can only go on this section," Gretchen said, gesturing to the countertop farthest from the food preparation area. "Right here on the corner."

"Anyway, you should work on your own psychic abilities."

"If you're so good, why haven't you solved Martha's murder and found my mother?"

"It doesn't work like that." Nina watched Tutu lick every last crumb from her bowl. "Sometimes I have a clear mental image of fragments of the past or future, but mostly I analyze my feelings through auras. An image of Martha's murderer won't pop into my head, but I might see an evil aura emanating from the killer if I encounter him."

"And have you seen any malevolent auras lately?" Gretchen picked up the canine's bowls and soaped them in the sink. Wobbles jumped to the ground, challenging the two dogs to rush him. They kept their distance, although Nimrod wagged his short tail ferociously.

"To tell you the truth, my energy connection seems to be on the fritz lately," Nina said. "To make it work I have to clear my mind and concentrate, and there's too much turmoil right now to see through the haze. That hanging doll, for example." Nina shivered visibly. "I don't have to be a psychic to read that message."

"I agree," Gretchen said. "Steve's going to be away from Boston for a few days, and it doesn't make sense for me to go home now. I can't leave you here alone with some psychopath running loose."

She hoped Nina wouldn't pursue a discussion of Steve. She wasn't anxious to share her confused feelings with her aunt. Her emotions were too close to the surface, and she needed time to think about what she wanted to do next.

Nina was too delighted when she learned of Gretchen's change of plans to follow up with any comments about Steve. "Let's get started then. The key, obviously, is important. Important enough to risk breaking and entering."

"But the thief wants us to know he's angry."

"Or she," Nina said. "I still think we need to watch April more carefully. My aura might be off, but every time I'm around her, I get mixed signals and a confusing blend of colors."

"And how about Bonnie?" Gretchen said. "She was lying about the Rescue Mission."

Nina held up her copy of Martha's hidden key. "Let's start with April and Bonnie and see if this fits in either one of their door locks."

A flash of lightning struck nearby, and Nimrod's ears flattened to his head. His tiny poodle body shook violently, and Gretchen picked him up. "It's storming outside. Can't we wait until it passes?"

"During monsoon season in Phoenix?" Nina said. "It'll

continue to storm at least until midnight. Besides, we can use the rain and darkness as cover."

"Great. Just what I want to do. Stand in the rain."

"Slink around in the rain," Nina corrected her, ignoring the sarcasm. "We are going to slink like an Arizona rattlesnake."

They drove toward Tempe, taking one detour after another to escape entrapment in flooded washes. On the left side of the road, coyotes appeared in the Impala's headlights, gaunt, running loosely in a pack, eyes red and glaring. Their heads swung in unison to look at the car, but they continued moving on through the spears of rain.

The windshield wipers slapped against the window in high gear. Occasionally, Nina pulled over to the side of the road until visibility returned. At times, all they could see ahead of them were taillights and streams of water rushing down the windshield.

April's modest home came into view through the descending gloom. Nina parked across the street and killed the lights, and Gretchen saw April's car parked in the carport. Through the rapidly fogging windshield of the Impala they watched an undulating glow behind April's front curtain.

"She's watching television in the dark," Nina said, rubbing her palm in a circle on the driver's window to clear her view. "This isn't going to be as easy as I thought."

Gretchen clutched the key. "Only one of us needs to go," she said, watching April's window for movement.

"You can," Nina said, looking away.

"Who's idea was this in the first place?"

Rain hammered on the roof of the car, reminding Gretchen of one Boston hailstorm so intense that it pounded circular dents into the hood of Steve's Porche.

"I have an umbrella," Nina said, reaching onto the backseat floor and pulling out a long white umbrella with pink polka dots. She handed it to Gretchen.

"Pink and white? How can I hide with this?" Gretchen cast a dubious expression Nina's way. She tossed the umbrella into the backseat and quickly jumped out into the rain. *Sometimes,* she thought, *you have to take a deep breath and plunge in, like a dive into frigid water. The longer you wait, the harder it is to go through with it.*

Her flip-flops splashed through sheets of water, and her hair hung from her face in dripping strands even before she made it to the first porch step. She clomped under an overhang and flattened against the brick wall, wiping water from her face and listening to the sound of the television, muted by the pounding rain. The light through the window flickered.

She edged over and risked a peak between the curtains. April's enormous frame covered her sagging sofa, and in the glow from the screen, Gretchen could tell that she was fast asleep, eyes closed, mouth hanging wide open.

She wiggled back to the front door, careful to stay under the protection of the eave, although she wasn't sure why she bothered, since she was soaked to the skin. She tried to slide the key into the lock.

It didn't fit.

In one mad rush, she lunged back to the car. Nina, encased in fogged windows, searched Gretchen's face. "Well?" she said.

"It isn't April's key."

"You didn't try the back door."

"The back door?"

"We have to be thorough," Nina said.

"We?" Gretchen was annoyed by Nina's use of a plural noun to describe a singular act. It wasn't as though Nina was making a significant contribution. "We?" she said again. "Remember what you said? We are going to slink around in the rain like a rattlesnake. Your turn."

"Don't be silly," Nina said, crossing her arms in protest. "You're already wet. And rattlesnakes know better than to slink around in the rain."

Gretchen climbed up on the seat and reached into the back for the umbrella. "April's sleeping. I'm through slinking."

She made her way carefully over the AstroTurf in April's yard and circled around the back. Lightning struck nearby, too close for comfort, and Gretchen hoped her umbrella wasn't the tallest structure in the vicinity. Not a single tree or large shrub grew near April's yard. Aside from an antenna on top of the house, she held the only other lightning rod around. With her recent streak of bad luck, electrocution was a distinct possibility.

She hurried to the back door and transferred the umbrella to her left hand, hooking it with her thumb, which protruded from the cast. The umbrella swayed and tipped out of her hand, falling to the ground. Abandoning it, she fumbled in her pocket for the key, retrieved it, and tried it in the lock. It didn't fit.

As she bent in the rain to pick up the umbrella and make a speedy exit, she heard the back door squeak open. She straightened. April's face loomed in front of her.

"Thought I heard something out here," April said. "What you coming to the back door for when the front's so much closer? And look at you, you're soaked through. Come on in." April held the door open.

"I'm too wet," Gretchen said. "I'll come back later."

"Nonsense, girl, I'll get you a towel. Well, come on."

While April went for the towel, Gretchen stood in front of the window, hoping Nina was paying attention and had spotted her. She turned and swept her eyes over the clutter in the room. Miniature dolls scattered over the tables, empty bags of chips, a collection of soda cans on the coffee table.

Overnight bag still on the floor with its contents thrown carelessly on top.

Gretchen realized that the overnight bag could have been on the floor a long time. Judging from April's nonexistent housekeeping skills, her earlier assumption that the bag had been used recently could have been wrong.

"How are you feeling?" she asked when April handed her the towel.

"This valley fever has me feeling awful," April said, coughing and sinking back into the sofa. She looked ashen and languid, and Gretchen couldn't help but believe that she really was ill. April probably did suffer from Phoenix's infamous lung infection. She hadn't been away on some furtive mission after all.

While toweling dry the best she could, Gretchen told April everything—about the break-in, Martha's bag, the key, and the hung doll. As she talked, April sat up straighter.

"Hanging a doll is scary business," she said. "You better go back to Boston until this is cleared up. You might be in danger."

"Someone is trying to scare me off. I can't let them win. I need to know who else you told about Martha's bag."

"Not a soul," April said. "I'm not a blabbermouth."

"I didn't mean to offend you, April. I don't care if you did tell everyone you see, I'm just rounding up suspects."

"Well, you'll have to look someplace else." April blew her nose. "I have something to tell you that might help, though. I finally got a look at that doll the police found in your mother's workshop. I'm proud of my appraisal skills and consider myself one of the best around. I base most of my analysis on market research like actual sales from shops and shows and on what's hot at the moment. Right now its all-bisque dolls, but that parian, even though it's not on the hot list, is so rare, I took awhile to estimate its worth."

Gretchen gently dabbed the towel on her wet arms and legs. "What did you decide?"

"The doll has a unique hairdo, for starters. Real elaborate. And it has flowers and jewels molded in the bisque. Pierced ears, too. The other appraiser said three thousand, but my guess is it's worth an easy five thousand and could sell for a lot more. And I'm being conservative. One fine doll, that one."

"Because of her repair business, my mother works on rare and valuable dolls all the time." Gretchen folded the towel over a chair and returned to the window. "That's how she makes her living. She isn't a thief."

"Nobody said she was." April coughed. "Martha's the one I'd peg as a thief."

"Martha was an enigma," Gretchen said. "From what people tell me she kept everyone at a distance. She had few confidantes, if any. No one really knew her."

April grunted. "A nasty woman. She used to call me Chubby Checker. Hey, Chubby, she'd call out every time she saw me, and then she'd laugh. She had nicknames for all of us. Bonnie was Pippi Longstocking because of her stiff hair. She called your mother Cruella De Vil from that Dalmation movie, because of her silver hair. Right to our faces, too."

"Alcoholism is a disease," Gretchen said, remembering Julia's own complaints about Martha's name-calling. The Tasmanian Devil was Martha's term for Julia, she'd said, sounding hurt. "She probably couldn't help herself."

"There's no excuse for cruelty."

"Are you feeling well enough to work out tomorrow?" Gretchen asked.

"Doctor says I should get a little exercise as long as I go slow and don't overdo."

"Good. I'll see you at Curves."

April shifted her weight and slung a leg onto the coffee table. "Speaking of Curves. It's a social event for our little group. We've been working out together for the last year or so, and we touch on a lot of subjects while we try to shed some fat." She patted her midsection and sighed. "I suppose I'd lose some weight if I'd watch what I eat, but I work up a real appetite after all that exercise. They have a diet plan I'm going to look into."

"You'd feel better," Gretchen agreed.

"What I'm trying to say and taking the long way to say it is that Bonnie's been dropping hints about Martha's dolls. She knows more than she's letting on."

"What kind of hints?"

"She says things like, what if Martha stashed her collection someplace. Or, what if some of the Phoenix Dollers were hiding Martha's dolls for her. Bonnie's the club gossip, and she has a secret she can't hardly keep. Give her a little shove, and she'll spill."

April's face turned rosy red when she realized what she had said, and she lifted a pudgy hand to her mouth. "I didn't mean it to sound like that. After what happened to Martha I shouldn't be telling you to give her a little shove." April reached for a box of tissues. "Bonnie's always up real late. She won't mind if you stop by right now. Just don't call her before noon. She's a late sleeper."

Gretchen lifted the umbrella and worked it through the front door. "Thanks for the information, April."

"Let me know what you find out," April called out. "And say hi to Nina out in the car."

Caroline wondered if she had made a mistake by placing an early bid and alerting other bidders to her presence. Web traffic through the doll listing was extremely heavy. As antique dolls became more difficult to find, their worth increased by volumes, and the bidding for the French Jumeau Bébé proved it.

The bidding war that Caroline had hoped to avoid had begun. The current bid flashed across the screen for the doll with the unique eyebrows designed by the world-famous French designer: $12,000.

Every doll collector yearned for at least one Jumeau, but few could afford to purchase a doll selling for thousands. At this price, how many different collectors were actually bidding? Two? Four? Certainly no more than ten.

Caroline wondered how long the seller would risk exposure. A stolen doll. A murdered collector. The seller must be motivated by uncontrollable greed or bold arrogance. Or desperation.

Using both hands she pulled her silver hair away from her face and neck and twirled it on her head. She gazed outside. Soon the planes overhead would cease flying for the night, only to start up again a few hours later at sunrise. Orange lighting from the parking lot shone into the drab room, and she could hear a television playing in the room next to hers.

Caroline rose and closed the heavy, smoke-laden drapes. She felt a small shiver of excitement, tasted the thrill of the auction on her tongue. She welcomed these new emotions, which until now had been masked under her own sense of desperation. Refreshing after days of extended panic. *Pretend you're in Vegas,* she thought, *where time is meaningless. Where light and dark merge into an insignificant gray.*

Good and evil. Light and dark. Were these and concepts such as justice and retribution subjective in nature? Caroline had always been able to see both sides of an issue, empathize with each point of view, rarely taking a firm stance. Everything a hazy shade of melded colors. Until now.

"Play to win," she whispered aloud. "At closing time, you must be the highest bidder."

The motel phone rang shrilly, the harsh and unexpected sound startling her, and, after a pause to still her pounding heart, she picked up the receiver.

A voice spoke soothingly to her in flawless French, and she smiled.

"You know I don't speak French," she said.

"Take a small break and eat something, cherie. What can I do for you?"

"Stall," Caroline said. "I need more time."

22

A new hobbyist interested in collecting dolls should start out by joining a local doll club. There are as many types of clubs as there are different dolls. You can join a Barbie club or an antique doll club, but a general doll club that welcomes all types of collectors will present the most variety. Clubs offer educational opportunities as well as experienced advice and an appreciative audience to share new acquisitions with. Active doll club members develop durable bonds and consider themselves part of a large extended family.

—From *World of Dolls* by Caroline Birch

Bonnie Albright sat at her kitchen table combing out her red wig and looking nothing like the presiding president of the Phoenix Dollers club. The small table overflowed with hair rollers in various sizes, bobby pins, a pile of brushes and combs, and a can of heavy-duty hair spray.

Gretchen tried not to stare at the mass of tangled red hair sitting on its wig stand or at the tight red wig cap covering Bonnie's head. She tried not to stare at her eyebrows, or rather her lack of eyebrows, since the penciled lines had been scrubbed away.

Nina's mouth hung open. "I never guessed you wore a wig. All these years . . ." Her voice trailed off.

"You should have called first," Bonnie said, annoyed, tufts of steel gray poking out from the wig cap, lips thin and pale without lipstick.

She spritzed the inside of the wig with Lysol, and Gretchen looked away.

Kewpie dolls lined a shelf in the dining room. Classic Kewpies, Action Kewpies waving and crawling, one of Kewpie's companion dogs—Doodle Dog—a Kewpie bank, and two Kewpie Thinker paperweights.

Teddy bears in every imaginable pose overflowed from bookcases in the adjacent living room. Nina had been right about teddy bear collectors. The bears resembled Bonnie with their big red bows and colorful faces.

"We were in the neighborhood and need to talk to you," Nina said, struggling to compose her facial features and avoid hurting Bonnie's feelings. "We had a break-in tonight, and someone hung one of Caroline's Shirley Temple dolls with a noose and poured red paint over it to look like blood."

"Oh my," Bonnie said, her hand slowing as it worked the rat-tail comb through the wig, picking out tangles.

"We need to know who else knew that we had Martha's bag," Gretchen said. "The burglar took the bag."

"I didn't tell a soul," Bonnie said, her knuckles white around the comb.

Nina pulled a chair out and sat down. She leaned across the table. "I've known you a long time, Bonnie, and you don't keep secrets well. You must have called someone, told someone."

Bonnie continued combing, looking down at the wig. "Do you know why I wear a wig? Because I'm practically bald on top of my head, that's why. Just like a man. You know how embarrassing that has been for me. And wearing a wig requires special attention. I have to watch out for rotating fans and revolving doors. I live in constant fear that my wig will fly off and expose me for what I really am."

Nina rolled her eyes to the ceiling, and Gretchen waited patiently beside her.

"I'm sure it's been hard for you," Nina said, sliding her eyes back to Bonnie. "But we are talking about breaking and entering and destruction of property, and we need answers."

"I kept my wig a secret, and I kept Martha's bag a secret, too."

"We never asked you to keep it a secret," Gretchen said gently. "You can tell anyone you want to tell. Why did you think it was a secret?"

Bonnie jabbed the wig on her head, roughly adjusting it, the hair still matted like a Barbie doll's crown of knots after making the rounds through a group of toddlers. A trapped look formed in Bonnie's eyes. "I didn't tell anyone because Martha had my key and I've been trying to get it back and I thought it might be in that bag and I didn't want anyone else to know. There. Are you happy?" The words came fast, spilling over each other in one long breath.

Gretchen gaped at Bonnie, wondering if she had heard correctly. Detective Albright's mother? What surprised Gretchen the most was the ease with which they had forced the truth from her. Bonnie crumbled with little resistance. Detective work might be easier than she originally thought.

Nina found her voice first. "You broke in, stole the bag, and hung Caroline's doll?"

Bonnie held her hands up in protest. "No, of course not. I don't know why anyone would do that. I wanted to get my key back before it surfaced and I became a suspect, too. Matty would be so angry. But I never went to Caroline's house. You have to believe me."

"I do," Nina said, and Gretchen wondered if Nina's aura analysis skills were working again. She also wondered what color Bonnie's aura would be. Red, she guessed, to match her hair and teddy bears' bows. "The key *was* in the bag, Bonnie. But why would anyone else steal it?" Nina asked.

No one said anything.

An idea dawned on Gretchen, and she wanted to thump her head with her cast. What little mind she had left could fit inside the French fashion doll's beaded purse. *Dense. Dense. Dense.* "We didn't tell anyone what we found in the bag," she said. "So maybe the thief expected to find something else. The strangled doll might have been an angry afterthought."

Bonnie nodded her snarled head in agreement. "That makes sense."

"It's possible," Nina said.

"Tell us what happened, Bonnie," Gretchen said. "Why did Martha have a key to your house?"

"If I tell you, you have to promise not to tell anyone."

"We promise," Nina said.

Bonnie looked at Gretchen. "You, too?"

"Me, too."

"About a week before Martha died," Bonnie began, "she came to my house, disheveled and agitated. At first, I thought she'd been drinking, and I had reservations about even letting her in, much less doing her a favor. But Martha insisted repeatedly that someone was stealing from her and that she needed a safe place to store something that meant a lot to her."

"She wouldn't tell you what it was?" Gretchen asked.

"She said she would tell me when she brought it over. That she had to find it first. She said she needed several hiding spots, not just one, because one hadn't worked before. I felt sorry for her. She cried and carried on like her closest family member had died, and in a weak moment, I told her where I keep a spare key in case she came back when I was gone. Behind that little Hummel picture inside the screen porch, I told her. That's where I keep it. Or kept it."

"What happened?" Nina asked.

"A few days later, the key disappeared. I didn't find anything hidden in the house, but she was the only person I ever told about the key, so I know she took it. Then after she died, I forgot all about it until Matty started saying he thought she had been murdered, and by the time I remembered, the opportunity to tell him about it seemed to have passed. You know how sometimes you put off telling someone something important, and the longer you wait, the harder it gets until you don't tell them at all?" Bonnie sniffed, and tears formed around the rims of her eyes.

"That's why you went to the Rescue Mission?" Gretchen asked. "To find Martha's friends and to retrieve your key?"

Bonnie wrung her hands. "No one there would help me. It scared me to think that some homeless people might have a key to my house. And I didn't want Matty to know how foolish I'd been."

Nina cupped Bonnie's hands in her own. "You have to tell your son what you just told us."

"I did. I told him all about it. Well, except for the key. But I told him everything Martha said to me about her dolls." Bonnie glanced sharply at Gretchen. "It certainly doesn't clear Caroline. In fact, it casts more suspicion on her."

Gretchen thought the same thing. Bonnie's story only confirmed the existence of dolls worth stealing, worth killing for. If only Martha had mentioned a name, things might have turned out differently. Her furtive actions and evasive words could destroy an innocent person and allow the guilty one to escape.

Gretchen took her copy of the inventory list out of her purse and handed it to Bonnie. "This is a list of the dolls Martha used to own. It's becoming clearer that she had at least some of them in her possession when she died. We don't know whether she actually owned them or if she was in the process of stealing them. Take a look at the list. Have you ever seen any of these dolls? In the past or recently?"

Bonnie slipped on reading glasses and bent over the list. "These here," she said, pointing at the list. "I saw these years ago."

Gretchen pulled the list over and read the description. "Kammer & Reinhardt 101 Character children, composition and wood jointed bodies, sixteen inch and seventeen inch, c. 1916."

"Beautifully made dolls," Bonnie said, taking the list back. "German manufacturers. Kammer & Reinhardt were the first to popularize character dolls, you know. Quite wonderful dolls. I remember them well."

"Pictures of the dolls would be helpful," Gretchen said, always amazed when collectors could identify a doll by such a brief description. The picture of the French fashion doll flashed through Gretchen's mind. Once she'd seen a picture, the doll would remain in her memory forever. Martha had catalogued her dolls with such detail. Why wouldn't she have taken pictures?

"Anything else look familiar?" Nina asked.

"Noooo . . ." Bonnie said, reading intently. Then she gasped, a little puff of air escaping from pursed lips. "Maybe this one. I'll read it to you." She looked up over her reading glasses. "You know I like Kewpie dolls. Actually, I'm obsessed with them. Listen to this." She cleared her throat. "Blunderboo laughing baby Kewpie, Bisque, c. 1915, O'Neill mark on feet, original red heart label."

"What about it?" Nina demanded. "What's familiar about it?"

"I saw a Kewpie fitting this description at Joseph's Dream Dolls." Bonnie pounded the table with an open palm. "That has to be the same doll. No question about it."

"When did you see it?" Gretchen asked.

"Two days ago," Bonnie answered. "I couldn't afford to buy it. He had priced it right, considering the age and condition, which was excellent, but I'm on a fixed income, and the price was out of my budget."

Around in circles we go, Gretchen thought. *Like musical chairs. The music stops, players scramble for seats, and I'm left standing in the middle staring at the same faces and asking the same questions.*

What had today's intruder expected to find in Caroline's workshop besides a bag of old clothes? Another doll from Martha's original collection? If Gretchen could believe April and Bonnie, they hadn't shared news of the discovery of Martha's bag with anyone else. That left only a handful of people who knew about it and had the opportunity to steal it. But why risk exposure by taking the bag if it contained nothing of value? And why draw more attention by hanging the Shirley Temple doll? Quite dramatic.

"Wait a minute," Bonnie said, still concentrating on the list. "I've gone over this inventory twice, and it isn't here."

"What isn't here?" Nina said.

"Martha showed me several dolls. This was long before the bank repossessed her house, and I had gone over to solicit donations for the Phoenix Dollers annual fund-raiser, which by the way is coming up again soon, and I hope I can count on you two for a contribution. Anyway, she showed me the character children, and she showed me another doll. A Madame Rohmer. I remember how surprised I was at the time, because she never let anyone see her dolls. But this group was new to her collection, and she was very excited."

Nina swung the list around to her side of the table, and Gretchen watched her index finger underline each entry. "No Madame Rohmer," she announced.

"That's so odd. It had a darling blonde wig." Bonnie posed both hands lightly on top of her own wig for emphasis. "And the cutest little cream dress with a blue feather pattern."

"Maybe she sold the doll and revised the list," Gretchen suggested. "But from what I hear, she refused to sell anything from her collection."

"That's right," Bonnie said. "Even at the end, she wouldn't sell any of them. They were like her children. She never had children of her own, you know, and I think she transferred all her pent-up affection onto the dolls."

"That's so strange when women do that," Nina said, missing the connection between a childless woman and her own four-legged forms of compensation. Everyone needed to love somebody, and it didn't matter whether they chose children or dogs or dolls. But children and dogs, and—yes, cats—loved you back. Inanimate objects like dolls couldn't reciprocate.

No wonder Martha felt compelled to finish out her life in a lonely state of inebriation after her lifelong partner had died.

"She must have loved her husband very much," Gretchen said, "to have fallen so far."

Bonnie nodded, and the unsecured wig slid to the side of her face. She straightened it. "You have no idea what his death did to her. A match made in heaven, we all said. I hope they finally found each other." Bonnie looked upward.

Gretchen, caught in a relationship that was quickly spiraling downhill, tried to imagine total and unconditional love with a husband of her own. She loved her mother that way, but could she say the same about her feelings for Steve? Would her world fall apart without him? Would she become a homeless drunk destined for a life of degradation and excess?

Hardly, she thought. She was stronger than that. If they failed to work out their problems, she would go on. Maybe that was the true test. If she wanted to fling herself from the top of Camelback Mountain, would she pass the test of love?

Maybe, after all the speculation and information gathered to the contrary, Martha had simply soared from the mountain heights in an attempt to rejoin her husband.

"It's possible that she forgot to include the new doll in her inventory," Gretchen said. "Everyone makes mistakes occasionally."

Caroline knew that some doll collectors refuse to participate in online auctions. They worry that the seller will exaggerate the condition of the doll and they will unknowingly purchase one of inferior quality. Some say that they must hold a doll in their hands, prod for flaws or misrepresented repair work, look into the doll's eyes, make a connection.

Watching the computer screen, Caroline again admired the valuable doll. She had already held this particular Bébé in her hands, had examined it from every angle. She knew it was in mint condition, not a single imperfection, and it wore its original white muslin dress and matching bonnet.

Her requirements for purchasing the doll were not the same hands-on connection that some collectors demanded. The doll was superfluous to her. The seller was her target.

Four hours and twenty minutes left in the auction, and twenty-seven bids registered. Caroline watched her e-mail in-box intently for new bids, the auction house alerting her each time another buyer outbid her. She rapidly and expertly moved between screens, from e-mail to auction.

Two thirty in the morning, and Caroline felt her resolve slipping as her need for sleep increased. Anxious worldwide buyers were bidding on the same doll. What time was it in London? In Rome? She cursed the seller for accepting international bids but recognized it as a brilliant maneuver to remove the doll from the United States. Crucial for the seller, but she refused to allow it to happen.

Caroline decided to check the auction bid one last time, then break for a few hours' rest. She needed sleep desperately, her thoughts too loosely connected and ineffective without it. She watched as the auction screen lit up, and her eyes grew wide with urgency. The Buy It Now icon flashed across her screen, the signal that the seller was ready to end the bidding at a certain set price. Usually this option wasn't available after the bidding began, and Caroline hadn't expected it.

The price shown under the listing for the Jumeau Bébé caused Caroline to pause momentarily. Twenty-two thousand dollars, a princely amount.

Her fingers flew on the keyboard, intent on beating another bidder to the treasure, hoping they had been caught off-guard also. All she needed was a lead of a few seconds. Faster fingers.

She hit Enter and sat back.

Something must have frightened the seller, too much attention on the site perhaps, or an unforeseen problem in waiting out the remaining four hours. She sensed a change in plans, a quiet desperation.

She punched in her e-mail address and smiled weakly.

"Congratulations!" appeared on the screen.

· 23 ·

Doll clothing is big business. With a sewing machine and expert sewing skills, a doll repairer can mend cloth bodies and reattach arms. She also can make reproductions of original costumes, remembering the ethical value of honesty when representing such work. Knowledge of period costumes is invaluable in determining originality, which gains importance with the age of the doll. Collectors remember clothing. Who can resist a perfectly fashioned two-piece satin jacket dress, a vintage white organdy, a pink cotton dress with pleated bottom, or a boy doll with red cummerbund and brass studs? The clothing, some say, makes the doll.

—From *World of Dolls* by Caroline Birch

Gretchen rolled out of bed early Wednesday morning after a restless night's sleep and painfully pulled on a pair of socks over her burnt feet and tied up the laces on her hiking boots. Glancing in the mirror, she noticed that her facial coloring remained a crispy, flaky red, and she dabbed on more healing lotion.

Nimrod, ready for high-energy puppy action, bolted his breakfast, while Wobbles savored his meal one morsel at a time. After eating, Wobbles nimbly sprang to the floor, and Nimrod proceeded to run in circles around him in a vain attempt to entice him into a game of chase. Wobbles looked on with disdain, his eyelids hooded and watchful. Eventually, he sauntered over to the protective height of the washing machine.

Gretchen drank coffee and ate what remained of last night's Chinese meal, wistfully remembering the enormous all-American breakfasts of her past. As she approached thirty, she'd been forced to change her eating habits to reflect her slower metabolism and the accompanying ease with which she gained unwanted weight. No more breakfasts of eggs, bacon, toast, and fried potatoes for her. Ruby red grapefruits and plain yogurt from now on.

She had jealously observed that Arizona women were fit, trim, and golden tan, and she hoped to model her unemployed self after them rather than eat her way through mounds of seven-layer self-pity.

She also noticed that she had more commitment to self-control and strength in the mornings than later in the day, when most of her determination faded.

A hardy hike up the mountain before the sun began to scorch the earth would solve the metabolism problem, at least temporarily. Last night's storm had moved toward the coast, and the arid desert heat had already begun to absorb the large quantities of fallen rain. In the next short, sunny hours, all evidence of flooding would evaporate, and the land would appear parched again.

On the day Gretchen arrived in Phoenix, the local news had recounted the rescue of a dehydrated, heat-stricken hiker. Gretchen planned a cautious, safe climb to protect herself from embarrassing media coverage. Water bottle, hat, and an early ascent were essential.

As an afterthought, she grabbed a pair of binoculars in case she spotted a new bird to add to her growing life list of bird sightings.

Taking the footpath to the trailhead, she veered to the left onto Summit Trail and began the rugged one-point-two-mile uphill climb, periodically stopping to rest and to glance at the summit, almost three thousand feet above sea level, according to a sign below. A Harris antelope squirrel darted along the rocks, tail curled across his back, and disappeared into a tangle of mesquite.

Halfway up, Gretchen paused at the hand railing and listened to the high-pitched trill of a rock wren. She felt rejuvenated by the fresh air and the open expanse of the desert mountain. She saw nesting holes bored into a saguaro cactus by a gila woodpecker and daydreamed about life as a bird. Free and mobile. It seemed a peaceful existence compared to the complexities of human relationships.

She looked back down the steep trail toward the trailhead, now a tiny spot in the distance, and out over the city. She saw someone moving up the path toward her with a familiar gait. She held the binoculars to her eyes and watched Matt Albright making the steep climb. He wasn't doing too badly, considering how unprepared he was for the hike. He didn't wear a hat, which is the very first hiking rule, and didn't carry water, as far as Gretchen could see. Obviously, a beginner. Or perhaps he hadn't anticipated climbing a mountain today. Had he been watching her all along? Following her from home?

Matt looked up in her direction, and she reluctantly waved, wishing instead to slide down and flatten into the rocks. He hadn't exactly been the bearer of good news lately. Matt lifted a hand as a shield from the sun and waved in return. She watched him pick his way through the rocks.

"You obviously never joined the Boy Scouts," she said, when he stopped before her, breathing hard. Lines of perspiration ran down both sides of his face, but he managed one of his dazzling smiles. He could make a living as a tooth model.

"Their motto is *Be prepared*," she continued, handing him her water bottle. "You're a classic dehydration victim and potential buzzard food." She watched him tip the bottle back and take a long drink.

"The fire department needs the extra business," he managed to say. "They'd be happy to come up and get me." He sat down on a boulder. "I should have trained for this assignment. Keeping up with you isn't easy. A triathlon would be less work."

"I see you're a walking advertisement for social issues," she said, pointing at his T-shirt, reading the inscription *Follow Your Own Path—Leave Only Footprints.* She remembered the Indian Youth Fund T-shirt he wore a few days ago. "A cop with a social conscience."

"You make it sound like we aren't human. Maybe I can prove you wrong."

"My cousin, Blaze, is a sheriff in a little town in the Michigan Upper Peninsula. He kind of gives the profession a bad name, He's Neanderthalish and loudly self-righteous. I'm going to the top. If you want to make sure I don't commit a crime against Phoenix, like littering on one of your premier tourist attractions, you'd better go up with me."

Matt stood and gestured up the mountain. "After you."

Gretchen hiked fast, determined to make it to the summit as quickly as possible and start the descent before the sun crested over Camelback. "I was hoping to see a gila woodpecker," she called back, noting that the gap between them had widened. "I've seen the holes in the cacti, but I've never seen the bird."

"They have zebra-striped backs," he called up to her in short, choppy words. A period punctuated every word, each a sentence of its own. "I didn't know you were a birder."

"I've never considered myself one. I just like to look. It's an excuse to be outdoors." She stopped and waited for him to catch up.

"There are eighteen species of hummingbirds in Arizona," he said, looking miserable, his smile subdued and strained. "Arizona is a bird haven in the winter."

"Why are you following me?" Gretchen asked. "You aren't a hiker, at least not at this skill level. You could have waited at the base for me."

"I could, but I like the challenge." He lifted his shirt to wipe his face with the edge of the cloth, and Gretchen glimpsed a well-toned midsection. Too much weight lifting and not enough aerobic conditioning, she thought.

"Sapsuckers, whiskered owls, quail, Arizona has it all," he said. "In answer to your question, your Aunt Nina mentioned that you like to hike. When you weren't home, I thought I might find you here."

"On the way down you can tell me why you're visiting so early in the morning. Come on, let's go."

He smiled with relief. "You've made my day. I thought I'd have to finish the climb to get your attention. I'll buy you breakfast to show my gratitude."

The Waffle House was crowded, but the waitstaff knew Matt and found them a table almost immediately. Gretchen, her early morning healthful dieting resolution temporarily forgotten, dove into an enormous platter of pecan waffles.

"Nina says you're peladophobic," Gretchen said between bites. "Is that true?"

Matt laughed. "Are you asking me if I have an unnatural fear of bald people or are you asking me if I have pediophobia?"

"The fear-of-dolls one."

"Pediophobia." Matt poured more syrup over his waffles and handed the bottle to Gretchen. "It's weird, but I've always had a problem. I'm surprised you spotted it, since I go out of my way to hide behind daring bravado." He thumped his chest. "You know, the big bad cop that's afraid of a little doll doesn't exactly improve my image. My mother tried to break me of it when I was young with no luck. Facing my fear, in this case, didn't work."

"Maybe she made it worse," Gretchen said, thinking of bewigged, gossipy Bonnie forcing dolls on her son.

"Maybe," he agreed pleasantly, not particularly concerned with resolving his issues or delving into the reasons. "But the symptoms mimic those of the flu—nausea and sweating—and I avoid those feelings whenever possible. I couldn't believe it when I was assigned to this case."

"Speaking of the case," Gretchen said, her waffle-filled fork midair. "Any progress?"

"That's why I came to see you," he said. "We have a suspect in custody."

Gretchen sharply lowered the fork, and it clattered to her plate. "My mother?" she said, not sure what answer she wanted to hear. She had little doubt that her mother was alive and well, but her physical presence would be confirmation, an erasure of that tiny bit of lingering doubt, unspoken and consciously ignored, yet there all the same. Gretchen craved living proof. On the other hand, she couldn't bear the thought of her mother behind bars, caged like a dangerous mountain lion.

Matt shook his head. "No, not your mother. Theodore Brummer turned himself in late last night. He confessed."

"I never heard of him."

"Well, he said he did it."

"He confessed to Martha Williams's murder?" Gretchen sighed with relief, noting the assertion in Matt's expression. It was over. Her mother could come home, and she could return to Boston and the life she had made for herself there. She tried not to think of the recent negative qualities of that life. She could put it back together again, find a job, salvage her long-term relationship. She would consider it a new beginning, a starting point for the next phase of her life.

"Yes, he could only communicate in Spanish, no English at all. He says he did it."

"Did he say why he killed her?"

"Apparently they knew each other from the Rescue Mission. He says he was drunk, she had a bottle of whisky and wouldn't share. A physical fight ensued, and he pushed her."

Gretchen's eyes narrowed, and her brows furrowed. Killed for a bottle of whisky? Something felt wrong about that. The homeless lost their lives occasionally, and sometimes they did lose it over a bottle of booze.

But Camelback Mountain was miles from the area the

city's destitute frequented. Why chase her all the way up a mountain and then push her off?

A disturbing thought struck her, and she knew the answer before she asked the question. She sensed what Nina would have called her special inherited talent, a certain unspecified intuition. Goose bumps dotted her arms as she braced herself to cross paths once again with a duplicitous transient.

"What does this Theodore Brummer look like?" she asked suspiciously.

"Scruffy, smelly. Usually the homeless are nondescript and tend to blend in, but this guy has a large lump on his head that distinguishes him from the rest, some kind of growth." Matt cupped his hand on the side of his head.

Gretchen stared at him.

She was right.

Nacho.

"What about the witnesses?" she managed to ask. "The ones who saw my mother on the mountain when Martha died?"

"If you're asking if their sighting is credible, it is. She's still wanted as an accomplice based on their accounting. She was on the mountain, and she's guilty of something. Maybe not murder, but certainly she withheld information and obstructed the pursuit of justice. I'm not buying his motive. He didn't kill Martha Williams over alcohol. And there's still the possibility that your mother conspired with Brummer."

Gretchen pushed her plate away, having suddenly lost her appetite.

"I suspected him all along," Nina said. "Doesn't surprise me at all."

They drove toward Scottsdale Memorial Hospital through typically heavy traffic on their way to visit Daisy. Nina's menagerie—Tutu, Nimrod, and the volatile Enrico—rode in the backseat, and Gretchen again felt gratitude for her cat and his independent character. His only requirements were a

constant source of food and water and a warm body to
cuddle with at night. Dogs, on the other hand . . . She let the
thought go, resigned to the present situation and present,
doggy-breath company.

The back windows were crusted with accumulated drool.

"Nacho didn't implicate her," Gretchen said, repeating
the rest of the information supplied by the detective. "In
fact he insisted that my mother had nothing to do with it.
He was adamant, maintaining that he acted alone."

"That's good news."

"The police still have a warrant out for her arrest based
on the description from the hikers."

"That's not good news."

Something still didn't feel right about Nacho's confession, but Gretchen was confident that her questions would
be answered eventually. How, for example, could Nacho
have been responsible for Daisy's car accident? He didn't
even own a vehicle, so how could he have forced her off
the road? And his concern for Daisy had seemed genuine.
Why would he try to harm her?

However, his sneaky manner and covert actions made
his guilty plea plausible. And he admitted to the murder.
Case closed. Or almost. Maybe the reason for Daisy's
crash was simpler than it appeared. Daisy, inattentive or in-
experienced, could have lost control and driven off the
road. It was possible that, as the detective had conjectured,
no one had tail-ended her.

"I don't understand his penchant for speaking Spanish,"
Gretchen said. "He refused to speak English, and as far as
I know, he isn't even Spanish. At least he doesn't look
Spanish. And we know he's fluent in English. What's the
significance of the Spanish?"

"You think too much," Nina said. "Accept his confession at face value."

"And ignore the fact that he didn't break in and steal
Martha's bag?"

"How do you know he didn't?"

"Because he's the one who gave the bag to us."

Nina swung into the hospital parking lot, and all three dogs tumbled to the right side of the car. "Seat belts for you guys unless you learn to brace better for turns," she warned.

"How are we going to fit Daisy into the car?" Gretchen said in exasperation. "There isn't room."

Nina slid the gears into the park position and turned off the engine. "It was your idea to take Daisy home with you," she said. "I don't approve of letting a vagrant take over Caroline's home, but it's your decision. Now, when you're robbed blind, I'll know exactly who did it."

"You're stereotyping," Gretchen said. "I thought you were more open-minded than that."

Nina grinned. "In answer to your question. We have plenty of room for Daisy because you can ride in the back with the pooches."

Gretchen got out of the car and slammed the door.

Caroline didn't flinch at the exorbitant amount of money she had paid for the doll. Thanks to the increasing popularity of plastic and the credit card service's unethical tactics that trapped the impulsive consumer into a lifetime of interest-paying servitude, she had been allowed to spend more than she could reasonably repay. Usually outspoken about the evils of excessive credit debt, Caroline, in one single transaction, had joined the multitudes of overextended debtors.

She smiled with satisfaction.

Until now she had carefully avoided leaving a paper trail. In fact, she still practiced extreme caution. Watchful eyes would find no easy path to her temporary door. She had used only cash until the final moment when she had no other choice. The evasive maneuvers, however, would end soon enough.

The terms of a private auction were strictly adhered to, Caroline knew from her own experience with online selling.

Bidders' e-mail addresses were not disclosed, a distinct advantage for Caroline that effectively concealed her identity from the seller. Of course, this seller, she knew, also requiring anonymity, had used another identity and an escrow service to manage the transaction.

Full contact information could be requested only after winning the auction, and only the seller and the highest bidder were notified via e-mail when the auction was over.

Caroline keyed in her request for the seller's identification and settled in to wait for the response. The information she was about to receive would be well worth the thousands she had spent moments earlier.

She thought of Nacho, her friend back in Phoenix, with a mixture of fondness and reserve. Her accomplice. One of life's enigmas, the erudite outcast, fluent speaker of multiple languages. All the knowledge in his head couldn't save him from his struggles with the bottle. Lucid for long periods of time until the next inevitable alcoholic binge and the rapid descent from lucid to lurid.

Caroline hoped he could maintain his focus long enough to continue to be of use to her. He was the only one she could trust. Their mutual cause bound them together like two foot soldiers huddled in a foxhole.

She rubbed her tired, dry eyes and opened them again at the same instant that the monitor changed.

The "Receiving mail" message flashed across the bottom of her computer screen.

For the collector who enjoys a bit of the macabre, a line of dolls has been created especially for you. Living Dead Dolls come, not with a certificate of authenticity, but with a death certificate. One possible choice for the avid collector is Died & Doom, a gruesome bride and groom. All dolls are accompanied by morbid rhyming histories and original individualized coffins. Blood spatters and glow-in-the-dark are available as well. They have a certain freakish appeal for mystery and horror fans.

—From *World of Dolls* by Caroline Birch

Daisy settled into the spare bedroom with her meager supply of toiletries, furnished by the hospital, and with the clothes on her back, several layers of mix-and-match items that were all mix, no match. Didn't the woman appreciate the extent of the high summer temperatures? Couldn't she feel the sweltering, relentless heat rising to a boil under all those layers? Gretchen felt hot just looking at her and adjusted the air-conditioning upward.

"I'll say this again," Daisy said, the top of her head bandaged and the surrounding hair shaved to stubble. "I'd rather stay with Nacho. All the Hollywood scouts hang out in downtown Phoenix. What are my chances of being discovered way out here behind this ugly clump of dirt you call a mountain?"

Nina sighed heavily. "How many times do I have to say it? Nacho's house swept away in the last flood. I saw it with my own eyes. It's gone."

Along with my phone, Gretchen thought. Somehow there hadn't been time to visit her phone service and purchase a new one. She felt naked without it and experienced a moment of pampered privilege for her thought. Daisy had absolutely nothing in the world, while she clung to all the modern, convenient trappings, every one of them.

Nacho wouldn't need his cardboard home any time soon, but she hadn't told Daisy about his incarceration yet.

"And my clothes," Daisy continued to complain. "I can't function without my shopping cart."

"We'll find the cart later today. Your clothes and the rest of your things are in Nina's trunk," Gretchen assured her, watching Nina make a face at the thought of Daisy's foul-smelling odds and ends arriving inside her sister's home. "Or we can buy you a new outfit or two," she said, hoping to appease Nina's sensibilities. "Would you like that?"

"I'll pay," Nina offered enthusiastically.

The tiny trio of dogs sniffed at Daisy's ankles. Enrico hadn't barked or growled at Daisy, not once, which Gretchen took as a good sign. Anyone who connected with animals had to have redeeming qualities. Even Wobbles, usually reserved around strangers, stalked back and forth before Daisy, rubbing up against her legs and purring.

Gretchen remembered her first encounter with Daisy on the streets of Phoenix and Daisy's fascination with Nimrod as he rode contentedly in his embroidered poodle purse on her shoulder. The homeless woman obviously loved animals.

Daisy lifted Enrico into her arms, and Gretchen watched in stunned surprise as the normally whirling tornado licked the top of Daisy's hand in beastly gratitude for her attention.

"Well, doesn't that beat all," Nina said. "He likes you."

"I have a certain way with doggies," Daisy said, looking down at Wobbles. "And kitties. When are we going to bring in my stuff from the car?"

"Not right now," Nina said with annoyance. "Let's get

you a few new things first. Then we can decide what to do with the rest."

"Great," Daisy said, stuffing Enrico in Nimrod's purse. She slung him over her shoulder, and Enrico peeked out, perplexed by the change in mobile homes. "Grab the other two and let's go. What are you waiting for? Where are we going for my new outfits?"

Nina, a pained expression on her face, packed up the pooches without responding. She silently consigned Nimrod to the Chihuahua's purse and gave Gretchen a withering glare after Gretchen announced that she would remain at home.

"I have a few calls to make," she said. "You go ahead and have fun. Happy shopping."

"You can't do this to me," Nina whispered out the corner of her mouth.

"It will do you good to make a new friend. Look how she gets along with Enrico. Daisy's a natural." She hustled them out the door, Nina blustering and Daisy discussing the requirements for her new wardrobe.

"Red and purple," Gretchen heard her say as she left. "Like those Red Hat ladies. I like those colors."

The phone rang as Gretchen finished straightening up the kitchen.

"Somebody's been in my house," Bonnie screeched. "Since we were talking about my key only yesterday, I've been more watchful than usual. And I know somebody's been in here."

"What was taken?"

"Nothing that I can see. But I'm meticulous. I can tell if one little thing in my house has been moved. And a dresser drawer in Matty's old room is open just a smidge. I didn't leave it that way."

"Are you sure?"

"I'm sure, because after I saw the open drawer, I started paying more attention to details. Things have been moved around. Whoever stole the key from your house came here."

Bonnie sniffed. "It's a horrible thing to know a stranger vi-
olated the sanctity of my home without permission. It gives
me the creeps."

"Are you positive that they got in with the key?" Gretchen
dropped the dish towel onto the table.

"Nothing is forced open or broken, and I always lock up
because you can never be too careful these days. Criminals
prey on women living alone. There are only two keys—one
on my key chain and the one you had. I never replaced the
spare behind the Hummel."

Gretchen didn't think it necessary to mention the copies
she had made for Nina and herself. "I don't know," she said
doubtfully. "A slightly open dresser drawer seems like
flimsy evidence."

"That's exactly why I didn't call Matty," Bonnie whined.
"He would say the same thing. I have a locksmith on the
way over, and the lock will be changed. That'll solve the
problem quick enough. I just thought you'd like to know
what happened."

"I appreciate the call. I really do. Are you okay?"

"I'll live." Bonnie sniffed again.

Gretchen thought about Martha and the disappearing key.
Martha had taken the key but never delivered the package. Or
had she? Had she hidden a doll inside Bonnie's house without her knowledge? Did she enter Caroline's house as well,
with practiced stealth? Maybe Martha had hidden the doll
that the police confiscated. And who else could have had
enough information to search Bonnie's house? And what
would be the point of hiding dolls in other doll collectors'
homes?

Questions raced through Gretchen's mind with no easy
answers following behind.

"When did this happen?" she asked.

"I was out this morning for a few hours," Bonnie said.
"In fact, I'm in and out of the house every day with my
part-time job at Saks and all my errands."

Gretchen experienced a rising sense of alarm. Nacho couldn't possibly be responsible for a break-in that morning, since he had turned himself in to the police sometime during the night.

"But I haven't been in that room for two or three days," Bonnie continued, effectively placing Nacho back as primary suspect in the lineup. "I've got to go. The locksmith is here."

Gretchen hung up and remembered a certain uneasiness right after she arrived in Phoenix, when she'd noticed the open patio door, unlocked when she was sure she had locked it.

Her mother's pink bracelet on her wrist caught Gretchen's eye, and renewed anger at her mother's silence washed over her. Why hadn't she returned by now? In Gretchen's opinion it was time to resurface and to refute the charges against her. Exactly one week since Martha died, and now with Nacho arrested for the murder and a full confession, where was her mother?

Only one explanation occurred to Gretchen. The Bru French fashion doll and its incredible value must have tempted her mother into her current situation. It didn't really matter whether Martha or Caroline had placed the parian doll in the workshop. The French fashion doll, dressed in a green silk costume and a straw hat, and the doll trunk filled with original costumes and accessories, played a critical role in the murder. That doll was the beginning. Or the end for Martha.

Gretchen had lost her direction. Her plan to find the French fashion doll had been forgotten in the anxious moments of the noose-necked Shirley Temple and the deceitful actions of members of the Phoenix Dollers. Joseph hiding his family ties, Bonnie's covert visit to the homeless, and April's suspicious illness. All had distracted Gretchen. Then Daisy's accident in her mother's own car and Nacho's surprising confession.

All had diverted Gretchen from her path to the French

fashion doll, and she realized with a sinking sense of helplessness that she had no idea how to go about finding it. Perhaps her mother had the doll with her, and it would never reappear. Maybe they were both gone forever.

What did her mother know that had caused her to flee? Could a doll gain such importance for her that she would abandon her comfortable life in Phoenix for the uncertainty of a life in hiding, cut off forever from her friends and career and family?

Why did Gretchen have this awful premonition that her mother wasn't coming back?

Close to tears, she heard the phone ringing again, slicing sharply through her tumultuous thoughts. She wouldn't accept her mother as an accomplice to murder or as a common thief, she decided.

Longing to hear her mother on the other end of the line, she hid her disappointment at the sound of Larry's voice. "You must be keeping on top of my mother's work," she said. "No one has been around here threatening lawsuits for unfulfilled promises."

"Anything to help. I thought I'd invite you out to lunch," he said. "You must be ready for some company after spending the last few days with your aunt."

The morning's pecan waffles were a distant memory, but the knowledge that she had eaten an entire day's worth of calories in one sitting lingered. She really didn't want to be home when Nina and Daisy returned, craving time away from the large entourage that accompanied Nina everywhere.

Besides, she might enlist Larry in her search.

Gretchen laughed. "Only if you promise not to bring any dogs along."

"Deal," he said.

The menu at Garcia's Mexican Restaurant, situated at the base of Camelback Mountain on a busy stretch of Camelback Road, featured some of Gretchen's favorite foods, and she found it difficult to decide what to order. The menu read like a good book—cheese quesadillas, one of the best guacamole dips in the valley, chicken tortilla soup—the endless list tempted and teased. A perfect pick-me-up after her close call with the onset of major depression. Dieting could wait.

She ordered shrimp tacos and a nonalcoholic margarita and Larry followed suit.

Gretchen briefly wondered how Nina and Daisy were getting along. She hoped Nina wouldn't be too distressed when she read the note Gretchen carefully remembered to leave for her explaining lunch with Larry.

She missed her cell phone terribly.

Larry apprised her of the status of the repair work. He had offered customers the option of waiting for Caroline to return, and many had opted to do exactly that, insisting that no one else could handle the work as well as she could. Many had heard the rumors and expressed concern for her safety.

"She has a loyal following," he said. "Three customers were in a panic because they had committed the dolls to shows or to one of their customers. I finished the last one yesterday. Do you think she'll come back soon?"

"I have no idea. She still hasn't contacted me. Have you heard about Nacho?"

"Nacho?" Larry's squinty eyes blinked rapidly.

"I mean Theodore Brummer. Nacho is his nickname. He confessed to Martha's murder."

The surprise on Larry's face surpassed her own astonishment when she first heard. "You're joking," he said. "Someone actually came forward and admitted to it?"

Gretchen filled him in on the details she had learned from Matt, careful to exclude any mention of keys or doll lists or burglaries. Mainly because she had lost the energy to revisit them, their stories too complex and convoluted. Perhaps later when she felt stronger, Larry's opinion would be helpful.

"Caroline can come home now," he said. "And clear her name."

"That's my hope."

"If you hear from her, I'd like to know."

"You'll be one of the first," Gretchen assured him.

A whippet-thin, golden blonde carrying a Prada handbag walked by as Gretchen bit into her third shrimp taco. She placed the rest of the taco on her plate, abruptly reminded of her commitment to lose a few pounds, and used her napkin to dab at the corners of her mouth.

"I'm free for awhile," Larry said. "Julia said I was underfoot and gave me the boot. She's in the middle of inventorying supplies in the back room, and she's in a terrible mood. I'm at your service until it's safe to go home. Where would you like to go?"

Gretchen considered her options. With Nacho in custody for Martha's murder, she could direct all her efforts into locating her mother. But where to start? Then she remembered the laughing Kewpie doll that Bonnie had seen in Joseph's shop, the one Bonnie insisted matched the description from Martha's inventory. It wasn't much of a lead, but it was the only one she had.

"Do you mind taking me to Joseph's Dream Dolls?" she said. "He has a doll I'd like to see."

"Not at all," Larry said. "I'm always interested in what the competition is up to. Wheeling and dealing is the name of the doll seller's game."

"Can I use your phone?" Gretchen asked. "Sorry to ask, but mine's gone."

Larry pulled a phone from a holder on his belt. "Help yourself."

Gretchen called her mother's house, but no one answered. She left a message on the machine so Nina would know that she was going to Mesa to visit Joseph. She smiled to herself at the image of Nina and Daisy shopping together and wondered where Nina had taken her newfound buddy. Probably not to the Biltmore Fashion Park where she might run into Bonnie. A chance encounter would supply Bonnie with enough gossip material for the next week.

No, Nina would select a shopping mall far from the doll collecting crowd, one with the least chance of meeting a familiar face. South Phoenix or Glendale, most likely. She'd be away for most of the afternoon.

Gretchen felt slightly guilty for ditching Nina, but her aunt slowed her down and, more than anything, Gretchen wanted this whole affair resolved as soon as possible.

She tried Nina's cell phone, but the voice mail prompt answered immediately, indicating that Nina was out of range or that she had turned off her phone. She left the same message on the cell phone's voice mail as she had at the house, but this time she included a hearty wish for a successful shopping trip.

Caroline leaned forward and stared at the computer screen. On the run for so many days, rushing toward this precise moment while recklessly disregarding her own safety, she was aghast at the image before her and recoiled from the bitter truth.

Blood drained from her face and, in the mirror hanging above the desk, her face appeared the same color as her silver hair, ghostly white, filled with pale fear.

She dialed numbers—Gretchen's cell, Gretchen's Boston apartment, Nina's numbers, Steve's office and home—pounding the keys and finally, after listening to multiple mechanical voices suggesting that she leave a message, she threw the offending phone against the motel wall.

Get a grip on your emotions, she thought. *You're exhausted, but now is not the time to collapse.*

Caroline stumbled through the motions of packing up her few belongings, tossing the phone into her purse, and closing her laptop. She dialed the front desk and requested a cab while planes roared overhead. Tucking her silver hair under the baseball cap, she refused to worry about Nacho or Nina or her daughter, earlier fear of the unknown transforming into intense anger.

She was on her way back to Phoenix with the proof she needed to save her life and to avenge Martha's death.

· 25 ·

Recent Market Report on French Fashion Doll:

*I'm always cautious about determining prices for dolls, be-
lieving that this inexact science is best served through published
pricing guides and current market demands. However, I can
report at the time of this writing that the French fashion doll,
particularly those manufactured by Bru and Jumeau, have experienced a resurgence in popularity and are considered hot
dolls. They paved the way for the modern fashion doll we all
know and love—the Barbie—and today's collectors couldn't be
more bewitched by this captivating antique doll.*

*I have personally had the opportunity to witness an exquisite
rare specimen selling at auction for six digits!*

—From *World of Dolls* by Caroline Birch

Gretchen couldn't help measuring the success of the two
doll dealers. Larry struggled to keep his business open, and
the physical stress showed on his face as a nervous twitch.
Joseph, diamonds glistening in his pierced ears and wearing flamboyant garb, enjoyed a thriving business and enormous success, if the number of customers in his shop was
a reasonable indicator.

Location, location, location.

It really did matter.

Joseph's Dream Dolls was part of a booming new shopping mall in a bustling section of Mesa with heavy walk-by
traffic. Who could resist a front window brimming with
smiling dolls?

On the other hand, Larry and Julia's China Doll Shop sat in a near-empty outdated mall with a straggle of aging but loyal customers.

Gretchen wished the best for Larry and Julia and made a mental note to visit their shop soon and make a purchase. Perhaps it was time for them to consider moving to a better location.

Larry and Joseph eyed each other like boxers in a ring, and Gretchen thought it must feel strange for Joseph to know that his competition was taking in all the details of his shop and assigning a grade. Gretchen thought Joseph would earn the highest score possible, a ten on a scale of one to ten.

His store had pizzazz. He knew how to set up his displays to show off his dolls to the best possible advantage.

The first thing he mentioned after greeting them was Nacho's arrest, having learned the news through a courtesy phone call from Detective Albright. "Relieved to finally put an end to the whole awful business," Joseph said. "Maybe now they can release her body."

His fingers fluttered over a display, edging pieces into new positions, moving a doll over by a space so infinitesimally small Gretchen wondered why he bothered. "I knew your mother was innocent," he said. "I just knew it."

Larry wandered away, studying the shop with intensity, stopping to observe the woman behind the cash register who wore a bright bow in her hair and looked like an Ideal Tammy doll herself. Details everywhere, even in the staffing, not a trick of the trade missed.

Gretchen lowered her voice and said to Joseph, "I'd like to look at your Kewpie dolls. I'm thinking of one as a gift for Nina."

Joseph looked surprised. "I didn't know Nina collected dolls. Well, that's marvelous. I always wondered how she could survive as a member of your family without taking part. Right this way."

Smiling Kewpies covered a section of the back wall.

Kewpies in every imaginable pose, lying down, holding baskets, wearing costumes.

"There's a strong market for Kewpies," Joseph said. "It's a good choice for a gift, because it will never depreciate."

Gretchen scanned the grouping without finding the Blunderboo that Bonnie had described. "I was hoping for something very special. She's done a lot for me."

"I have just the thing over here in a locked cabinet with all my distinctive pieces. It's costly though. I'm not sure you should spend that kind of money for a first-time collector." Joseph laughed. "Listen to me, trying to talk a customer out of a sale."

Larry joined them as they approached a large glass cabinet. Gretchen spotted the Blunderboo immediately, its laughing baby face lighting up the entire grouping, the red heart label prominent on his naked, chubby body.

Joseph unlocked the cabinet and carefully deposited the Kewpie in Gretchen's hand. "Blunderboo, the clumsy Kewpie," he said. "Forever tripping over himself."

"It's marvelous. Where did you acquire it?" she asked.

Joseph turned away, refusing to meet Gretchen's eyes, and began to arrange the other dolls within the cabinet. "At an estate sale," he muttered. "Most of my dolls are purchased through auctions or estate sales."

Was Bonnie mistaken? Or had the doll really belonged to Martha at one time? Why would Joseph tell her that the doll had been purchased at an estate sale if Martha had given the doll to him? He'd have no reason to misrepresent the facts.

"Someone told me that Martha had owned a Kewpie like this one," she said.

Gretchen thought she saw Joseph flinch.

"Who told you that?" Larry said from behind Gretchen.

"I don't remember," Gretchen said.

"Well," Joseph said, "it wasn't this Kewpie."

Gretchen glanced at the price tag and handed the doll to Joseph. "I'll think about it," she said. "He's beautiful."

Joseph locked the Kewpie in the cabinet and placed the key in his pocket.

"I'm still looking for my mother," Gretchen said. "If you have any ideas where she might be, please let me know."

"Sorry, Gretchen. I haven't heard a thing."

Walking out into the intense sun, Gretchen knew that Joseph had lied to her. He'd lied the first time she visited the shop when he claimed no knowledge of the disposition of Martha's dolls, and he'd lied again today. Joseph was worth serious consideration as a suspect in Martha's murder. Had he killed his aunt for her doll collection? Was that why he had become successful? By selling off Martha's valuable dolls?

Nina pulled up to the curb with Daisy in the passenger seat wearing a purple sundress and a floppy red hat that covered her bandaged head. She rolled the window down and waved. "Look at me. I'm like a new person, real movie star material in this getup."

"What are you doing here?" Gretchen said, bending down and peering at Nina.

"We got your message," Nina said, not looking especially happy. "And we were shopping right down the street."

"You came all the way to Mesa for your shopping spree? I thought you'd head in the other direction." Gretchen grinned and turned to Larry. "Thanks for lunch. I'll hitch a ride home with Nina."

Larry blinked rapidly in the glare from the sun, continuing to stand on the sidewalk, apparently reluctant to return to his own shop and Julia's battlefield tactics.

"I've got to go now," Gretchen said.

"See you ladies later," he said, walking slowly to his car.

"Get in the back," Nina said to Gretchen, and she slid in with the dogs, accepting her punishment for forcing Daisy's company on Nina.

Nina slung an arm over the back of the seat and stared solemnly at Gretchen. "You have the blackest aura surrounding you that I think I've ever seen around a human being. Are you feeling okay?"

"I'm fine."

"If you aren't feeling it yet, it must be a gathering force. The outlook is scaring me."

Gretchen felt cold in spite of the heat and in spite of her personal opinion about Nina's psychic experiences. None of her predictions had exactly panned out so far. If Nina were an oilfield geologist, they'd be drilling a multitude of expensive dry holes.

"I agree with you about Gretchen's aura," Daisy said to Nina as they pulled out. "And I see exactly what you mean. It's a bad one."

Nina looked over at Daisy and scowled.

"What if . . ." Gretchen said, scrubbing at the red paint crusted on the workshop floor with paint thinner and an old rag, "we've missed the meaning of the note found in Martha's hand."

"The one with Caroline's name on it that said to put her away?" Nina leaned back against a stool and watched Gretchen clean up. Daisy, exhaustion etched across her face, had gone to the spare bedroom to try on her new outfits and rest. "By the way," Nina said, "I decided to shop in Mesa, the opposite direction of the Rescue Mission, so I could tell Daisy that we didn't have time to pick up her shopping cart, that we were too far away. She got so excited over the clothes that she didn't even mention the cart."

"The police assumed Martha left the note as an accusation," Gretchen said, focused on her line of thought, concentrating so Nina wouldn't distract her. "What if my mother was helping Martha? The note could have referred to putting away the French fashion doll. We know she had the doll because she wrote it in the note to Nacho. She said she had it but he had to hide the trunk because it was too large for her to hide easily. If she didn't take it with her, where would she have hidden it?"

Nina hopped from the stool, excitement flushing her face. "I have a feeling about that. It's getting stronger." She cocked her head to the side as if listening to something beyond Gretchen's range of sound and clapped her hands together. "The doll is close by, probably somewhere in the house."

"Where in the house?"

"You're expecting way too much detail," Nina said, exasperated. "Isn't it enough to know we're on the right track? Let's start looking."

"The police searched the workshop thoroughly. It wouldn't be in here."

"Caroline's bedroom then. Come on."

Gretchen and Nina attacked the house with gusto, Nina driven by her need to prove that her psychic abilities were real. Gretchen's personal belief was that her mother had the doll with her wherever she had gone, but Gretchen had run out of options. Searching the house kept her body in motion, made her feel as though she was moving forward instead of stagnating.

The search moved slowly, both women working together fluidly but without results. With one room left to search, Nina tapped gently at Daisy's door. She opened it a crack when she didn't receive a response. Daisy was sprawled across the bed, sound asleep.

They tiptoed in and searched the room without awakening Daisy. "She's still recovering from the surgery," Nina whispered. "I shouldn't have kept her out as long as I did."

Before they finished, Gretchen moved close enough to satisfy herself that Daisy was still breathing. She hadn't moved since they started the search. Gretchen watched her chest rise softly.

After a thorough search of the last room in the house,

they collapsed on the living room sofa with nothing to show for their efforts. The only consolation, Gretchen thought, is that Arizona homes don't have basements or attics. Otherwise they'd be at it the rest of the day and all night with possibly the same discouraging news in the end.

Nothing. They had unearthed absolutely nothing.

Zip, nada, zilch, zero.

Nina pulled off her shoes and rubbed her feet. "I really thought I had it right this time."

Gretchen scratched the part of her left hand protruding from the cast and assumed the intense itching inside the cast meant her wrist was healing. "Why are we bothering to look for it anyway? Nacho has confessed. My mother will come home eventually, and the police will drop the charges against her. It's simple. There is no urgency anymore."

"Ha," Nina said, mockingly. "Your aura is still black. We have to continue what's begun, and we have to understand it, or you're in big trouble."

"Okay, then," Gretchen said to humor Nina. "Put on your shoes and follow me."

The pool water glistened in the sun, reflecting patterns and images cast by the towering palms and exotic shrubbery. The only sound came from the hum of the air-conditioning unit as Gretchen padded along on her way to the cabana. The July sun sizzled on her skin, and she found herself struggling for breath in the hot, airless vacuum.

The water mesmerized Gretchen, reminding her of the recent trek through the flooded streets and the skill with which Nacho had concealed his home. She noted a chameleon lounging on the side of the adobe wall, its skin color fusing into its background, effectively hiding it from watchful predators.

She remembered again the Easter basket hunts of her youth. If Caroline had hidden a doll somewhere in her home, no one would be able to find it.

No one except her daughter, who had played this arcane game with enthusiasm and appreciation.

The silence and emptiness of the cabana weighed on Gretchen. One section of the room she'd been so fond of now resembled a storage unit, filled with her mother's boxes of sale dolls. The room brought back memories of her past visits. She longed to return to one of those times, to pretend her mother was busy in her workshop, humming while restringing an old doll after giving it a renewing bath. She imagined her mother putting away the doll repairing tools and seeking out Gretchen, conversations filled with love and caring and companionship.

"We've already gone through the boxes," Nina said, bringing Gretchen back to the moment. "It isn't in any of them."

"I know," Gretchen said, scanning the room, her eyes sweeping over clay pottery and potted cacti. She bent and peered up the chimney, then pulled a small television set from a built-in shelf and checked behind it. She walked into the bathroom.

Nothing here except stationary bathroom fixtures and an overhead cabinet set above the sink. Two towels rolled up, stacked neatly inside the cabinet, entirely filled the space. Gretchen removed the towels and stared at the back of the cabinet. Her heart pounded, because she remembered everything about the cabana and she remembered the cabinet. Plenty of room inside, last time she visited, for a large stack of assorted towels, bath, hand, and face.

Her fingers pushed gently on the back of the cabinet, pressing and exploring, and she felt the wall give slightly. She pushed on a corner, and the backing moved.

Gretchen heard Nina gasp behind her as she forced her fingers under the false wall and pulled the backing toward her, exposing a compartment.

Like Nacho's hidden home, the cabinet interior had been designed to deceive the casual observer, to dupe the unaware.

From behind the wall, Gretchen removed a package

wrapped in fabric the size of the doll she sought, along with another parcel, smaller and denser.

Gretchen had found the French fashion doll.

The landing gear whined into place as the plane rapidly descended over the familiar desert landscape. Caroline braced herself and waited for the plane to touch down. Finding a flight home had been more difficult than she'd anticipated. The first flights she checked were filled to capacity. In July, she thought. Who flies willingly into Phoenix in July, where the day's temperature, according to the pilot, hovered around one hundred and seventeen degrees?

Her plan was simple. A cab ride home, since she assumed her car had been properly disposed of. She would remove the hastily fashioned wall containing the French fashion doll and the accompanying pictures and inventory. Those items and the information stored on her computer were the only things she needed.

The Inspector had been caught unaware, and the end was near.

· 26 ·

I hope I have managed to remove some of the mystery from the expansive world of doll collection. You can decide for yourself what level of participation you want to actively pursue. Many of you won't start out with the ferocity and intense focus of the truly addicted collector. But mark my words; eventually you will become caught up in the pageantry and intrigue. With this book I have given you the tools you need, and so my job here is done. May your dolls bring you years of boundless joy.

The End

—From *World of Dolls* by Caroline Birch

The picture hadn't done her justice. A photograph, in Gretchen's mind, was never able to re-create the splendor and beauty the photographer hoped to capture.

The doll's delicate bisque features, unflawed in any way, shone with charm, her green cascading costume sumptuous and accurately portraying the dress fashion of her historical era. A circle and dot on the back of her neck established her Bru heritage. Gretchen marveled at the craftsmanship and at this rare opportunity to hold the doll in her hands.

Nina unwrapped the second package, and photographs spilled out onto the kitchen table.

Gretchen carefully laid the French fashion doll down on the sofa and picked up a sheet of paper. "Look," she said. "Martha's old inventory of dolls. And pictures of each." She shuffled through the photographs, noting bisque dolls from various French and German makers, several fashion dolls, Bébés, character dolls, dolly-faced dolls, cloth dolls, wooden dolls. Gretchen was stunned by the number of quality dolls in the collection. Reading the inventory days ago didn't have the same impact that viewing the pictures did.

She turned over a photograph. The doll's written description, transposed from the inventory list, was scrawled across the back of the picture. Gretchen studied the date stamp on the back, the same as the date stamp on the back of the French fashion doll photograph. Picking up the inventory list, she scanned it, running her index finger along the entries. She stopped at a listing.

"Nina," she said, breathlessly. "This inventory list is different from the one the police found in the workshop."

"How do you know?" Nina asked. "What's different?"

"Well, to begin with, the Bru French fashion doll is listed right here." She dragged the paper across the table, careful to keep her finger placed next to the appropriate listing. "It wasn't part of the other inventory. I remember commenting on that at the time. We thought Martha must have forgotten to update the list."

While Nina looked it over, she hurried to her mother's bedroom and returned with her copy of the inventory. A cross-comparison of the two lists exposed several inconsistencies, aside from a difference in the font used to print the lists. The list found in the cabana appeared to have been composed on an old-fashioned typewriter; the one found in the workshop was laser-printed from a computer word processor.

The fashion doll wasn't the only doll excluded from the first list. "A china Madame Rohmer wearing a cream dress with blue feathers is also missing," Gretchen said. "And a French Jumeau Bébé holding a Steiff monkey." Gretchen continued along the list. "Here's the Kewpie that Joseph said he purchased through an estate sale."

Nina shuffled through the photographs. "I found pictures of those three," she said, holding up the pictures.

"But why aren't they included in the list from the workshop?" Gretchen said, confused. "Why two different lists?"

"Maybe the second list is a more current inventory," Nina suggested.

Gretchen shook her head. "If that were true, the dolls' descriptions missing from the first list would be entered together at the end of the second list. They aren't. The list is in order by dates of purchase. The French fashion doll was purchased early in her collection. She wouldn't have forgotten it." Gretchen laid the two lists side by side. "No. Someone tampered with the first list, the one the police found in the workshop."

Nina picked up the fashion doll and gently touched the white daisies on her straw hat.

Gretchen found another conflicting entry. "Here's another one that didn't appear on the first list. She read the entry out loud. "Jumeau Triste doll, circa. 1875, composition and jointed wood body, real hair wig, thirty-three inches." She shuffled through the pictures, checking the back of each until she found the matching description. The dark-haired doll with the thick eyebrows must be worth a nice sum, she thought.

"Let's assume that Nacho planted the parian doll and the inventory list to throw suspicion on my mother," Gretchen said to Nina. "For some reason he wanted the police to view her as the prime suspect, so he hid the dolls and made an anonymous call to the police."

"There isn't any other explanation, since we know she's innocent," Nina said.

"Right," Gretchen said. "And let's assume that Martha Williams saved her entire collection after all."

"That's a stretch," Nina said. "Look at how she lived. She wouldn't have lived that way if she had thousands and thousands of dollars' worth of dolls."

"She would have lived that way if she was emotionally disturbed, and the indications are pretty strong that she had emotional issues. She also had a drinking problem. And she was obsessed with her dolls."

"Okay, let's pretend that she managed to keep her dolls when she lost her house. Then what?"

"Nacho knew she had them and wanted to steal them," Gretchen said. "She was killed for her dolls, not for a bottle of whisky, as he said. And he wanted to frame my mother for Martha's murder."

"And the reason for two different lists?"

Gretchen frowned as she stared at one picture after another. The explanation had to be in her hand.

"Because he didn't want anyone to know about those five dolls."

"That doesn't make sense."

"Yes, it does. I'm not an appraiser, though. We need to get April over here, but I'm guessing that the dolls excluded from the first list are the most valuable dolls in the collection. Only he doesn't have those dolls for some reason. Otherwise he'd be gone instead of breaking into collector's homes. Those dolls are missing. And those are the ones that matter to him. He doesn't want anyone to know they exist."

"So Nacho was searching for the French fashion doll and these other dolls you just mentioned."

"Correct," Gretchen said. "Is my theory holding together so far?"

Nina nodded, lost in thought.

"Nacho turned himself in for the murder," Gretchen said. "And since we're assuming, let's assume that he did kill Martha. His motive is much greater than he'd like us to believe, but why continue to hide information after he admitted that he killed her? To tell you the truth, even with a recorded confession, I have a hard time accepting his guilt."

"Why," Nina asked, slowly, "would he go to all the trouble of planting evidence against Caroline, almost kill Daisy, and then turn himself in?"

"Because he didn't do it," Daisy said from the doorway, her head wrapped in bandages and tears in her eyes. "He wouldn't do it."

* * *

Daisy slumped over the worktable, her head held in her hands as though it was too heavy to carry, and listened silently while Gretchen repeated what she knew of Nacho's confession and arrest. The dogs wandered in, spotted Daisy, and bounded over, with Wobbles following at a discreet distance.

Daisy perked up at the sight of them and bent to stroke each one.

"Nacho wouldn't harm Martha," she said. "He loved her more than anything in the world. Not that she deserved it."

"How can you be so sure he didn't kill her?" Nina said.

"Because he's the gentlest human being I've ever known. He helps everybody he meets, and his only problem is his drinking. He speaks all kinds of languages, which is pretty amazing. He's not so gruff once you get to know him. He wouldn't hurt a flying cockroach."

"Maybe he drinks because of that cancerous tumor on his head," Nina suggested.

"That isn't cancer," Daisy said. "He says he's had it his whole life."

"Why would Nacho confess to a crime he didn't commit?" Gretchen asked, lifting each picture and studying it before adding it to a pile on the worktable.

"He's protecting someone," Daisy said with confidence, confirming Gretchen's own suspicions that he was creating a smoke screen. Possibly so the real culprit would remain undiscovered.

Something about the dolls' pictures bothered Gretchen, tugged at her memory in a disturbing way. What was she missing?

"Have you heard of somebody called the Inspector?" Nina asked Daisy, scooping Nimrod onto her lap. "Martha complained about someone she called the Inspector."

Daisy waved dismissively. "Martha had names for everyone. She called me Marilyn Monroe because I want to be in the movies." She knit her brow in concentration. "I don't remember any Inspector though."

"Maybe she meant April. She's an inspector of dolls, if you think about it." Nina stared into space. "Gretchen, let's not get April over here to see this collection until we can eliminate her as a suspect. The more I think of it, the more likely it is that April was the Inspector. Are you paying any attention, Gretchen?"

After hearing her name for the second time, Gretchen glanced blankly at Nina. "There's something about the pictures," she muttered, tossing those in her hand onto the table. "Something familiar. I've seen some of them someplace before."

"Yes," Nina said, gesturing to the French fashion doll. "Like this one, for example. And the Kewpie at Joseph's store. And the one the police hauled away. You *have* seen some of them."

Gretchen frowned. Of course, Nina was right.

"We've managed to do it again," Nina announced. "We found more evidence against Caroline, digging her grave by the shovelful. This is one more thing we can't show to the police because it only proves what they already believe."

"With friends like us . . ." Nina said.

"Who needs enemies," Daisy added, and they finished in synchronization and high-fived each other.

Gretchen stared out the window at Camelback Mountain. She had tentative answers for many of the problems surrounding the death of the alcoholic doll collector. But she didn't have an explanation for one important question burning in her mind.

Two witnesses saw her mother on the mountain when Martha died.

What was she doing up there?

Nina drove off for a prospective client appointment with all the dogs in tow, leaving Gretchen to ponder the pictures before her in an attempt to find solid answers to fluid questions. Daisy, appearing worn and pallid, shuffled off to her room.

Gretchen rummaged on the lower shelf of the workshop cabinet, removed the doll trunk, and gently reunited the doll with its trunk. She closed the lid as the doorbell rang.

Gretchen smelled Chrome cologne as soon as she opened the door, wondering what bad news the detective carried with him. She had his number. He lured her in with feigned concern and a dazzling smile, then zapped her with the current turn of affairs, which was never advantageous for her. She cringed to think of what he had to say this time.

Yet she had to know.

She panicked briefly when she thought of the French fashion doll's trunk and the assorted pictures lying in plain view in the workshop, but then remembered his phobia.

He'd be the last one to suggest they meet in a workshop brimming with dolls and assorted doll parts.

"Since you seem to thrive on exercising in horrific heat," he said. "I thought you might like to take a walk. As long as we don't go that way." He motioned up at Camelback Mountain. "Uphill and hot don't mix well with me, but there are two kids selling lemonade down the street, and I'd like to buy you one. My treat."

Gretchen slid through the door and closed it behind her. "Sounds like just the thing."

They walked up the street, turned the corner, and bought two lemonades from the young entrepreneurs. The sun, slowly descending in the west, filled the sky with streaks of brilliant orange. Gretchen wondered where the day had gone and checked her watch. Six thirty. It would be dark in an hour. They started walking back to the house.

"Any word from your mother?" Matt asked, sipping from a straw.

"No," Gretchen said. "Sometimes I'm filled with dread thinking she's dead and will never return. Other times I think she's okay and expect her to walk in the door any minute. I can't understand how she could simply disappear without contacting me."

"Your feelings aren't unusual," Matt said. "In my job I see people all the time who are dealing with the same issues you are. Besides, I have irrefutable proof that your mother is alive."

Blood rushed to Gretchen's head, and her heart began to beat so loud she thought he would hear it. "Tell me."

"Caroline Birch requested a credit card transaction for a large sum of money. So large that the credit card service required verbal approval from her. We traced the call to a motel near O'Hare International Airport."

"She went to Chicago?" Gretchen was incredulous.

"She purchased a doll online for an exorbitant amount of money."

Anger flashed through Gretchen. After the relief of knowing her mother was safe, Gretchen felt an intense anger toward her. "She's out buying dolls while I'm worried sick about her?"

"Everything I'm telling you right now is confidential," Matt said. "I'm giving you a heads-up because of our family friendships, but you can't interfere with the arrest process."

"Aren't you worried that I'll find a way to warn her?"

"She's on a plane as we speak," Matt said, glancing at his watch. "She can't receive phone calls in the air, and she'll be landing in less than an hour. Two plainclothes agents are waiting at the gate, and they have orders to arrest her quietly. We don't want a spectacle in the airport."

Gretchen felt light-headed, and her steps slowed.

"This is her opportunity to clear her name," he said quietly.

A squad car slid along and parked in front of the house, and an officer got out and hitched his belt.

"He has orders to make sure you stay in the house until further notice." Matt nodded to the officer.

"You can't hold me hostage," Gretchen said, aghast. "This isn't a police state."

"Arrest her if she tries to leave," he said to the officer and hurried to his car. "I have to go to the airport to meet your mother when her plane lands."

The Inspector, Gretchen thought, watching the blue Chevy make a U-turn. Isn't that what the English called their detectives?

Gretchen's eyes were riveted to the empty workbench. The French fashion doll, the trunk, the inventory list, and all the pictures were gone. That explained why the patio doors stood wide open and hot air billowed in. Someone had entered the house through the back.

The air-conditioning unit whirled into motion to compensate for the increase in temperature. Then Gretchen saw it. She picked up a rumpled piece of paper lying where the fashion doll had lain a short while ago.

Meet me on the mountain. You know where. I'll
explain everything. And hurry.
Mom

Gretchen felt an enormous weight crushing her chest and concentrated on breathing slowly. The handwriting appeared to belong to her mother, although obviously rushed. How could Matt have been so wrong about her time of arrival? She must have eluded his efforts to spring the trap by taking an earlier flight.

Gretchen sprinted to the bedroom, grabbed her binoculars, and returned to the workshop window. The few hikers on the mountain, aware that the sun was rapidly setting, descended from the heights and began traveling earthward. Only one climber continued upward, and Gretchen sighted in the binoculars for a clearer view.

The departing sun's shadows splayed across the red cliffs of Camelback Mountain, darkening Gretchen's visibility through the binoculars. But she made out one distinguishing feature. Her mother's shoulder-length silver hair gleamed in a ray of light as she climbed with her back to Gretchen. The light shifted away, the color in her hair faded, but her daughter had recognized her in that brief moment.

Gretchen struggled to understand her mother's actions.

Why did she take the doll and climb the mountain? What was going on?

The only path to the truth was up. She had to meet her mother and demand an explanation, had to hear her reason for running away. Then she had to convince her to turn herself in. With a good lawyer and Gretchen beside her, they would overcome this obstacle just as they had survived the cancer scare.

She remembered the police officer stationed outside. The only way out of the house would be through the backyard and over the adobe wall. Gretchen sized up the wall, a good six feet high, and frantically looked around for something to stand on or to climb with.

A kiva log ladder in the living room with a decorative runner draped over its rungs would work perfectly. She flung the cotton runner aside and hurried past the pool with the ladder in her good hand.

Bracing it against the wall, she climbed the rungs, then, with incredible effort, given her broken wrist, she pulled her body the rest of the way up and dropped over the other side. She loped up to the trailhead and passed the posted safety warnings while scanning the ledges above her.

The last of the straggling hikers passed as she veered to the left and began the steep climb up Summit Trail. The only thing on her mind was her reunion with her mother.

Twilight descended quickly in the desert, but Gretchen's eyesight adjusted readily to the change. Perhaps her mother didn't realize the dangers of being on the mountain after dark. They would have time to descend safely as long as she hadn't gone all the way to the top. Gretchen doubted that. The few times they had hiked the mountain together, their goal had been a point on the enormous boulder. The same one that attracted all the tourists and offered a splendid view of Phoenix and the valley below.

The boulder towered ahead, rising like an obelisk before her. She scurried up until she stood on its highest point. Her mother was nowhere in sight. Right when she decided she must have been wrong about their meeting place, she heard a voice softly call her name.

She twirled around on the ledge and stared with dawning terror at the image before her.

It wasn't her mother standing back in the shadows of the mountain.

Too late, she remembered where she had seen one of the dolls in the picture.

· 27 ·

Acknowledgments

I'd like to thank the Phoenix Dollers for their overwhelming contributions to this book, especially April Lehman, doll appraiser extraordinaire, Bonnie Albright, who manages to keep the club members on task and supplied a wealth of valuable information, Rita Phyller for her extensive Barbie doll expertise, and Larry and Julia Gerney, owners of the China Doll Shop. They took me under their wings and shared many secrets of their success.

I am eternally grateful for the love and encouragement of two wonderful women: my sister, Nina, who can make me laugh even when I want to cry, and my daughter, Gretchen, who remains, always, the light of my life.

—From *World of Dolls* by Caroline Birch

Gretchen stared in horror as Larry Gerney stepped from his protected position against the mountain rocks, a gun hanging loosely at his side. Strands of hair from the silver wig he wore blew in the gentle breeze, reminding her of her mother.

Or a caricature of her mother.

The picture should have warned her.

She remembered picking up the Schoehut wooden doll and admiring it in the back room of the China Doll Shop. At the time, she had noted the slight crack around its nose, and she remembered that Larry had watched her intently.

The wooden doll's picture was among those she had found hidden behind the false cabinet wall.

One of Martha's.

Larry's financial problems and the threat of losing his doll business could be strong motives for stealing valuable dolls and murdering Martha.

His talent for making human-hair wigs was exhibited in the intricately fashioned replica of her mother's own hair that he wore on his head. The hikers who had witnessed Caroline's descent from the mountain must have pointed accusatory fingers based solely on the color of her hair.

As Larry walked toward her with a gleam of triumph in his madly blinking eyes, everything fell into place.

He was the Inspector.

Another epiphany realized too late.

Inspector Dreyfus, Clouseau's boss in *The Pink Panther*, had been driven crazy by Clouseau's bumbling antics, resulting in wildly twitching eyes just like Larry's. Martha had made a mockery of Larry's involuntary facial spasms by comparing him to a slapstick comedy character.

"You had to interfere," Larry said without emotion. Quietly. "You couldn't leave well enough alone."

"All I want is to find my mother. I don't care about the dolls." Gretchen stole a glance at the ledge she stood on. Too close to the vertical drop. She edged away from the precipice toward Larry.

"The dolls. Yes, thank you for finding the French fashion doll. I searched Caroline's house several times and couldn't find it."

Gretchen thought of the times Larry had offered to check on the animals as she sat at the hospital waiting for news. Of the unlocked door and her personal items slightly out of place. Of how easily he could have planted the parian doll while feigning concern. "You tipped off the police," she said. "You told them about Martha's doll and the list."

Larry grinned, pleased with himself, while Gretchen tried not to stare at the gun in his hand. "Martha entrusted all her dolls to me while she slowly drank herself to death. Always talking about how she'd get a place of her own again and take them back. My business dying with well over a million dollars' worth of dolls wasting away in the storage room."

Larry's mouth contorted in contempt, and he shook his head. "I sold one of her dolls to pay the rent and keep afloat a little longer. I didn't expect her to notice, but she did. She started stealing them back, if you can believe that, and I had to stop her."

"What does any of this have to do with my mother?" Gretchen asked.

"Caroline helped her. I got that much out of that drunken sad excuse for a human being." Larry's eyes flickered; his hand that held the gun seemed unsteady. "The pathetic woman begged me to let her go, thinking she could buy her life in exchange for information. She told me she had hidden the Jumeau Triste doll at Bonnie's house one day when she was away. I don't fault Bonnie for that. But Caroline . . ."

Larry looked off over the city lights. "Caroline willingly aided Martha in destroying me, and now it's my turn to destroy her. I followed them one night when they drove out to Joseph's, and I saw them give him the Kewpie. Caroline should have minded her own business, just as you should have."

"So you made the silver wig and wore it when you killed Martha." Gretchen felt cold fingers of fear. Pale, chilly fear.

"I thought I could get to Martha before she gave the doll to Caroline, but I was too late. Caroline had already hidden the most valuable doll in the collection. I don't care about the rest of the dolls. I'll wait until this all dies down, and I'll sell them in the future, one by one. I can wait. But I need some cash to get by, and the French fashion doll is my ticket."

That's why he needed to alter the list, Gretchen realized. He needed to sell off some of the dolls, and he didn't want them traced back to Martha's collection.

He came closer. "I thought I killed Caroline when her car left the road. I thought, *What a break to see her on the highway. What an opportunity. Eliminate the prime suspect in the murder investigation. Closed case with all the pieces in place.*"

"It must have been quite a surprise to find out you almost killed Daisy." Gretchen glanced around for an escape route or something to use as a weapon. She was trapped between the ledge hanging over a sheer drop and a determined killer with a gun.

"It doesn't matter anymore. Caroline strikes again, as you can see." Larry patted the wig with his hand. "A double murderess. Or make that triple, because I hate to inform you, but your dear aunt is next. I assume she knows about the French fashion doll as well, and I consider that deadly information."

"My mother's been arrested," Gretchen said desperately. "You won't get away with this."

"It's time for you to take a little dive." Larry smirked, gesturing with the gun. "I dislike noise, and would prefer not using this little toy, but I found it in Caroline's closet. Wasn't that convenient for me? One more piece of incriminating evidence against her."

Gretchen thought she saw movement in the gloom, a flash of motion behind Larry. Coyotes would be on the prowl as darkness swept over the desert. And mountain lions.

A dark shadow loomed up behind them, and Gretchen hoped it wasn't a mountain lion. The cougars were known for occasional attacks on humans, usually young children and dogs, but occasionally an adult.

A fist-sized rock flew through the air and hit Larry on the side of his head. His head snapped forward, surprise registering on his face as he raised his left hand to his face.

He spun away from Gretchen and fired.

Another rock flew out of the gloom, soaring straight and true, striking Larry in the face.

Gretchen, aware that this might be her only chance, hit

the ground and rolled away from the ledge toward a pile of rocks. Larry fired wildly into the dark, unable to see his attacker.

Another rock. Another direct hit to his face.

Larry had temporarily forgotten about Gretchen, intent on stopping the assault.

He fired several more times.

Gretchen's hand found a jagged rock the size of her palm, and she rose and hurled it, striking him in the back.

Another large rock sailed from the shadows.

The onslaught drove Larry backward toward the ledge, and Gretchen continued to edge away.

His head jerked in her direction, and he aimed the gun at her. She flinched as he pulled the trigger.

Gretchen heard a click.

He tried to fire again.

Another click.

Realizing he had used the last bullet, he flung the gun at Gretchen, then took a step in her direction, stumbling to find a solid foothold.

Another rock flew, and Gretchen saw movement. Silver hair shone in the rising moonlight, and she expected to hear the moaning howl of a werewolf rising from the apparition. The vision approached with the wrath of a mother bear protecting her cub. Then Gretchen saw a goddess running forward, Gretchen's oasis in the desert sands.

Gretchen's hand found another rock, and she put everything she had into launching it.

"I'll kill you both," Larry shouted, his face puffed with rage.

He took a step back, then another, lifting his arm to protect his face, teetering on the brink of the abyss. Another rock hit him, and he flung his arms overhead, struggling to maintain his balance. His foot slipped from underneath him, and Gretchen watched as he fell backwards over the edge.

His screams reverberated through the aptly named Echo Canyon as her mother's arms encircled her.

Gretchen cried for the first time since arriving in Phoenix, all the anguish of the last week rising inside her and exploding outward. She clung to the warmth of their shared embrace even after they began their descent from Camelback Mountain.

"Larry's going to live," Gretchen said when she hung up the phone, incredulous that anyone could survive that fall. "His back is broken, but he was conscious, and he confessed. They released Nacho this morning."

Gretchen sat at the kitchen table with her mother and Nina. Dogs and cats scampered underfoot.

Caroline clamped her hand to her chest. "You can't imagine how frightened I was when I saw Larry's car parked next to the trailhead. I knew he killed Martha, and I was afraid of what I would find up there. I never dreamed it was you." She cupped Gretchen's hands in her own.

"You saved my life," Gretchen admitted. "I don't know why I missed his car when I started the climb. I must have run right past it."

"You wanted so badly to believe that you were on your way to meet your mother," Nina said. "You weren't thinking about anything else."

Gretchen agreed. "I'm glad the police released Nacho. They could have charged him with obstruction."

Caroline took a sip of tea. "When I asked him to stall for time, I didn't expect him to take such a drastic step. But that's Nacho . . ." Her voice trailed off.

Gretchen frowned. "Why did Martha have a note asking you to hide her French fashion doll if you already had the doll?"

"I wondered about that also," Caroline said. "Martha left the doll in my workshop, and I think after she left, she must have realized that she forgot to leave the note. She ran into Larry on her way back, and he chased her up the trail, so she never had the chance to return and leave the note."

"What about Joseph?" Gretchen said. "Why did he lie about the Kewpie?"

"I think he was simply afraid of involvement," Caroline said. "He didn't want his name added to the list of suspects."

"Poor Julia," Nina said. "She didn't know a thing about it. I don't know how she'll run the shop with Larry in prison."

"Julia's tough," Caroline said. "And the club members will help her through it."

Nina chuckled. "Daisy almost fainted when she heard that she slept through all the excitement."

Gretchen frowned in thought. "How did you get past the police at the airport? According to Matt Albright, officers were waiting for you."

Caroline smiled. "I expected a welcoming committee, and I really didn't want to explain from a jail cell so . . . let's just say that Larry isn't the only one who knows how to throw together a disguise. If Bonnie's son hadn't spent so much time drinking lemonade with you, he wouldn't have been late, and he certainly would have recognized me the moment he saw me. I managed to scoot right past those other officers."

"I think he likes you," Nina said.

Nimrod gave a little yip from his poodle purse on the doorknob.

"Look who's awake," Nina exclaimed. "He needs a home, Gretchen. His family is still away, and they've decided a dog is too much commitment, since they travel extensively. They asked me to find him a good home." Nina stared at Gretchen with pleading eyes.

Gretchen slid a peek at Nimrod, and his ears perked forward. Wobbles sat contentedly under Nimrod and purse, watching over Tutu and Enrico.

"Look." Nina pointed out. "Even Wobbles likes Nimrod."

Gretchen, amazed that she would even consider owning a purse dog, grinned at Nina. She pushed back her chair and lifted the curly black teacup poodle from his traveling home. "Okay," she said. "If Wobbles says he approves."

Wobbles, reserved with his comments, looked on.

"He said yes," Nina said. "I heard him through a special energy field."

Caroline laughed, a deep, throaty roar. "It's good to be home."

"I have a new helper," Nina said. "Daisy's interested in learning to train purse dogs. You're right, Gretchen, she's a natural."

Caroline laughed again. "Things have changed so much in one week. Gretchen's here, we have a new houseguest in the spare bedroom, and the house is full of pet life."

"I hope you don't mind," Gretchen said, realizing what an imposition she must be.

"Not at all. I didn't know how lonely I've been until I saw the house brimming with activity." She glanced at Gretchen. "Why don't you stay? We can clear out the cabana for you. I have more repair work than I can keep up with, and you're looking for a job. Stay and be my partner."

Gretchen smiled awkwardly. Could she exchange her life in Boston with its East Coast sophistication and changing seasons for eternal heat and sun and transient neighbors? She'd lived her entire life in Boston, born and raised, and all her connections and roots were there. Except for her mother, who had yanked her roots up without a backward glance.

"Steve wouldn't appreciate it," Gretchen said lamely.

Nina sighed deeply. "You two have to make the next step or change direction. I'm all for dumping him and starting over."

"Nina," Caroline said. "This isn't your business."

Gretchen left her mother and aunt bantering at the table and slid through the patio doors. She sat on the edge of the pool, dangling her toes in the lukewarm water, the sun already a burning glow above.

She dialed Steve's cell phone and was surprised to hear his voice when she expected to connect to his voice mail.

"My mother's home," she said. "It's over."

"Has she been arrested?"

"No. The real murderer confessed."

Steve blew a sigh of relief over the airwaves. "I'm sorry I didn't show more support, but I had to distance myself until it was over. If your family had been involved in that murder, it would have destroyed my chances for partnership. You know how much that means to me."

Gretchen knew exactly how much the partnership meant to him. It meant enough that he had abandoned her at a time when she needed him the most.

Seven years of work on this relationship.

How much did it mean to her? How much was she willing to sacrifice? And what about Courtney, the intern?

Was Steve willing to put the same effort into the relationship as she was? As much as she wanted to believe that he was committed, his actions spoke against him.

Gretchen stared up at Camelback Mountain.

"Steve," she said, closing her eyes, "I'm going to stay in Arizona for awhile. I need to sort out my priorities and decide what I want to do with my life."

The rest of the conversation was predictable. Steve, the divorce attorney, gave a brilliant closing argument.

"No," Gretchen said, surprising herself with the force of her conviction, with the forcefulness of the small word.

Aunt Gertie's parting words popped into her head. *"Stay strong."*

"My mind is made up. I'm staying."

Turn the page for a preview of the next
Dolls to Die For Mystery,

Goodbye Dolly

Coming soon from Berkley Prime Crime!

Jennie H. Graves created the Ginny doll in the late nineteen-forties. Her small home business quickly grew to become the Vogue Doll Company. Ginny's popularity sent other companies racing to emulate the eight-inch plastic play doll. The most innovative feature of the new doll was its separate clothing. Ginny came wearing underwear and ready to dress in costumes designed by her creator. And what wonderful costumes they were.

—From *World of Dolls* by Caroline Birch

Gretchen Birch stood next to the flatbed trailer parked in the driveway leading to the house and eyed the mounds of dolls. Howie Howard, the auctioneer, worked the crowd like a harmonica tongue slap, all swinging elbows and agile, fluid mouth movements. Gretchen had a first-timer's knot of nerves in her stomach the size and weight of a Sunkist grapefruit.

"Do I hear twenty? There's a two oh. Thirty. Forty. Fine box of dolls." Howie's head bobbed like one of the swivel-head dolls boxed up in Gretchen's doll repair workshop. "Fifty? No. Forty going once . . . Sold for forty dollars."

Gretchen glanced at the stucco-and-tile house where Chiggy Kent, the once-vibrant founder of the Phoenix Dollers Club, had lived. Dragging an oxygen tank connected to her nostrils, Chiggy had finally succumbed to the persistence of her concerned neighbors and the ravages of lung disease and now resided at Grace Senior Care. But

Chiggy would have forced them to haul her out kicking and screaming if she'd had the breath to resist.

Chiggy's doll-making skills hadn't improved with experience or with advanced age. At least six hundred handmade dolls cluttered the open-bed truck and Gretchen winced at the poor workmanship. Dolls' eyebrows wisped in unlikely directions, painted with heavy, awkward strokes; eyelashes that would have impressed the legendary Tammy Faye, notorious queen of eye art.

The doll clothes were worth more than the dolls that wore them, but many of the shoppers bellied up to the truck weren't serious collectors and couldn't tell the difference between an original and a poor reproduction.

Howie Howard wasn't about to clue them in. "Here's a priceless imitation of a German Kestner. Full of character. Who could resist? Do I hear ten?" The words melded together, strung without the briefest pause, and Gretchen smiled at his singular ability to sell certifiable junk.

A man beside her lifted a doll from a heap and made space on the flatbed to prop it up. He smoothed the doll's bright blue gown and rearranged the curls framing her face, then stepped back and snapped a picture. Gretchen watched him move along the truck from doll to doll as he repeated the process again and again.

The camera, a Leica digital, looked expensive—too expensive, considering his gaunt, unshaven face and the faded T-shirt stretched over his protruding stomach.

The sun beat down on Gretchen.

She glanced around for a shady spot in which to stand. The last day of September was hot and dry, and Gretchen needed respite from the intensity of the Phoenix sun. One lone palm tree cast a pencil-thin shadow across Chiggy's now-barren yard, not nearly enough for protection.

Where did I put it? Gretchen dug through her purse for the list of dolls her mother had wanted her to bid on. She must have left it at home. *Now what?* She didn't have time to search for it. *No choice but to wing it.*

She hoped Howie wouldn't auction off all six hundred of these handmade copies before moving on to the real reason she stood there suffering from the heat. Chiggy's private collection. The real dolls.

Gretchen recognized several serious collectors in the crowd and a few impatient doll dealers looking for bargains. She edged closer to Howie.

"Change of pace," he shouted, as though reading Gretchen's mind. "We can't sell everything one at a time or we'll be here through Sunday. Let's dig out something new. What we got, Brett?" He turned and accepted a cardboard box from his assistant. "Box of Kewpie dolls." He held one aloft. "Cute little things. Whole bunch made by the same talented doll artist, Chiggy Kent." Howie held up a three-inch Kewpie. "Who wants to start . . . ?" And he was off and running.

Gretchen was fascinated by the speed with which Howie flew through the bidding process. She had sorted through the Kewpie dolls before the auction and noticed that almost all were bad reproductions. Gretchen saw imperfections in the molded bodies, amateurishly shaped topknots and tufts of babyish hair.

Someone was actually bidding on this mess?

"Sold for thirty dollars." Howie's voice slammed through the group, and Gretchen craned her neck to see the successful bidder.

Him again. He slapped his knee in delight. She'd watched the shriveled old man bid several times. Who could miss his stooped shoulders, full head of white hair, and Groucho Marx eyebrows? He waved his registration number with gleeful abandon.

Howie's assistant, Brett, continued to bring items to the auction block. A collection of paper dolls, then an Aston Drake Little Red Riding Hood.

Gretchen tried to imagine the list her mother had composed. No paper dolls. She was sure of it. Or was she?

Why do I have to be so forgetful and disorganized?

Brett continued lugging boxes out of the garage.

". . . Ginny dolls."

Gretchen snapped back to the call of the auctioneer. Ginnys were on the list. Here goes. Her body felt clambaked, and her hair, hard to manage on a good day, frizzed out from her damp scalp.

Someone pushed past her, another bidder positioning for the same round. Gretchen's palms felt sweaty and she grasped her number firmly, waiting for the opening volley. *Calm down. This is like a horse race. You don't have to start out in the lead to win.* She remembered her mother's coaching. Don't look desperate. Lay low. Wait for the right moment.

Gretchen gulped and felt the thrill of competition. Right this minute she wanted that collection of Ginny dolls more than anything in the world. Was this how it always felt? What a rush of adrenaline! No wonder her mother always covered the auctions and left her to handle repairs.

The dolls that Gretchen lusted after were eight-inch Vogue vintage dolls from the late forties and early fifties, all in their original boxes. They came with a variety of costumes—hats, dresses, purses, and snap-shoes.

Howie's voice sliced the sun-scorched air. "This is it," he said, his words coming fast. "The finest of the fine . . ."

Gretchen's heart sank into her stomach and settled next to the grapefruit-sized nervous lump. Why did he have to call special attention to the dolls she was interested in?

Her eyes never left him as his voice rang out.

"Who'll give me fifty?"

Gretchen raised her number against her sweat-laden halter top. So much for her mother's sound advice to lay low. Howie trained his eyes on her, acknowledged the bid, and worked it up. From the rapid sweep of his head, she guessed that three or four others were placing bids.

"One hundred. We have a cool crisp bill." Howie kept going, and Gretchen felt the sting of impending defeat.

One of the bidders dropped out and Gretchen held up her number again.

Another bidder dropped out.

Yes. Gretchen slapped an internal high-five at the dwindling competition.

The Ginny dolls whispered her name and she did the math in her head. Twelve dolls. She could sell them at the doll show for at least fifty each. That would be a total of six hundred dollars.

She still had some leeway.

The current bid shot past two hundred.

But some of the dolls needed work. Her mind flicked through the supplies in the repair workshop. She was sure she had extra Ginny doll parts. Arms and legs, even some original dresses, a wig or two.

"We have two eighty."

Gretchen signaled.

"Three hundred." Howie's red face beamed in anticipation of his growing commission. "Do I have three fifty?" His eyes darted behind Gretchen, his eyebrows one big question mark.

Silence. Howie waited a millisecond, then shrugged.

"Sold," he shouted, pointing at Gretchen.

Brett, who was standing behind Howie holding the next box, managed to give her a thumbs-up.

She felt like she'd won a million-dollar lottery.

Howie didn't miss a beat, intent on pounding through the remaining items as quickly as possible. Gretchen worked her way out of the crowd and stood at the back. She'd spent all her money on twelve dolls but she couldn't help grinning. They were worth it.

Had she paid too much? Her mother's request included at least six or seven different dolls. Even if she hadn't forgotten the list, she wouldn't be able to bid on any others.

After Gretchen paid for the dolls, Brett had her box ready at the side of the truck. He slapped her shoulder. "Good job."

Gretchen tuned out Howie's theatrical voice when he presented another round of Chiggy's badly painted dolls to the crowd. She sat down on a white plastic lawn chair and placed the box beside her. Her registration number and the word "Ginny" were scrawled across the top in black magic marker, the handwriting almost illegible.

The photographer strolled her way, camera strapped at his side, and his hand stretched out to her. Gretchen accepted the business card and glanced at the name. Peter Finch.

"I'm putting together a collection of doll photographs and selling them on eBay," he said. "Photo gallery, you know. A hundred and fifty pictures for thirty bucks. A steal."

"You're including photos of Chiggy's handmade dolls?" Gretchen was incredulous.

"Check it out," he said, moving off, offering his card down the line.

Gretchen tucked the business card in her white cotton purse embroidered with black poodles and red bows, a gift from Aunt Nina.

She bent over the box and removed the cover.

A heap of poorly produced Kewpie dolls grinned impishly up at her astonished face.

Just great.

The boxes had been mixed up. The stooped man with the bushy eyebrows who won the Kewpies must be walking around right now with her Ginnys.

Grabbing the box, she hurried back to the truck and scanned the crowd.

Then she heard tires squeal and a car horn blare. Someone screamed. Gretchen, along with everyone else in Chiggy Kent's yard, rushed toward the street.

"Back up. Quick." A man's voice sounded panicked.

Gretchen scooted between two parked cars, still holding the box of Kewpies.

She saw a woman get out of a Ford Explorer that had stopped in the middle of the street. "I didn't see him," she said to the people gathering around. "He flew right out between the cars. I didn't even have time to brake."

Several people crouched in front of the SUV.

Gretchen gasped and almost dropped the fragile Kewpie dolls.

Howie's assistant, Brett Wesley, lay crumpled in the road.

• 2 •

The ambulance pulled away slowly, without the need for wailing sirens and flashing lights. The police finished questioning possible witnesses and released the remaining auction attendees. People stood in small groups, talking quietly. Cars began to pull away. Everyone would drive with extra care for the rest of the day.

The auction came to an abrupt close. Howie Howard had lost his business partner and close friend and was incapable of continuing. No one seemed interested in dolls anymore. Gretchen watched Howie get into a blue pickup truck, his face the color of Arizona adobe. She guessed he would follow Brett's body to the morgue.

She felt a wave of nausea each time she thought of Brett lying dead in the street. How quickly life can be snuffed out by a misstep between parked cars. An image of the car's tire slamming across Brett's torso forced its way into her thoughts and she tried to block it from her mind.

One of the registration workers slapped a sign on the side of the flatbed trailer: All remaining handmade dolls would sell for ten dollars each. Help yourself. Pay at the register.

The notice reminded Gretchen that she still carried the wrong box of dolls. She looked around for the stooped man but didn't see him.

A chunky woman with brassy blond curls sat at the registration table. Gretchen approached. "I know this isn't really important considering what just happened," she said. "But I have the wrong box of dolls."

"Nothing I can do about it, sweetheart." A single sob

escaped from the woman but she quickly composed herself.

"I think I know who I need to contact," Gretchen said. "Can you check the records and tell me who bought a box of Kewpie dolls?"

"I suppose." She scanned the registration sheet. "That would be Gretchen Birch."

"Well, I'm Gretchen Birch and I bought Ginny dolls, not Kewpies. Can you tell me who bought the box of Ginny dolls?"

"Name's Duanne Wilson. Here's the address. You'd better write that down now."

Gretchen dug in her purse for a pen and paper and copied the name and address.

"Shame about Brett. I can't hardly believe it," the woman said, tears in her eyes. "He was a good guy."

Gretchen nodded, close to crying herself. Other people's sorrows always set her off. If she caved in now, she'd be a basket case for the rest of the day. "Thanks for the information," she said, in a hurry to get away.

Most of the cars in front of Chiggy's house had cleared out. Gretchen didn't see the Ford Explorer or the woman who had driven into Brett. *That poor driver. How awful*. She stowed the box of Kewpie dolls in the trunk of her car and eased away.

Gretchen fought back tears and considered the accident. Apparently no one had seen Brett step in front of the car. Amazing, considering the number of people mobbing the trailer. Of course, everyone's attention had been riveted on Howie and the auction. The driver of the SUV had insisted that Brett literally flew into the street. Why had he been in such a hurry? Shouldn't he have been working beside the auctioneer?

Brett had probably been the one who mixed up the boxes. Gretchen sighed heavily. At the moment, the last thing she cared about was the doll mix-up. But three hundred dolls was a lot of money. She had to correct the mistake.

After asking for directions twice—two months in Phoenix and she still couldn't find her way around—she turned onto Forty-third Street and searched the apartment buildings for the number she had written down. She drove around the block and tried again.

No number matched the one she'd been given.

Gretchen frowned in annoyance.

Maybe she had written it down wrong? No. She remembered double-checking the numbers with the teary blonde.

She pulled to the curb in front of the only apartment complex within several blocks. This had to be where the man lived. She pulled open the first set of doors, entered, and tried the second set. Locked.

She scanned the names on the mail slots. No Duanne Wilson.

She waited, hoping someone would come along and open the door. Maybe a manager's office inside would give her the correct apartment number.

No one came.

Standing on the sidewalk, she looked up and down the street. *What now?* She had three hundred dollars invested in those dolls.

Then she noticed the sign. Gretchen dug her cell phone from her purse, and dialed the number on the sign that announced a vacancy in the building.

After a few holds and redirections, Gretchen had her answer and she didn't like it.

No such person. No such place.

Duanne Wilson had vanished along with her Ginny dolls.

DEB BAKER spends as much time as possible in Phoenix, Arizona, the setting for her Dolls To Die For Mysteries featuring Gretchen Birch, and in the Michigan Upper Peninsula, home of her Gertie Johnson Yooper Mysteries.

She lives in North Lake, Wisconsin, with her husband, their two teenagers, two border collies, and two wayward cats.

Visit Deb's website at www.debbakerbooks.com.

The Scrapbooking Mystery series from

Laura Childs

Carmela Bertrand owns a scrapbooking
store in New Orleans—and can't help but solve a
murder every once in a while.

Keepsake Crimes
0-425-19074-9

Photo Finished
0-425-19434-5

Bound for Murder
0-425-19923-1

**Free scrapbooking tips
in each book!**

Available wherever books are sold or at
penguin.com